Waiting to Love You

A Secret Baby Small Town Romance

AJ Alexander

WAITING TO LOVE YOU by AJ Alexander

www.authorajalexander.com
aj@authorajalexander.com

First E-book Publication: May 2024
Photo provided by: Cadwallader Photography, LLC
Cover Designer: Wildheart Graphics
Developmental Editing: Made Me Blush Books
Line Editor: The Ryter's Proof Editing Services
Proofreader: Crystal Clear Author Services

dedication

To all the military brats and spouses that are holding down the fort while their loved one protects us all.

one

seth

"Why am I doing this again?" I mumble as I make my way down Main Street.

"Because my friends are your friends." Brady smiles, slapping me hard on the back before turning his attention back out the window.

Brady and I have been practically inseparable since they placed us in the same bunk about five years ago. On the surface, Brady and I have nothing in common. He's from Tyson's Creek, has two parents who practically adore him, and the support of an entire town around him. I chuckle to myself as I remember the first time I came home with Brady while on leave after deployment. The entire town was decked out in American flags with signs welcoming their local hero home. We couldn't go anywhere in town without someone wanting to shake his hand and ask him how he was doing.

At first, it made me uncomfortable, but after coming back to visit a few times, I understood that this was just how the townspeople were. They took care of their own, for better or worse. They were more like one enormous family instead of a town. Everyone looked out for each other and wanted the best for every person who came into town. That's something I've never had before, especially growing up in the foster care system.

"And why is that again?" I snicker, knowing that everyone probably asks him the same thing after meeting me.

Brady is outgoing. The guy loves to be around other people, while I'm the quiet type, who would rather bury my nose in a book than go out and party—his polar opposite. But somehow, he got it into his head that we were going to be the best of friends and wore me down until I agreed. Being friends with Brady has brought me a peace that I haven't known since my parents died, not that I would tell him that. His acceptance of me and all my issues has made it easier to breathe over the past few years.

"Because you love me. But mostly because my momma makes the best smothered pork chops, which she makes you every time you come to visit."

"True. I am very food motivated." I laugh as we make our way toward the center of town.

The streets are lined with people, but no one is rushing around or in a hurry to get anywhere. Tyson's Creek looks exactly like you'd envision a small southern town being. There are a few mom-and-pop shops lining the street and no major chain stores in sight. As I make my way down the familiar street of my second home, I notice someone changing the marquee on the only movie theater in town, The Flickhouse. There's a small bookstore tucked right next to it, with Tyson's Hardware on the other side. Across the street from the theater is Just the Drip, a small bakery and coffee shop combo, which is the place to be in Tyson's Creek. There are tables scattered in front filled with people, the peach-colored umbrellas open and casting shade over each table to protect the occupants from the sun.

"Pull in right there," Brady points to what seems to be an empty store a few feet away from Just the Drip. "Walker and Riggs said they'd meet us here."

"Where is here, exactly? This place looks deserted," I question as I turn off the car and we both climb out.

"This is where the studio is going to be, but it's not open yet. Walker said something about Bristol needing to do some practice classes or something to get her certification," Brady replies as his phone chimes in his pocket, and he pulls it out. "It seems Walker and Riggs are running late, but Bristol should be inside. They said to go on in."

"If you say so," I respond skeptically as we approach the storefront.

The entire front is covered in windows, allowing natural light to fill the space. As we get closer, I notice the outline sketch of a logo on the front door with the words *Nurture Space Yoga Studio* outlined in black in a serif-type font. "Someone needs to get a better sign if they plan on bringing in more business," I mumble to myself as I pull open the door and motion for Brady to head inside first.

The space is larger than I expected as we enter a small waiting room off to the right. There is a small desk tucked into the corner, with a small computer screen and a few succulent plants sitting on the edge. The walls are painted a calming shade of green, with light-colored wooden boxes strategically placed near the door for easy access. Inside each box appears to be an assortment of yoga mats filling each one. Directly below the boxes on the wall is a two-tiered wooden shelf, about the same size as the desk. Each shelf is filled with neatly rolled white towels, and a fancy water dispenser sits on the top of it, surrounded by more plants.

"Nice place," I say before taking a seat in a chair positioned under the windows as I continue to examine the rest of the studio.

Directly across from the seating area is what can be best described as a shoe storage cubby bench to keep everyone's shoes organized before walking through the small glass door to enter the studio. There is a large cutout in the wall above the bench, giving us the perfect view into the studio.

The entire back wall is covered in windows, with natural light reaching almost every corner of the room. There is a breathtaking view of the same hills that are on the outskirts of Tyson's Creek. There are several houses sprinkled in the distance, and I notice a small wooden bridge that likely leads to another part of town.

A soft breeze brushes against my skin, causing me to turn toward the door. Walker and Riggs come strolling inside.

"Next time, I'll drive. You drive like a damn grandma." Riggs snickers as he gives Brady a one-armed hug before reaching down and giving my shoulder a squeeze.

"I drive at a safe speed, not like a man with a death wish like you do." Walker walks into the reception area behind Riggs. "If you wouldn't have overslept, none of this would've happened."

I met Walker and Riggs the first time I came home with Brady to visit his family. Riggs seems to be the least serious of the two, choosing to waste his days giving Walker's sister, Leia, a hard time instead of just telling her how much she means to him.

"Stacy wore me out last night. What can I say?" Riggs chimes in, causing me to shake my head in disapproval.

We all know how Riggs feels about Leia and has for years. Although I've only known him for a few years, I can see the way his entire face lights up the moment she walks into a room and how he orbits around her like she is the sun. However, whenever they're in the same room with each other, he riles her up. Choosing to push her buttons with his sarcastic comments and sexual innuendos instead of sincerely letting her know how he feels.

Walker says this has been going on for years, ever since they all became friends as kids. While Brady and Walker had a perfect childhood, Riggs wasn't so lucky. I don't know much about his past, just that he swears he can't be with Leia because she's too good for him. I don't know how he still believes this, especially with Walker doing everything he can to push the two of them together.

"Cut the act, Riggs. We all know you sat at home, searching for a way to get into Leia's good graces," Brady reaches for Walker's hand and gives it a firm shake.

"I did not," Riggs grumbles, running his hand through his dark-colored hair. "In all honesty, I slept through my alarm."

"Dreaming about my sister?" Walker questions, his expression calmer than I would expect when talking about his friend's feelings for his baby sister. I don't have any siblings, but if I did, I doubt I'd be so calm if someone was dreaming about my little sister.

"Maybe." Riggs winks at Walker before dropping

into the seat beside me. "So, why exactly am I here again?"

"Didn't he tell you we were taking a yoga class?" I ask, turning my body towards him. My eyes flick toward Brady and Walker standing a few feet away, deep in conversation.

"He may have, but the only thing I heard was Leia's name, and I agreed immediately," Riggs' eyes flicking toward the back of the studio like he's searching for someone.

"She isn't here, man. She had to take my dad to the doctor," Walker chimes in as Riggs's shoulders sag slightly.

"Damn, you have it bad." I snicker, clapping him hard on the shoulder. "Maybe if you stopped acting like a five-year-old, she might give you the time of day."

"I've been in love with Leia Armstrong since we were kids. I made one mistake and instantly ended up on the top of her shit list. A place I've remained to this day."

"What the fuck did you do to Leia to earn that position? And why the hell haven't you kicked his ass for pissing your sister off that badly?" I question, wondering why I never asked this same question in the years that I've known them.

"Oh, I kicked his ass, all right, but then I got over it. Riggs is an idiot and has some weird idea that Leia would be miserable if they were together. However, that hasn't stopped him from pining after her all these years either."

"Yes, you did." Riggs chuckles, gripping the back of his neck. His eyes look slightly unfocused, as if he's lost in the memory of what happened. "He broke my nose, and I had two bruised ribs, but I deserved it."

"You did, but that doesn't mean she'll never forgive you. You just need to explain things to her. I'm sure she'll understand that you aren't the same person you were back then."

"I wish it were that easy." Riggs scoffs before pushing to his feet and changing the subject. "When are we going to get this party started? Crawdaddy's is calling our name."

"Crawdaddy's?" I question as my eyes narrow in my friends' direction. "Strange name for a bar."

"You're in a town sitting right near the Tennessee/Alabama border, the home of the crawdad. It's also Beckett's pride and joy," Brady smiles proudly. "That place makes the best crawfish dishes in the area, hence how it got its name."

"It's also the best place in town to grab a cheap beer and focus on something other than how much is going on in your life." Riggs throws his arm over my shoulder motioning his chin toward Brady and Walker." We try to stop by whenever we're into town. It has a great atmosphere. Definitely a good place to unwind after a long day.

"Bristol is here somewhere, probably in the back doing something." Walker strolls through the glass door and into the open studio area before turning left and opening a door.

"Crawdaddy's is a good idea. I've been dying for one of Beckett's famous burgers," I respond, my mouth beginning to water.

"I could go for a good local microbrew. The shit they usually have at the bar on base tastes like piss," Brady chimes in, causing Riggs and me to laugh loudly.

We barely get our laughter under control before Brady shifts his attention over my head, a bright smile blooming on his face. "Look who finally graced us with their presence."

"I was in the back the whole time with my headphones in. There's no way I wouldn't have heard your big mouth otherwise."

I turn my attention toward the voice and freeze, my eyes connecting with the most beautiful woman I have ever laid eyes on. Her red hair lays over her shoulder in an intricate braid, with a few stray tendrils of hair framing her face. As she comes closer, I notice there are streaks of blonde in her hair brought out by the halo of sunlight behind her head. My eyes continue to wander down her body, taking in the fitted green top covering her curvy frame and the way her apple bottom fills out a pair of black yoga pants. Images of sinking my teeth into that ass as I take her from behind fill my mind, creating a rising problem in my pants.

Her face lights with happiness as she throws her arms around Brady's neck and squeezes tightly. He chuckles softly, lifting her in the air before placing her feet back on the floor. She doesn't even get a second to breathe before Riggs wraps her in his arms and spins her around, causing her to let out peals of laughter. Jealousy shoots through my veins as I jump to my feet, my entire being vibrating with the need to rip her from Riggs's arms. I've never had this reaction to a woman before, let alone one I just met, but my body is moving before I stop myself. I have no idea who she is, but I plan on remedying that as soon as possible and learning everything about her.

Unable to contain my desire to meet this woman, I step between her and Riggs, causing her to take a step back.

"Hello," she replies as she raises her eyebrow in question.

"Hi," I reply awkwardly, suddenly at a loss for words. Flecks of gold sparkle in her emerald-green eyes as she looks me up and down, probably making many assumptions about me and my manners.

I hold out my hand, shoving it in her direction. "Hello. I'm Seth."

The gruff sound of my voice surprises me as I clear my throat loudly, causing all three of my friends to snicker softly. I've always been slightly socially awkward, but this time it's different. It's like I've forgotten how to speak. Words are stuck in my throat as I try to make sense of what is happening right now. I've never been a person who believes in love at first sight, but right now, I do.

"Hi, I'm Bristol," she responds tentatively as she looks down at my outstretched hand before grasping it in hers.

As soon as our skin connects, an electric current sizzles up my arm. Her eyes widen in surprise as she pulls her lip between her teeth. The two of us remain standing there, frozen, staring at each other. My heart aches as my hand moves on its own, brushing along her cheek. Her eyes drift closed as she leans into my touch, a soft sigh escaping her lips as I tuck a stray piece of her hair behind her ear. We stare at each other, neither of us moving, trapped in each other's gaze until Brady clears his throat and breaks the spell.

He gives her his trademark grin. "Excuse him, Bristol. This is my friend, Seth; we are in the same unit together."

Bristol's demeanor immediately changes, her eyes hardening in my direction before plastering on a fake smile. "Nice to meet you, Seth. Are you guys ready to get started?"

"Sure thing. Lead the way, darlin'," I motion toward the glass door separating the waiting area from the main studio. She flashes me a tight smile before spinning on her heels and walking through the glass door.

"What the hell just happened?" Brady's eyes are focused on her retreating form.

"I don't know, but the temperature in the room dropped by a thousand degrees the minute Brady said you were his friend," Riggs retorts, a confused look crossing his face.

"Do you and Bristol have something going on?" I growl, my fists tightening at my side.

"Calm down, Seth. Bristol and I are just friends, nothing more. What did you do to piss her off that quickly? You only said three words to her."

Riggs and Brady are right. I highly doubt that I could have done anything, but there must be a reason for her sudden change in behavior. I just don't understand why she would shut down so quickly after hearing Brady and I are friends. Does she have a thing for Brady he doesn't know about? Is it because I'm in the military? No, that can't be it, especially with how she reacted to Brady.

Out of the corner of my eye, I notice Bristol moving around the studio, laying four beige-colored yoga mats on the floor as she gets ready to start our class. "I'm not sure, but she doesn't seem like she wants to talk about it right now."

I take a step forward to enter the studio but feel

someone tugging on my arm. I turn to find Walker eyeing me skeptically.

"What?"

"You need to tread lightly with her, Seth," Walker warns as he releases my arm, his eyebrows pulled down in concern as he examines my face. "Bristol is Leia's best friend from college, but..." he begins, but shakes his head. "Never mind, just be careful, okay?"

Walker strolls past me and into the studio, Riggs right on his heels. Brady gives me a slap on the back. "Don't think too much about it. Talk to her and ask what her deal is, then we can proceed from there."

My eyes instantly shift to Bristol again, a soft sigh escaping my lips, which causes Brady to laugh. "You're hooked, aren't you?"

I pause for a moment and consider what he just said. Am I hooked on a girl that I've never laid eyes on before today? I don't know, but I do know one thing. If there's one woman I would trade my little black book in for, it would be her.

I shake my head, trying to clear my thoughts before shrugging my shoulders. "There's just something about her that calls to me."

"That's always how it starts." Brady squeezes my shoulder before shoving me softly toward the door. "Let's make it through this class, then you can ask her if she wants to come to Crawdaddy's with all of us."

"Good plan," I respond before walking through the door and taking a mat right next to Riggs.

Bristol is all business. She immediately shows us the right way to perform various stretching poses. Soft classical music plays in the background as she shows four grown men the right way to stand and stretch their muscles before finishing the class with a short meditation.

"Thank you for attending my class today. I hope you leave a little more relaxed than when you arrived," Bristol says cheerfully as my eyes open and flick toward her.

She's in the front of the room, her legs tucked beneath her, as she smiles brightly at Brady, Walker, and Riggs. The moment her eyes lock with mine, her smile disappears, and she pushes to her feet.

"You can leave the mats where they are. I need to wipe them down before putting them away," Bristol says over her shoulder before disappearing into a small room tucked into the back corner of the studio.

"Seth can help you. Then you can meet the four of us at Crawdaddy's to celebrate a successful class," Brady shouts loud enough for her to hear him.

"That's okay. I can handle it. Besides, I have plans to meet up with Leia after this, anyway."

"Leia is meeting us there, too," Walker pulls out his phone, winking in my direction. "Does an hour sound good?"

"Sure." Bristol sighs as she comes strolling out of the room, a small spray bottle full of a clear liquid and a roll of paper towels in her hand. "That gives me enough time to shower and head over there."

Walker says something to Brady before clapping him on the shoulder and striding through the open door.

"Since Seth is staying to help you clean up, I'm gonna catch a ride with Riggs and Walker." Brady turns on his heels and hurries after Walker, likely afraid of getting left more than anything.

"See you two later." Riggs winks in our direction before following the other two men out of the room. I hear the small bell above the door chime softly as they exit the building.

"Just spray this liquid on the mats and then wipe it off. I'm going to make sure everything is locked up before turning off the air. Shouldn't take me too long."

"No problem, darlin'," I reply, with a little more twang in my voice than usual. I reach for the bottle, and my fingers brush against hers. Another zing of electricity shoots up my arm as Bristol's cheeks turn a delicious shade of pink.

"There's no need for any of this, Seth. I'm not interested in whatever it is you want," she mutters, taking a step away from me.

"I don't believe that one bit, Bristol."

"And why is that?"

"I know we just met, but you have to admit there's something here between us. It might be nothing, but it might also be everything. I only want a chance to find out."

"I can't." She turns to leave, but I grip her arm, pulling her to a stop.

"Why?"

"*Why?* Can't you take no for an answer?" she huffs, wrapping her arms around her waist as if she's trying to protect herself from some unknown threat. Her eyes remain focused on a spot on the floor, and my heart aches at the thought of not being able to catch another glimpse of her beautiful eyes. My hand moves on its own, resting my finger below her chin and forcing her to look at me.

"You haven't actually told me no yet, darlin'." I grin, my eyes searching her face for any hint as to why she's fighting so hard to resist the connection between us.

"You're a Marine," she blurts out, taking a step away from me and turning around. "I refuse to tie myself to a man who will come in and out of my life every few months. Been there, done that."

"But..." I begin, wanting to tell her that the separation is only temporary. The end of my contract is coming after our next deployment. We can take our time finding out where things might go between us and then decide together whether this is something worth pursuing, but I don't get a chance. Bristol immediately cuts me off.

"But nothing, Seth," she snaps, not even bothering to turn around. "Thanks for offering to help me clean up after class, but I got it from here."

I open my mouth to say something but decide against it. My mind is racing with a million questions, wanting to know who hurt her so badly that she doesn't even want to take a chance to see where things would lead with me.

"See you at Crawdaddy's, darlin'," I mutter, planting a soft kiss on the back of her head before turning on my heels and striding out the door.

I know in my heart that there is something between Bristol and me. I just need to figure out how to help her see how good we can be together. I'm only going to be a Marine for another two years, and then, who knows? Right now, the only other thing I want to be is hers.

"Are you sure we can't just stay here and watch *Golden Girls*?" I ask Leia as I grab one of the many outfits she's picked out for me and pull it on before turning toward the mirror. "With how many people I know your dad invited, no one is going to miss us."

Leia called me about an hour ago and told me she was on her way over before hanging up on me. This isn't anything out of the ordinary for Leia. If it wasn't for her, I'd spend most of my time at home, watching *Golden Girls* reruns and eating peanut butter out of the jar with a spoon. I know it's not the healthiest of food options, but it's my favorite.

The moment Leia walked through the door, she shoved me towards the bathroom and demanded I take a shower because we were going out. I grumbled for a few minutes but eventually headed towards the bathroom, where I found Leia on a video call with our other friend, Audrey, trying to choose the perfect outfit for me to wear on this mysterious outing.

"No. You need to go somewhere other than Nurture Space every once in a while." Audrey snorts as she rolls her eyes at us through the computer screen.

Audrey Wilde and I have been friends since right after my dad was stationed at the military base in New Orleans. My family rented the house a few blocks down from hers instead of living in base housing. My dad had promised my mom this would be the last move, and we would finally put down roots as a family, but as always, he was lying.

Honestly, if I had known that we were going to move again in a few years, Audrey and I probably never would have become friends in the first place, but I'm glad that I didn't. Audrey and I needed each other back then. I knew the minute I saw her standing at the bus stop with her dark curly hair pulled into a messy bun at the top of her head and her body enveloped in clothes that were obviously two sizes too big that she needed a friend as much as I did.

She tried to keep me at arm's length, especially when we were at school, but slowly, I convinced her to lower the walls she had up around her heart and slowly let me in. After a few months, she told me she was pregnant by the most popular guy in school and that he wanted nothing to do with her or the baby. Instead of pushing her aside like she expected, I wrapped her in my arms and promised to babysit whenever she needed help.

My parents were the same way, especially after her parents were killed in a car accident. Neither of them hesitated to offer Audrey a place to stay with us, making sure she and her daughter felt as if they were a part of our family, because they were. My parents told her she was welcome to stay for as long as she needed.

But, of course, duty called, and my father was transferred to Tennessee shortly after Love's first birthday. I begged Audrey to come with us, but she was determined to make a life of her own for the two of them. The two of us have stayed in touch with weekly video calls and almost daily phone calls, even through college. We are as close as two people can be, with hundreds of miles between us. We tell each other everything, even our deepest, darkest secrets.

"Starting a business from scratch is hard," I retort before pulling off my outfit and reaching for another one off the bed.

After graduating college, instead of chasing my parents around the country until my dad retired, I came back to Tyson's Creek with Leia. Once I got my bearings, I combined my love for yoga and a business degree to open a yoga studio. Business has been all right—nothing too spectacular, but steady—thanks to all of Leia's family for their support. I'd love nothing more than to have

Audrey right here with me, helping to run the business. It would be a win-win for everyone involved.

"You could always move here. Love and I would love to have you live closer to us," Audrey retorts quickly.

"She isn't moving there. I'd miss her too much." Leia grabs the set of clothes I'm holding and shoves another into my hands. "You could always move here. Audrey."

"Yeah, what she said."

Audrey is currently living in San Antonio, Texas, with her daughter, Love, although I try every time we chat to get her to move here to Tyson's Creek. I know she says she's happy there with her current boyfriend, Ian, but something feels off about their relationship. Something I can't seem to put my finger on. Ian seems to be the perfect guy for Audrey, but there is this nagging voice in the back of my head that keeps waiting for the other shoe to drop.

"Not this again." Audrey sighs loudly. "Love has a life here and friends. I don't want to uproot her just because I miss being near my best friend. And there's also Ian..."

"Oh, yeah, Ian." Leia huffs. "How's this amazing boyfriend of yours?"

"He's fine. On another business trip to the East Coast, but he should be home this weekend." She grimaces slightly before plastering a fake smile on her face.

"What's wrong?" Leia and I ask in unison.

"Nothing," Audrey eyes looking anywhere but at the two of us.

"Do we need to call Selina, too? I'm sure she'll convince you to tell us what's going on."

Selina is the other person missing from our friend group. Leia and Selina grew up here in Tyson's Creek together but didn't get close until after their friend, Lydia, passed away during childbirth. Currently, Selina is living her dream as a ballerina in the New York City Ballet after graduating from Juilliard. She doesn't come back to town at all to visit, but we all stay in touch through our weekly video calls.

"No. Besides, she's at practice. She won't be able to answer anyway." Audrey huffs before sighing loudly. "Everything is fine. I promise. You four would be the first to know if it wasn't."

"We better be," I respond quickly with an affirmative nod before stripping down to my underwear and changing clothes for the second time.

"And don't forget, we know places to hide a body. Just say the word."

"You know that makes it premeditated, Auntie Leia, right?" Love shouts from somewhere off-camera, causing Leia and me to laugh loudly.

"Yeah, I know," Leia replies before checking the

time on her watch. "Not that I don't love chatting with you two, but if we don't get Bristol dressed and out the door soon, my brother might send a search party."

Before I met Leia in our junior year of college, I kept to myself. Sure, I had a few friends, but I wasn't close to anyone besides Audrey. I chose to keep people at arm's length as much as possible so that when I had to leave them, it didn't hurt nearly as much. However, Leia wasn't having it. After we were partnered up for a project in class, Leia continued sending me text messages and asking me to hang out. I ignored all of them, hoping she would get the hint and leave me alone. But she didn't. Instead, she started sitting next to me during class, asking me to have lunch with her, and even planning study dates for the two of us. After a while, Leia started asking me about my family and friends, both subjects I rarely spoke to others about, and I found myself telling her everything. It was as natural as breathing, just like my friendship with Audrey. With Leia came Selina, and the four of us all became fast friends. I never had a close-knit family, but these three are the family I always dreamed of having. I know deep down that these ladies will have my back, no matter what happens.

"Why didn't you say so?" I shout with glee. "Gotta go, Audrey. Love you, and give Love a kiss for us."

Leia doesn't even have time to say goodbye before I slam my laptop shut and grab her hand, pulling her toward the door. "You should've told me this was just us hanging out with Walker. I would've been dressed and ready to go hours ago."

The first time I met Leia's family, I was nervous. She grew up living in the same place her entire life, nothing like the way I grew up. Sure, we found something in common while we were at college, but I wondered if things would be different now that we weren't in our little insulated bubble at college. I know it was silly, but I was worried I'd no longer have anything in common with her.

That all went out the window after meeting her dad, her older brother, Walker, and her younger sister, Skye. Yes, you read those names right. Leia and her siblings are all named after *Star Wars* characters. I don't know the entire story, but her mom came to Tyson's Creek to see some comet or something and never left. Her parents met when her mom was on that trip, and the rest is history.

"My apologies." Leia huffs, blowing a loose tendril of her blonde hair out of her face as I shove her out the front door and pull it closed behind me. "Who knew that all it took was mentioning my brother was home to get you out of the house?"

Walker Armstrong is two years older than Leia and me and has become just as much my brother as he is Leia's. The moment he smiled down at me, I felt safe and cared for. Not romantically, but how a brother looks at his sister. That moment was when I became his Bri Bri, and it's been that way ever since. He lives a few hours away in Rose Hill, a small town in Magnolia County, where he's the fire chief. If he isn't busy saving the townsfolk of Rose Hill from fires and rescuing kittens from trees—Leia's description of his job, not mine—he's volunteering at the local community center or building homes for the homeless. Basically, he's the male version of Mother Theresa—again, Leia's description, not mine.

"That's not the only way, but it helps. You know I love hanging out with your family, so leaving the house is an easy decision. If you were forcing me to go to a bar or on a double date, that would be a different story," I make my way down the driveway toward her car. "But just for that, you can drive."

"As if you weren't going to make me drive anyway."

"True." I snort before stopping suddenly. "If this is just a dinner with the famjam, why did you have me put on a fashion show and go through so many outfits?"

Leia's cheeks turn bright pink before she scurries to the other side of the car. "Look. We really need to get going."

"Leia. What are you up to?" I question as she ducks into the car, and I pull the passenger door open and climb in.

"This is the first time Walker has been home in months, and he decided it would be a good idea to host a BBQ to thank the staff for all the extra work they did while Dad was in the hospital."

"That's not the worst idea in the world," I say as she pulls away from the curb and heads toward her dad's place in the hills a few miles outside of town.

Leia's dad grew up on his family farm right outside of Tyson's Creek, but after her parents were married, her mom helped him take things to the next level. It's tucked into the lush and rolling hills just outside of town, but instead of being just a working farm, there's now a warm and inviting inn, spa, and even a rustic farm-to-table restaurant. The story goes that the family farm suffered a drought or something right after Leia's grandfather passed away suddenly from a heart attack, and the family had to survive. It was then that Leia's mom came in with a fresh perspective on things. By turning part of the acres of land into tourist destinations, they could generate revenue for the entire town and save the farm, as well. And the rest is history, as they say.

Now Tranquility Retreat is one of the hottest resort destinations in all of Tennessee. People come from all over the country for a chance to take in the views of the mountains at sunset and learn what it's like to work on a farm at the same time.

"Walker wants to keep it as low stress as possible. He's hoping to have some time to relax while he is home. Work has been very stressful lately."

"How much does he plan on relaxing? I thought he was coming home to help you take care of your dad?"

"He is, but we can't very well tell my dad that." Leia huffs as she turns the corner and heads down the covered bridge road towards the hills outside of town. "If it were up to him, he'd have been right back to tending to his bees the moment we pulled into the driveway."

"Didn't the doctor tell him it was time to slow down? He's almost seventy years old, for goodness' sake. It's not like he's the only person who works at the retreat."

"Yes, he did. I'm just worried that if he doesn't slow down soon, his next heart attack will be his last."

I reach over and give her shoulder a squeeze. "Your dad is as stubborn as a goat, but I doubt he'll do anything to intentionally damage his health."

"Maybe. Maybe not. If he would keep his behind in the office instead of trying to follow everyone around like he's still thirty years old, that would be amazing."

"We both know that won't happen anytime soon. Not unless he gives up some of his control over the business."

Leia has been begging her dad to retire since his last health scare a few months ago. The man is almost seventy years old. Any sane person would have retired by now, but Mr. Armstrong just won't let go. He still wakes up every morning to feed the cattle, check the fields, and do all the daily chores that need to be taken care of. They have plenty of staff with the tourist season being in full swing, so there is no need for him to be out on the grounds as much as he is. Leia has tried a million different things to convince him to take it easy and focus more on the admin side of the business, but he refuses, much to her chagrin.

The only person Mr. Armstrong seems to listen to is Walker, which, to me, makes no sense. He's the oldest, but he doesn't live here anymore and has no intention of moving back to town. Walker has a life and career in Rose Hill. I highly doubt he's going to give that up to come run the family farm, especially when Leia has been taking care of it since her mom passed away after we graduated from college.

"Maybe Walker can help you convince him to finally retire and turn the place over to you. You practically manage the entire operation on your own anyway."

"From your mouth to the Lord's ears. But that's not the reason for the fashion show..."

My eyes narrow as I stare at her, waiting for her to speak before turning and pinching her side.

"Bitch! That fucking hurt!" she whines, the car swerving slightly to the right as she flinches away from me. "You could've caused an accident!"

"There's no one on the road. Now tell me what's going on." I cross my arms over my chest before turning my entire body in her direction and waiting for her to answer.

"Walker invited Brady, Seth, and the bane of my existence, also known as Riggs Monroe, tonight."

"Oh," I whisper, trying not to let Leia know how much this news affects me. "Aren't Brady and Seth leaving on deployment again soon?"

"Yeah, they're shipping out in two weeks. Beckett's parents are having a huge going away party for them next weekend."

"That's great." I force a smile. "I'm sure everyone is going to miss them."

"Some more than others, I'm sure," Leia responds knowingly, causing my head to whip in her direction.

"Don't start with me." I huff before turning my entire body toward the door, hopefully ending the conversation.

Seth Williams is the last man I should be interested in, but apparently, my heart didn't get the memo. I met Seth and Brady before I finished my certification and opened Nurture Space about a month ago. I was working to get my instructor certification, and Walker, being my pseudo-big brother, took it upon himself to invite anyone who was available to help.

Brady, Riggs, and Walker played on the football team together during high school. However, instead of moving on to become a firefighter like Walker and Riggs, Brady joined the military, and that's where he met Seth. Which, for me, was a huge red flag. I promised myself I'd never date a military man, and until meeting Seth, I never thought about it. However, now I may be having second thoughts.

The moment I laid eyes on Seth, I was a goner. My eyes kept drifting to wherever he was in the room, attempting to commit everything about that moment to memory. The way the sun created a warm glow on his russet brown skin as I strolled through the door. The way his white T-shirt and dark-colored sweatpants hugged every part of his body as if they were painted onto him.

Ever since that day, my dreams have been filled with images of his soulful brown eyes, chiseled jawline covered in black-haired stubble, muscular build, and the most breathtaking smile. I spent nights wondering if there was a difference in texture between the skin on his bald head versus his face and arms. I know those are strange things to think about, but this is where I'm at. Seth Williams makes me think and want strange things. Thankfully, he is leaving town soon on deployment, which will put an end to these delusions.

"I'm not starting anything, Bristol. I just think you should give Seth a chance. He seems to be a nice guy and is completely gone over you."

"He barely knows me," I mumble, wanting to end this conversation as quickly as possible.

"That's easy to fix." She flashed me a knowing smile.

She isn't wrong. Every time we are near each other, Seth asks me questions. It's as if he wants to learn everything there is to know about me as soon as possible. At first, I tried to keep him at arm's length, letting him know there was no way we were ever going to be anything more than friends, but that's been almost impossible. The more time we spend together, the stronger the pull I feel to be near him gets, making it almost impossible to stay away from him. But I have to. There is no other choice. I refuse to come second in my significant other's life. I want to be the center of their universe. The sun to their moon, and there's no way that will ever be possible with someone who's in the military.

"I don't have time to date, let alone start a relationship with someone who's leaving in a few weeks."

"Who said anything about a relationship?" Leia quips. "There's nothing wrong with two grown adults blowing off some steam together. And what better person to choose than someone who is leaving town in a few weeks?"

I guffaw, which causes Leia to scowl in my direction as we pull up to a red light at the edge of town. "Look. I get you have issues with the military, but not all men are like your father. From what Brady has been saying, this deployment will be their last. No more deployments."

"I'll consider being more than friends with Seth if you stop giving Riggs such a hard time. Anyone can see that he's head over heels in love with you."

I know this is a sore spot for Leia, but desperate times call for desperate measures. Leia and Riggs have had this love-hate relationship ever since I've known them. Everyone else can see how much he cares about her, but I doubt either of them has noticed yet. Seeing these two interact is like watching a little boy pick on the girl he secretly has a crush on.

"Whose side are you on, anyway?" Leia scowls in my direction as she pulls into the long drive leading towards the family portion of the property.

"Yours. Always yours. I'm just saying that maybe if you were nicer to him sometimes, he wouldn't give you such a hard time."

"Bristol, I doubt that's even possible for him at this point. Riggs has been giving me a hard time since we were teenagers, and I don't see that ending soon. It's like he gets a sick thrill out of pushing my buttons."

"Some people might call that foreplay," I retort as Leia pulls her car to a stop in front of her dad's farmhouse, tucked into a corner of the property.

A large covered wraparound porch takes up almost the entire front of the house with a porch swing positioned to give you the perfect view of the sun setting over the mountains when you sit there. It's a warm butter yellow color with white framed windows practically covering the front of it and a manicured garden with perfectly trimmed bushes and a bright array of flowers, which gives it an even more welcoming feel.

"Well, I just call it fucking annoying." Leia sighs as I feel my door fly open, and a powerful set of arms comes around my waist, lifting me out of the car and into the air.

My entire body tenses for a moment until the smell of vanilla and sandalwood invades my senses, and the soft hairs of a beard rub against my cheek, causing me to relax. "Hey, Walker."

I giggle before lifting my legs to wrap around his muscular waist and throw my arms tightly around his neck. I use every muscle in my body to squeeze him tightly to me before leaning back and resting my chin on his chest. Walker hasn't changed a bit since he came back to town a few months ago. His dark brown hair is styled perfectly to give it that just-out-of-bed look without being too messy. His cerulean blue eyes are bright with happiness as he plants a kiss on my forehead.

"How's my Bri Bri doing?"

"You could at least let her get out of the car first." Leia groans as she smacks my captor hard on the shoulder, causing him to chuckle softly.

"I could, but I know the moment she and Seth lay eyes on each other, they'll be in their own little world."

My cheeks burn instantly as I unwrap my legs from around his waist and wiggle in his grasp. It only takes a few moments for him to realize what I want before he lowers my feet to the ground. It seems everyone has picked up on my attraction to Seth, which can lead to nothing good. I know they mean well, but pushing Seth and me together is a bad idea. He has his career, and I have my business to focus on. Neither one of us can pick up and move to be with the other.

Sure, long-distance relationships are a thing and work for many people, but I refuse to be second in the relationship. My mom used to kid around and say if the military wanted my dad to have a family, they would have issued him one with his uniform. Which may have worked for her, but not me. No matter how much my heart might want Seth, there's no way I can let that happen.

"Stop being so dramatic." I huff before taking a step away from him. I'm average height for a woman at 5'5", but Walker towers over me. I look more like a toddler standing near him than the thirty-two-year-old woman I am. "What the heck have they been feeding you, Walker? I thought people were supposed to stop growing in their twenties."

"I haven't grown at all. Maybe you're shrinking in your old age." Walker pats me on the head twice before

I swat at him. "And I'm not being dramatic, and you know it. When are you going to give Seth a chance?"

"Bristol doesn't have time for men right now. She's focusing on turning her business into a success," Leia says before wrapping her arms around his waist in a quick hug.

"And I don't recall Walker asking you." Riggs saunters down the front steps toward us, a devious smile spreading across his face.

"I don't recall speaking to you."

"Here we go again." I groan before pushing my door closed with my butt and leaning against it. There's no telling how long we could be out here for one of Riggs and Leia's verbal sparring matches.

Walker leans against the car beside me before crossing his arms over his chest. "I really wish there was a way to get my two favorite people to get along with each other."

Riggs's chocolate brown eyes sparkle with amusement as he stares down at Leia, a mischievous smirk plastered across his face. His muscular body leans slightly forward, as if there's a magnet pulling him closer to her. If it were anyone else, I would step in, saving my best from the torment, but Riggs is different.

"I was fine until he opened his mouth and started speaking," Leia retorts as she lifts her chin slightly and glares at Riggs.

Leia can't stand Riggs for some reason only the two of them know. Although, I have a feeling Walker knows, because why else would he keep forcing these two together? Whenever I ask her, I get a vague answer about him being immature and annoying, but never anything more. There must be some sort of history between those two, but after all these years, I've stopped trying to figure it out. If they want to fight with each other like children, so be it. However, I have a feeling that they don't hate each other as much as they'd prefer for all of us to believe.

"You have a thing for mutes? If I had known, I'd have cut out my tongue and given it to you as a peace offering years ago."

"I hate you."

"You love me; you just haven't figured it out yet." Riggs snickers, wrapping his arm around her shoulder and pulling her to his side.

Leia's entire body melts into his embrace as her eyes drift shut. For a few moments, she looks like she is in pure heaven, but then her face morphs into what looks like indifference before she pushes away from him. "I'm going to go check on Dad."

"He's inside on the couch. I asked him to stay inside until we got the fire going. It's supposed to get chilly tonight," Walker replies as Leia pushes off the car, and we all follow her toward the front door.

"Of course, all you had to do was ask. If I were here, it would have turned into World War III."

"That's mostly because I ask. You demand."

"Suck-up."

"Now, now, children. Can't we all just get along?" Riggs laughs as Walker bypasses the door and heads down the wraparound porch, disappearing around the right side of the house.

"Shut up, Riggs," Leia snaps back before pulling the screen door open and stepping inside.

"If you're trying to get her to like you, this isn't the best way," I say, just loud enough for him to hear me.

"Oh, I know, but it sure is fun." Riggs smirks at me before holding the door open and allowing me to step inside. "Walker and I will get the grill started. Have fun, you two."

I smile at Riggs before stepping through the door right into the main portion of the house. There is no entryway to this house, just a great room filled with cozy-looking furniture and a grand fireplace tucked into the back of the room. There are small groups of people scattered around the room, but my eyes are searching for one person. After a few moments, I find Seth sitting on the arm of the cream-colored loveseat positioned near the fireplace.

"Aren't you going to say hi?" Leia whispers into my ear, causing me to jump slightly.

"He's having a conversation with your dad," I

mumble, my eyes shifting toward Mr. Armstrong, who is animatedly talking to Seth about something.

"No, he is humoring my dad, waiting for you to come inside so he can whisk you away."

"I doubt that very much," I reply as Seth and my eyes lock with each other, and he pushes to his feet, striding toward me.

Seth is about the same size as Walker, but instead of every part of him seeming oversized, he has a leaner build. His broad shoulders fill out a dark-colored T-shirt that looks as if it were painted onto his body. My eyes continue to make their way down his body, taking in the way his jeans hug his legs before stopping at his black leather boots, tucked neatly beneath his jeans.

"Close your mouth, Bristol," Leia giggles as I snap my mouth closed moments before he comes to a stop in front of us.

"Hello, Bristol." His gravelly voice sends a shiver down my spine as my cheeks heat in embarrassment.

"Hi," I respond breathily, trying to calm my heart pounding behind my rib cage. We stand there for a few moments, the air becoming even more charged between us as I try to list all the reasons starting anything with Seth is a bad idea.

Seth is a Marine.

He is deploying in two weeks with no promise of return.

The Marines will always be his first love.

These are all excellent reasons why any type of relationship with Seth is a bad idea, but my heart has other plans. Maybe Leia is right. One night to get him out of my system should be enough. We can go our separate ways when he leaves, no harm, no foul. However, the little voice in my head keeps telling me that whatever this is between Seth and me is for more than one night. These are forever kind of feelings, but forever isn't in the cards for us.

The sound of Leia's voice brings me back to the present as she wraps her arm around my shoulder. "Hello to you, too, Seth. I forgive you for being so wrapped up in our girl to forget I was standing here."

"How can anyone forget you, Leia?" Seth's eyes sparkle in amusement as he says in a husky voice, "How have you been?"

"Great. How about you? Are you ready to leave for deployment?"

Seth's entire demeanor changes. The playful smirk that was on his face a few minutes ago disappears. "If it were up to me, I'd stay right here in Tyson's Creek and never leave."

My eyes widen in surprise as I notice the truth in Seth's words shining in his eyes. Seth and I have been doing this dance around each other for months now. Sure, we've flirted and spent more time talking to each other than our friends when we were together, but this is the first time he has even hinted at there being something permanent between us.

No, that can't be what he meant. Just because he wants to stay here in Tyson's Creek doesn't mean I'm the reason. He's told me several times that Brady and his parents are the closest thing he has to family. Of course, he'd want to stay here in Tyson's Creek to be near them. That can be the only explanation for what he said, right?

"It was great catching up, but I really should go check on Walker and Riggs at the grill. If I leave them unsupervised for too long, all the food will be ruined," Leia said.

"Please don't leave me alone with him," I murmur in Leia's direction, causing her to burst out laughing.

"Don't mind her. Sometimes the brain-to-mouth filter isn't fully engaged." Leia flashes Seth a bright smile before motioning toward the backyard. "Seth, do you mind grabbing some steaks out of the fridge and taking them outside? I'm gonna check on my dad one more time, and I'll be right behind you."

"Sure thing. It was nice seeing you again, Bristol." Seth smirks at me, then heads out the back door.

"That man is head over heels for you," Leia says as she pretends to fan herself.

I roll my eyes at her. "I don't know what you're talking about. Let's go say hello to your dad."

I try to focus on making it over to the couch, where Mr. Armstrong is sitting, without tripping over my feet, but I can feel Seth watching me as I walk past the French doors leading to the deck. His gaze caresses my skin as it travels down my body, like he's trying to commit my features to memory.

"He's just another pretty face. He isn't the first and won't be the last," I mumble quietly to myself as I take a seat on the couch beside Mr. Armstrong.

I'm not a bad-looking woman by any means, so Seth isn't the first man to find appeal in the way I look, but there is something about the way he looks at me that's different. It's as if he can see me, see my soul, not just the superficial parts most men search for.

"Are you sure you don't need anything?"

My head snaps to the right at the sound of Leia's voice. I watch her fuss over her dad, asking if he's warm enough or if we can get him anything, being her usual mothering self. However, Mr. Armstrong isn't having any of that.

"I said I was fine, Sugarplum. Don't worry so much."

"I'll always worry about you, Dad."

"It's my job to worry about you, not the other way around." He huffs, crossing his arms over his chest, which causes me to giggle softly.

My eyes instantly wander back toward the French doors, locking with Seth's over Riggs's shoulder. I lick my bottom lip as I watch him lift a beer toward his mouth and wink. The temperature in the room seems to go up a few degrees as we continue to stare at each other. Neither of us dare to look away. It's just like the first time we met. All the sounds in the room seem to disappear, making it feel like we are the only two people in the universe.

What the fuck is wrong with me?

I've never had such a visceral reaction to a man, no matter how gorgeous he is. But with Seth, it's different somehow. He calls to me in a way no other man ever has with just one look. It's as if my soul has finally found its other half.

Why the hell does he have to be in the military?

I know most people would think this is a ridiculous reason to keep distance between Seth and me. Especially since the chemistry between us is undeniable. But growing up, it was just me and my younger sister, Melissa, until Audrey moved in with us. My mom did try to be there for us and anticipate everything we needed but my dad was never around, choosing his military career over everything else. Sure, I get it. He has a job to protect our country. To make it safe for everyone, but what about our family? What about what we wanted and what was best for us?

We moved every couple of years, making it almost impossible to make friends or put down roots anywhere. With my dad being gone so much, he reminded me it was my responsibility as the oldest to help my mom hold down the fort when he was deployed, which was pretty much all the time. I had to help my sister with her homework, keep my grades up, and practically be the perfect child to ensure my mom had no added stress in her life. That's a lot of shit to put on the shoulders of a little girl, and it took me a long time and a lot of therapy to realize that it wasn't my responsibility. Sure, I should have been there to help my mom and sister when they needed it, but I was still a little girl. I had responsibilities to my family, but I also needed a chance to just be a kid. To make mistakes and learn from them.

This is one of the main reasons my father and I aren't as close as we used to be. He was supposed to protect us, just like he vowed to do for everyone else in the country, but he put pressure on me to be perfect. Gave me the impression that I needed to become an adult long before my time in order to be there for my family, practically robbing me of the chance to be a child for as long as possible. I know my father loved all of us, but he loved being in the military more, and that's a very hard pill to swallow. I refuse to be second fiddle in my relationship, so why even bother seeing where things between Seth and I could go?

"When are you going to stop kidding yourself, Bristol?"

"Huh?" My cheeks heat again as a deep chuckle

filters in through the open window. I narrow my eyes at Seth before turning my entire body toward Leia so I can focus on what she's saying to me.

"You haven't heard a thing I've said, have you?"

I open my mouth to answer before snapping it shut. Sure, I could try and lie to her, but what's the point? "Nope. Not a thing," I reply with a smile, causing her to giggle softly.

"Just talk to him and see where things go." Leia lays her hand on my shoulder, giving it a squeeze before spinning me around and shoving me toward the French doors. "Yes, he is a Marine, but he isn't your dad."

"I don't know..." My voice trails off slightly as I spin around to face Leia. I pull my bottom lip between my teeth as I try to find the right word to explain my hesitancy. "Seth has the potential to be more than just a fling, and I don't know if my heart can take being second in his life."

"Wow. Okay," Leia's eyes widening in surprise before she wraps me in a tight hug. "But what if you do nothing?"

"Then I can protect my heart from being broken," I reply quickly, not understanding where she's going with this.

She pulls away from me. A soft smile spreads across her face as she takes a step back. "And you could regret it for the rest of your life."

"I..." I begin, but Leia covers my mouth with her hand.

"Nope, it's my time to talk. I've never once heard you talk about someone of the opposite sex like this. You've had flings, but that's it. You've never worried about getting hurt or about what would happen when things went badly."

Leia is right. I've been dreaming about the perfect man to sweep me off my feet. Someone who will make me the center of their universe and the most important person in their life. Because of those dreams, you can imagine how hard it's been for me to date anyone. I've gone on dates and had my fair share of one-night stands, but nothing that lasted more than a few months at the most. I was always the one to break things off with them for a multitude of reasons, but mainly because I didn't feel that spark with any of them. The all-consuming need to be near them every chance I got. The same feeling I've felt any time I've been in the same room as Seth Williams.

"You can't spend the rest of your life worried about being hurt or you'll miss out on that great love you've been dreaming of. The chance for you to be the center of someone's entire universe."

"You're right, but there's no way I can find that with someone who's in the military. Besides, the last thing I need is to get tangled up with a man that I've only known for a few months."

"Maybe not, but sometimes fate has other plans," Leia laughs before grabbing my hand and pulling me toward the French doors.

I don't know what the hell I'm going to do about my attraction to Seth, but everything about him spells trouble.

three

seth

"Are you planning on talking to her, or just staring at her all night?" Brady slaps me hard on the back before handing me another beer.

"A little of column A and a little of column B," I retort, causing him to snicker.

I've been watching Bristol flitter around the party, running in and out of the house to make sure no one needs anything. At first, I thought she was trying to ignore me, especially after the way she practically ran away after saying hello, but now I'm not so sure. I watch as she throws her head back and laughs at something Vance says, letting out peals of laughter. If I didn't already know Vance was still head over heels in love with his high school sweetheart, Selina Grimes, I'd be beyond jealous of their interaction with each other.

"You've got it bad." Riggs shakes his head as he grabs a beer from the cooler beside me.

"As if you're one to talk," I snap back, motioning toward Leia as she comes through the French doors and strolls past us. Her eyes instantly narrow as she spots Riggs standing next to me before making a beeline toward Bristol and Vance.

"I know." Riggs sighs, taking a healthy pull from his beer. "But at least I've attempted to talk to Leia a few times tonight. It just didn't go as planned. It never does."

I nod my head in agreement as I think about both of our predicaments. Riggs and I are gone for girls who refuse to give us the time a day. However, instead of trying to have another conversation with Bristol, I've been standing here for over an hour, mesmerized by Bristol's arms waving in the air while she talks with Leia. No matter where I am in the house, I find myself attuned to her every movement.

"I talked to her, but I can't figure out how to convince her to let me in. She apparently has an issue with guys in the military, but I have a feeling there's more to it than that."

"No matter what her reason is, if you hurt her, we hurt you." Riggs stares down the length of his bottle before taking another sip. "Bristol is like a little sister to Walker and me, and we protect our own," he says, and I take a sip of my beer.

"Message received loud and clear, but I need to get her on board first."

"Are you sure it's the military thing?" Brady asks, his eyebrows pulling down. "Could it be an age thing? You're almost five years older than her."

"Chicks dig older men," Riggs replies without missing a beat, causing me to chuckle.

"I don't think our age difference is that big of a deal. She specifically told me she didn't date people in the military. She wants to be the most important person in someone's life, and for a Marine, the military always comes first."

"Once a Marine, always a Marine," Brady replies, taking another sip of his beer.

"Yeah, that's true, but it doesn't have to be my whole life forever. Eventually, I want to get out, settle down, and start a family."

"With Bristol," Riggs chimes in, motioning toward Bristol and Leia standing on the other side of the deck.

"What?"

"With Bristol. You want all those things with Bristol, right?"

"Maybe? I barely know her." I reach back, gripping the back of my neck, knowing I'm full of shit. I've been able to see my entire future with Bristol playing out before my eyes since we met a few months ago. I can't imagine doing any of these things with anyone but her.

"Sure, but that doesn't mean a damn thing, and you know it. How's that saying go? *The heart wants what it wants*, or something like that, right?"

"Something like that, I guess, but no matter how much I want her, she has to want me back for things to go anywhere between us."

"Now that's the easy part. Try being charming. Ladies dig that." Riggs winks as he strides toward Leia and Bristol. I follow behind him, wanting to be closer to Bristol. As I get closer, I hear the tail end of their conversation.

"You know what you need?" Leia says as she notices us approaching. "A one-night stand. A good, hard fuck with an insanely attractive Marine."

I shake my head at her antics. "What are you, my pimp now?"

"How do you know she was talking about you?" Riggs questions as he flashes the girls another smile, taking the time to wink at Leia for good measure.

"Do you see any other attractive Marines around?"

"Brady isn't too bad looking," Leia giggles, motioning toward Brady bending down to grab another beer out of the cooler. "I'm sure he knows how to treat a woman right in bed."

Riggs throws his arm over Leia's shoulder, pulls her tightly against him, and whispers, "I doubt Brady has what you're looking for."

Leia's cheeks instantly flush as she licks her bottom lip before she shoves him hard, causing him to stumble backward slightly. "Pig."

"You're the one who brought it up, and I aim to

please, Leia. Always." He winks at her before she storms off toward the house.

"She's probably going to ask Walker if he'll come kick your ass," Bristol snickers.

"Probably, but totally worth it," Riggs replies before he follows Leia, no doubt thinking of some way to push her buttons again, leaving Bristol and me alone.

We stare at the beautiful scenery surrounding the Armstrongs' home. The sun is setting behind the hills, giving the sky a pink hue. This would be the perfect opportunity to talk to her, to figure out exactly what her hang-up is about exploring things between us, but my mind is completely blank.

"Beautiful, isn't it?" Bristol murmurs, bringing my mind back to the present.

"It is," My eyes lock on her as I step closer, cupping her cheek and turning her face toward me. "You're the most beautiful woman I've ever seen."

"Seth." She whispers my name, sending shock waves of need down my body as I lean toward her.

"Bristol." I bury my nose into the crook of her neck. My senses are bombarded with the reminder of the first day of spring, a scent that is specific to her. Who could imagine that a simple smell could set my senses on fire? Bristol is the most gorgeous woman I have ever laid eyes on. Now, if I could just convince her how amazing we would be together, everything would be perfect.

"This can't be normal," she mumbles as I step further into her personal space.

She takes a step back, bumping into the railing.

"Nowhere to run." I lick my lips, barely resisting the urge to claim her mouth as I grip the railing, caging her in with my arms, bringing my face within inches of her rose-colored lips. "You feel it, don't you?"

Her emerald-green eyes flutter closed as my breath fans across her face. I hear her whimper as I grind my cock into her stomach, letting her know just how much I want her. A smile from her is all it takes to send fireworks shooting off in my body and make every cell yearn to bury my cock between her folds.

"You want me, don't you?" I run my nose down the curve of her neck, nipping at her porcelain flesh.

She doesn't say a word. She just wraps her arms around my neck and pulls me tighter to her body. I can feel her pebbled nipples through her shirt as they brush against my chest.

"I need to hear the words. Tell me what you want and it's yours." I pull her ear between my teeth, nibbling on it softly.

"Kiss me," she begs.

Fucking finally. I send up a prayer of thanks as I devour her mouth, nipping at her bottom lip until she grants me access. Our tongues connect, and we both moan in pleasure as I slide my hand into her hair, pulling her head back for better access.

When we break apart, both desperate for air, I stare into her eyes, waiting for her to tell me she needs me. That I'm the only person in the world who can quench the burning desire coursing through her body. I can see that she wants me too, but until I hear the words, I won't touch her. I want her to give herself to me freely and completely, putting us both out of our misery once and for all.

"I have to go," she murmurs before brushing past me and scurrying back into the house.

I know it would be easier for both of us. Give us both space to get our libido under control, but I can't. Not this time. There's something between Bristol and me, and I know she can feel it. I'd give my dying breath to have a shot with her, to show her how amazing we'd be together, even if only for one night. One night together to survive the next year before I get out of the military. But let's be honest; I'm willing to take whatever she'll give me. And then I'll show her how amazing we could be together. That I'd do anything to see her smile and for her to be the last person I see at night and the first person I see in the morning.

Having made up my mind, I follow Bristol into the house, completely ignoring our friends as they call my name. I watch her go through the kitchen, heading toward the back of the house where Leia's room is. Right before she's able to slip into the room, I grasp her wrist, pulling her towards me. I wrap my arms tightly around her waist before leaning down and whispering in her ear. "You need to stop running away from me, Bristol."

"I'm not running from anything," she growls, wriggling in my arms, trying to get free. "I just needed a minute."

"A minute for what?" I ask, spinning her around and forcing her to look at me.

"Why does it matter to you so much?" Bristol's pupils dilate as I inch closer to her, pressing my body into hers while she backs into the door. She wants me. This. Us.

"Why are you resisting this thing between us so hard? And don't give me a bullshit line about it being because I'm a Marine. There must be something more to it than that." I lean down, running my nose along her ear. "You want whatever this is between us, Bristol. I know it. Whether it's just for tonight or forever is up to you. But you can't deny the connection between us."

"I don't know what you're talking about, Seth. I find you attractive. Who wouldn't? But that's it," she concedes as I step closer to her, grinding my cock into her soft belly.

"I can make you scream," I whisper, nibbling my way down her neck.

She groans softly and arches her back. "You seem mighty full of yourself, Seth."

"I'd give you the world if you'd let me." I lift my

head and rest it against her forehead, inhaling her intoxicating scent. "You drive me insane without even trying."

"The same could be said about you, too," she taunts, smirking at me.

I can't take it anymore; I need to have her. I don't care that we're standing in front of her friend's bedroom or that anyone could come down the hallway and see us. I need her like my next breath. The yearning to feel the softness of her skin against my fingers fills my veins. I know she is afraid, but I don't know why. I should slow down, talk to her more, and find out why she is so hesitant about there being anything more between us, but I don't think I can. I know in my heart that there's something here between us, but the need to be near her slowly overwhelms me.

I swipe my thumb across her cheek, her skin feeling like silk beneath my calloused fingers. I stare into her eyes, committing this moment to memory.

"I don't think this is a good idea," she mumbles as I thread my fingers into her hair, pulling her closer.

"You'll never know until you try," I growl through clenched teeth, barely hanging on to my last bit of control.

"Please," she breathes before leaning in again and capturing my lips, finally putting an end to the longest game of foreplay I have ever taken part in.

I devour her mouth, nibbling and sucking on her

bottom lip until she opens for me, and we both give in to our desire. I get lost in the sensation of her lips and hands touching me.

"Seth," she moans as we break apart, gasping for air.

I lean forward, nibbling on her earlobe before whispering into her ear. "We can go slow. Get to know each other. All you have to do is say yes." I grip her leg tightly, wrapping it around my waist. "It will take an enormous amount of effort, but I'll turn around and walk back down the hallway and leave you be. I'll say goodbye to our friends and find where to take a freezing cold shower. But if you say yes, we're going to go back to your place, and you will let me worship your body. I plan to feel your pussy clenching around my cock before the end of the night."

I punctuate every phrase by thrusting my hard length into her core, rocking back and forth as the tip slides across her clit.

"We shouldn't," she moans as she wraps her arms around my neck, pulling me closer to her so I can feel her hardened nipples rubbing against my shirt.

"We should," I breathe.

Bristol's head drops back with a soft thump as it hits the door. I lean down and capture her ear between my lips, rubbing the lobe between my teeth. "I want to taste you more than my next breath. To feel your skin beneath my fingers. To wake up next to you in the morning."

"Yes," she finally whispers.

I waste no time lifting her in my arms and taking her lips with mine once again. My eyes travel her body, noticing her oversized shirt hanging off one shoulder, her mussed hair from my fingers, and her flushed cheeks. At this moment, she's the most captivating woman in the world.

I thought I had feelings for Bristol before, but at this moment, looking at her pressed against my body, ready to give herself over to me, I know this is more than just falling. I'm in love with her.

"You're beautiful," I say reverently, wanting to say something to convey my feelings toward her, the words I want to say on the tip of my tongue.

"You don't need to say that," Bristol brushing her lips against my neck.

"I don't say things I don't mean. When I say you're the most beautiful woman I've ever laid eyes on, I mean it." I slide my hands under her ass, gripping the apple-shaped globes tightly in my hands before grinding my cock into the seam of her pants.

"Fuck," she moans loudly, grinding herself onto my cock, causing it to harden further.

"Hey, have you seen Bristol? I can't... Oh." Leia's words stop as she stands frozen in place, just a few feet away.

"I knew this was a bad idea," Bristol mutters as she tries to unwrap herself from around me, but I'm not about to let her go.

I tighten my hold on Bristol before turning towards Leia. "We were just leaving."

"Okay. I'll tell Brady to find his own way home." Leia winks at me as I turn on my heels and stride down the hallway towards the front door.

I send up a silent prayer of thanks that the party has thinned out and there's no one sitting in the living room to witness our hasty exit. I quickly make my way toward my car as I click the unlock button, then wrench the door open before dropping Bristol into the passenger seat.

"Thank you," she replies, barely above a whisper, but I hear her.

"Having second thoughts?"

"I can't promise you anything more than tonight, Seth."

"I'll take it." I grasp her neck and pull her toward me, sealing our lips together in a searing kiss.

She may not be ready to admit her feelings for me, but they're there, and we both know it. I need to prove to her she means so much more to me than just a quick roll in the sack. I know there is a bigger reason she is so weary of starting something more with me. Maybe she was hurt badly in the past. Maybe it could just be that she isn't a fan of guys in the military. Either way, I need to figure out how to make her see that being a Marine is not my entire world. That it will be nothing more than a distant memory after this next deployment. Especially now that I have her. Just being near her completes me in a way I didn't know was possible. Now the only thing I need to do is convince her to take a chance on me. Not a hard task, not at all.

four

seth

six months later

I hit *end call* on the satellite phone I've been using.

"Maybe next time," I mumble to no one as I push off my bunk and head toward the mess hall.

There's been an ache in my heart ever since I deployed. I spend most of my time missing the only person I've ever given my heart to. Sure, we only spent one night together, but that night meant everything to me. I knew the moment the sun came streaming through the window that morning that my heart would only ever belong to her.

When Brady asked me to attend a yoga class to help a friend of his, I scoffed at the idea. Attending a yoga class, let alone any type of fitness class, never crossed my mind. Give me a couple of free weights and a treadmill and I'm good. But something deep in my soul told me I'd regret it if I didn't go, so I reluctantly agreed. And I'm glad I did because that day I found that thing—or, better yet, that *person*—I've been missing in my life. I knew the moment I laid eyes on Bristol that she was entirely too good for me. Her long red hair and brilliant smile could light up a room, but her eyes captivated me. When she looked at me, it was as if she was looking into the deepest parts of me, setting my soul ablaze for the first time in my life.

After that, I always found an excuse to head to Tyson's Creek with Brady. He knew something was going on but never once made a big deal out of it. He seemed just as eager to head home to Tyson's Creek as I was. It might have something to do with the beautiful girl I saw him with at his going away party before we left to head over to the sandbox for the next year. I'm pretty sure that something happened between them that night, but he hasn't said a word about it. I wish he would talk to me, but who am I to give advice to anyone about relationships?

The connection I feel toward her has only grown stronger since I woke up that morning. The moment I laid eyes on Bristol Reid, I knew she was someone special. The more time we spent together, and the more I got to know her, I could see our future playing out before my eyes. Bristol is the type of woman I can see myself settling down and starting a family with. When we are together, all my worries and troubles turn into nothing but background noise.

It took me months to get Bristol to admit the attraction we felt toward each other. To give me a chance to show her she meant the world to me, even if there was no guarantee that I'd return. I knew deep in my soul that if I didn't find out how delicious she tasted as I licked the salty sweat from her skin, or how it felt to have her pressed tightly to me as she moaned my name, I'd regret it for the rest of my life. However, now that I know all those things, the idea of never having them again tears me in two.

Bristol wanted one night together, no strings attached, but to me, it was so much more. I knew I was shipping out in a few weeks, but it didn't matter to me. I wanted—no, needed—to know everything I could about Bristol, or I'd have regretted it for the rest of my life.

"Finally decided to join the land of the living?"

The only response I give Brady is a grunt as I grab a tray and begin piling on food.

"So talkative today." He rolls his eyes as I head toward a table in the back.

I've known nothing but being a Marine, having signed up as soon as I was old enough. Being a ward of the state helped me cut through a lot of the red tape, making it easy to enlist a few months before my eighteenth birthday. Ever since my parents died when I was eight years old, I bounced around between foster homes, each one making the hope of finding a family a little more impossible, before being placed in a group home my freshman year of high school. I was old enough to take care of myself, and as long as I stayed out of trouble, they left me alone. Being part of the system taught me to keep my head down, but I always yearned to be a part of a family once again.

"Seriously, man. Who pissed in your Wheaties?" Brady asks, breaking me from my thoughts as he takes a seat across from me in the mess hall.

"Just trying to figure out what the hell I want to do when my contract is up," I mumble as I shove another bite of food into my mouth.

I've spent the last two decades in the Marines, trying to find my place in the world. I've traveled across the world fighting for my country, which gave me a sense of belonging for the first time since my parents passed away. But I always felt like something was missing. There was a part of me that was still searching for that one thing that would bring me back to life.

"You could always come home with me," he responds matter-of-factly, as if he hasn't just handed me my heart's desire on a silver platter. "My dad told me they're looking for guys at the station. Since we're in the military, all we have to do is pass the civil service exam and then attend the academy. Nothing too hard."

Having no family of my own, I had nowhere to go

during leave periods or holidays, so ever since I met him, Brady has always invited me to join his family. But I had no way of knowing that this last trip would change the direction of my life forever.

"Maybe." I try to remain calm as images of reuniting with Bristol again filter through my mind. She told me we couldn't be anything more because she couldn't live with not knowing if she was the most important person to me. That if given the choice, I'd choose her over everything else. Maybe this is my chance. "But don't you have to wait for a date to open?"

"Yeah, but I doubt you'd have to wait too long. Besides, maybe you could work at Ace & Hammer construction company with me until a spot opens at the station," Brady suggests.

I met Vance and Connor, the owners of Ace & Hammer, a few times during my visits to Tyson's Creek. Brady and I are a few years older than them, but it seems everyone in Tyson's Creek is friends or at least cordial with each other. The same was true for me. Connor and Vance didn't bat an eyelash when Brady brought me home on leave. The three of us became fast friends, much to Brady's delight. They seem like pretty decent guys, but they've both been dealt a pretty shitty hand in life.

Vance and Connor started a construction business after Brady enlisted in the Marines. They both started taking business classes while they worked on building their company from scratch. Since they were one of the few construction businesses in the area, they started small, keeping their prices affordable and working off word-of-mouth referrals, but their business really exploded after doing a job in Magnolia. I guess tearing an old farmhouse down to the studs and rebuilding most of it in about a week is good for business.

After getting to know each other better, Vance offered me a job. He said any friend of Brady's was a friend of theirs. At the time, I didn't think twice about it, but now, that offer seems even more appealing by the minute.

"What the hell do you know about construction?"

"Enough to get by," he answers quickly. "Honestly, I don't know jack shit either, but after being in the Marines for all these years, we have to do something physical. It's either that or lose our minds from boredom."

I nod in agreement. After being nothing more than a glorified grunt during my time in the Marines, manual labor is something I can get behind. I would even go as far as to say it's something I would excel at. Also, knowing that I am using my hands every day to give someone a place to call their own, something I never had in my life, sounds like the perfect job for me.

"Where am I going to stay?" I question, knowing I

have enough money saved to buy a small house somewhere, but I don't want to make any rash decisions.

"As if my parents will let you stay anywhere but with us. Besides, you can crash with me in the apartment above their garage. It's nothing fancy, but it's more space than we've had in a long while."

The Thomases welcomed me with open arms the first time Brady brought me home during a stand-down, a time of rest and recovery the command gives us after deployment, and they ensure I always feel like part of the family every chance they get. Hell, his mom even sends me care packages over here in the sandbox, claiming she wants to brighten my day just a little more.

"But seriously, where else are you going to go? I'm the only family you have." A mischievous smile crosses his face. "Besides, this will give you a chance to prove to your girl you're not going anywhere."

I made the mistake of telling Brady about what Bristol said after our first meeting. Instead of laughing in my face, he seemed to understand where she was coming from. We spent a few nights racking our brains, trying to find the perfect plan to convince Bristol that she was the most important person in my life, but we always came up empty. Maybe this is my chance.

"Bristol is not my girl," I mutter as I stand up, grab my tray, and turn toward the exit. "She made it perfectly clear she wanted nothing else to do with me after that night."

Brady grasps my shoulder, pulling me to a stop. "But you never told her everything, did you?"

I shake my head, wrenching my arm from his grasp. "She has no idea we're coming home for good in about six months."

"I'm sure someone has told her that we are coming home. Tyson's Creek is a small town; I'm sure someone has said something," he continues.

"That doesn't change anything," I mumble to myself as I empty my tray into the trash and stomp off toward my tent. Thankfully, Brady turns and heads back for the table instead of following me.

Bristol made it perfectly clear that she wanted more than just a man who would come in and out of her life every couple of months. Being a military brat herself, she saw the strain that the military lifestyle put on her mother. However, I've spent the last year thinking about her and how she stole my heart, hoping that when I finally got out of this sandbox, she'd give me a chance to prove to her I was nothing like her father.

"I wish it was that easy," I mumble as I throw the flap to my tent open and flop down on my bed, grabbing the phone that I left lying on my bunk.

I'm tempted once again to dial her number but decide against it, stuffing the phone under my pillow and closing my eyes. Maybe I can grab a quick nap before I have watch in a few hours.

"Damn it, Seth. Stop being so stubborn!" Brady shouts as he smacks my boots and pushes my feet off the side of my bed, then plops down in their place. "I've never known you to give up so easily."

"I make decisions that could cost someone their life almost daily. I have to be sure about them," I growl before sitting up and resting my elbows on my knees.

"Would it kill you to take a chance?"

Brady waits for me to answer, but I remain silent.

"I know how much she means to you. Ever since that party at Tranquility Retreat, you've been different. You've been looking forward to your life after the military."

"What the hell is that supposed to mean?"

"You've never thought about getting out. You've never once said anything about what you wanted to do after retirement until that night. Now you're trying to make plans for the future. Plans that could easily include Bristol if you let them."

"When did you become so fucking demanding, man?" I smirk in his direction.

It's hard to admit that he's right, but I know deep down that he is. Being a Marine is all I have ever known, but since meeting Bristol, I want something more out of life.

"Give that buddy of yours a call. I don't have any

plans for after my contract is up. Might as well keep bothering your ass," I concede.

Brady jumps up and whoops loudly. "I knew you just needed an excuse."

I shake my head and give him a forced smile. "No. I just want more of your mama's cooking."

"Best damn fried catfish you've ever tasted," Brady preens, and my mouth waters, thinking of the fish fry the Thomases had before we left.

"It's the only catfish I've ever tasted."

"Hence why it's the best." Brady slaps me on the back before hurrying out of the tent, probably wanting to call in that favor before I change my mind.

I throw both hands behind my head before leaning back on my bunk and crossing my feet at the ankles. I close my eyes and attempt to imagine what it would be like to run into Bristol again now that time is on our side.

If I managed to find some way to get Bristol back into my life, I could never let her go again, even if I tried. Brady is right; it's just a matter of time before we run into each other. Tyson's Creek is a small town, so we *will* run into each other, eventually. I just have to be patient. Not everyone is given a second chance to make an impression on the woman of their dreams, so I need to seize this opportunity and make the most of it.

I tried to say goodbye to her once, but now our paths are about to cross again. I'm sure she'll be shocked to see me at first, but if I play my cards right, maybe we'll be a couple before the year is out.

"Wishful thinking," I mumble into the empty bunkhouse as I give up on getting a quick nap before watch and decide to head toward the gym.

Maybe Tyson's Creek is where all my dreams will come true... or maybe I'm just setting myself up for another heartbreak.

five

seth

eleven months later

"Seth!" Brady waves his arms over his head as I pull into the driveway at his parents' house. "It's good to see you, man."

He smiles at me as I shut off my truck and open the door, and I step out and give him a manly hug.

"You act like you haven't seen me in forever."

"After waking up next to your ugly mug every day for the last five years, I welcomed the alone time," he quips.

"Aww, you missed me." I slap him on the back and slam my door shut. "How did you survive this long without me?"

"It was easy." He smirks.

It's been almost four months since we arrived back stateside and started our out-processing from the Marines. Since I didn't officially put my retirement paperwork in until halfway through our deployment, it took me a little longer to get things settled. Now I'm a civilian and ready to get settled into my new life in

Tyson's Creek, which I'm hoping will also include a beautiful redhead whom I'm already head over heels for.

We both chuckle as he throws his arm over my shoulder and leads me toward the house.

"You're just in time for lunch. Mama has been cooking up a storm since I told her you were getting here today," he tells me.

I smile as the screen door slams behind me.

"You're here!" Mrs. Thomas squeals as we round the corner to the kitchen, quickly wiping her hands on a towel before opening her arms. "Now come and give me a hug."

"Thanks for having me, ma'am," I say as she wraps her arms around my waist and squeezes. Standing at a little over five feet tall, she barely comes up to my chest, but she makes up for her size in strength. Her salt-and-pepper-colored hair lands loosely around her shoulders, and I wrap my arms around her waist and plant a kiss on the top of her head.

"How many times have I told you to call me Mama? Everyone else does." Her emerald-green eyes sparkle with mirth as she leans slightly away from me before swatting at my chest, causing me to laugh softly.

"Okay, Mama."

She gives me one last squeeze before stepping out of my embrace and walking back into the kitchen, and I take a seat at the table.

"I wasn't sure what you would like, so I made a bit of everything." Mrs. Thomas starts rattling off different dishes faster than I can keep up, but I choose something to eat.

"Jesus, Mama. It's lunchtime. I don't even want to know what you're planning for dinner," Brady teases as she finishes making our plates and places both on the table.

"I never said he had to eat it all right now. Eat what you like, darling. We can rustle up something for dinner from the leftovers." She steps toward me, cupping my cheek in her hand. "We're so excited you're here."

"Me, too," I respond wholeheartedly before digging into my food.

I've never had a place to call my own, but I can already see myself putting down roots in Tyson's Creek, even though I've only been here for a few minutes. They always say home is where the heart is, and right now, I'm here in search of the other part of mine. Here's hoping that she'll give me hers in return.

The closest thing I've ever had to a job interview was walking into the Marine Corps recruiting office. To say I have reservations about what to expect from my meeting with Brady's buddy, Vance, today would be an understatement.

I have a few weeks before I can sit for the civil service exam, but if everything goes well, I can be the next deputy in Tyson's Creek in a few months. I'm sure Brady's dad pulled some strings when we told him I was interested in joining the department.

"Don't worry," Brady tells me. "Connor and Vance are good people, always willing to lend a hand to someone in need. Just be your charming self and everything will work out fine."

"That's what I'm worried about," I admit.

No one's ever called me charming in my entire life. My straightforward, no-bullshit attitude was great for being a Marine, but I doubt it will transfer over well to the civilian world.

"I can always just kick their asses for you if you don't get hired." He flops down onto the couch beside me as I stuff my foot into a boot.

I wasn't too sure what to wear for an interview and went with a nice pair of jeans and a button-down shirt. It's a construction company, so I doubt they come to work in a suit and tie.

"Easy there, slugger. I can handle my own battles. Thanks, anyway." I finish lacing up my boots and stand. "I'm more worried about what I'm going to do if I don't get the job."

"Stop being so pessimistic." Brady pushes up off

the couch. "There are plenty of places to work in town. I'm sure you'll find something in no time."

I give him a tight smile before grabbing my keys off the hook beside the front door and heading out.

"Don't wait up," I call over my shoulder as I shut the door behind me and head toward my truck.

"Good luck today, Seth." Mrs. Thomas waves at me as I pass. "Not that you'll need it. Anyone would be a fool not to hire you." She flashes me a bright smile before getting back to her garden.

"Thank you," I grumble as I climb into my truck.

Brady gave me basic directions to get to the company's main office right outside of town, but I don't want to take any chances. I quickly plug the address into my GPS and pull out of the driveway.

Here goes nothing.

I've spent the last few weeks getting used to civilian life. Not having a predictable schedule every day has set my nerves on edge, and I've become restless. I sat around for the first day or two, unpacking my limited belongings and grabbing the few things I might need until I found a place of my own.

Brady took me around town, even though I knew most of the places he was pointing out. This isn't my first time being in Tyson's Creek, but it seems important to him that I know everything there is to know about my new home. We spent a little more time than he would've liked at the only coffee shop in town, which happens to be right next to Bristol's yoga studio. I'd be lying if I said I didn't plan on spending a lot of time there, trying to catch a glimpse of her, but I haven't had any luck yet. She's been in my thoughts and dreams since we spent that night together over a year ago, and now that I'm back in town, I don't know how much longer I can go without seeing her.

I've tried calling her a few times, but I have had no luck getting through. Brady says I should stop being a creeper and leave a voicemail, but every time I hear her voice on the other line, I clam up. How do you sum up all your feelings for someone in a one-minute voice message?

I need to know how she's doing. How has business at Nurture Space been? I want to know if she ever convinced her best friend, Audrey, to move to Tyson's Creek. I want to know everything that I missed while I was gone, every little detail. Not because it's important, but because it has to do with her.

Bristol is practically the only thing I could think about while over in the sandbox. I'd imagine what it would be like the first time we saw each other again. Would she be happy? Would she even remember me? Does she still feel the connection between us, the same connection I've been sure of since the moment I laid eyes on her? I know it sounds insane, but I know I'm falling for her. I was never one to believe in love at first sight... until I met her.

But what if she's with someone else?

That nagging voice in the back of my head whispers in my mind for the millionth time since I moved to Tyson's Creek to see if there can be something more between Bristol and me. But it's been over a year. I never told Bristol my plans, so why would she have waited for me? She's amazing both inside and out. A catch for any man that sparks her interest. Is it naïve of me to think she'd still be single after all the time?

The voice on my GPS brings me back to the present as it instructs me to turn right on Paradise Road. As I turn the corner, the construction company comes into view. I make my way down the dirt road, keeping my eye out for potholes, and turn into the first parking spot I find. I take a deep breath as I turn off the engine.

"If it's meant to be, it will be," I mumble to myself before pulling the keys out of the ignition. I open my truck door and jump out... directly into a large puddle of muddy water.

"Shit," I mutter under my breath as I slam the door, step out of the puddle, and shake the water from my boots.

Good thing I dressed for the job and not the interview. I look down and examine my boots, checking to see if my jeans are covered in mud.

"Sorry about that. We've been meaning to get the

lot paved for a while now, but haven't gotten around to it," someone says from behind me.

My head snaps up, and I spin around and notice Connor standing behind me. Connor looks the same as he did the first time we met. His dirty-blonde hair is cut short on the sides and the top like a military haircut, and his jawline is covered in stubble the same color as his hair. A smile spreads across his face as he reaches his arm out toward me. "It's great to see you again, Seth. Did you find the place okay?"

"Great to be here," I answer with a smile before grasping his hand in a firm handshake. "Thanks so much for allowing me to interview for a position with your company. I was worried I wouldn't find any place to work while I was trying to get on my feet. Moving to Tyson's Creek was kind of a last-minute decision."

"That's not what I hear." He chuckles, releasing my hand from his grip. "I believe a certain redhead may have had something to do with it."

"Maybe a little." I snicker softly before flashing him a friendly smile.

"Nothing wrong with that. When you find someone you care about, hold on to them with both hands," Connor replies before stepping around me and striding toward the single-wide trailer a few yards in front of us.

I don't know too much about Connor's story, but it seems like he's speaking from experience. Brady said something in passing before we left for deployment that Connor was a widower. His wife, Lydia, died during childbirth. They were high school sweethearts, and he was devastated when he lost her. I haven't had the pleasure of meeting his daughter, Jade, but I hear she's a spitfire. Jade and this business are his entire world.

I couldn't imagine what it would feel like to lose the love of your life. The one person you believed you were going to spend the rest of your life with. How does someone's heart heal from something like that? Hell, I've only been apart from Bristol for a little over a year, and each day has been excruciating. I tried not to think about her, but my mind always came right back to that night we spent together. I never forgot her, even though I tried. And damn did I try, but now I'm here in Tyson's Creek, hoping that she might give me a chance to see where things could lead between us.

"Let's get inside and get this interview out of the way—although it's just a formality at this point," Connor says, as I nod and follow behind him.

There really isn't much to their setup. There are another two trailers off to my left with a few backhoes and Bobcats parked next to them. A chain-link fence surrounds the entire area, more to keep people from getting in than out.

"Home sweet home." Connor swings the door open and walks in.

I stop for a moment and wipe my feet before

following him inside. There are two medium-sized desks splitting the center of the room, with filing cabinets lining the wall to my left.

"Take a seat." Connor motions toward the empty chair in front of his desk. "Vance is running late, as usual, but he should be here soon."

"Not a problem. I don't mind waiting for a few," I reply as I sit down.

"How are you settling in here in Tyson's Creek?" Connor doesn't waste any time asking the serious questions.

"Great. I've been to visit a million times over the years with Brady, as you know, but there's something about knowing this is my home that makes things a little different."

It's different because this is my home. Something that I haven't had since joining the Marines. I had a roof over my head and a place to sleep, but the barracks on base never felt like a place I could belong. I'd never felt that until I stepped foot into Tyson's Creek for the first time. There's just something about this town and these people that makes me feel at ease.

And it's not just the town. The Thomases are the closest thing I have to a family. When I needed a place to go, it wasn't even a question that I was coming to stay with them. Mrs. Thomas always told me I had a home here in Tyson's Creek, but I thought it was just for show. Something nice that you say to your son's friend, but the Thomases are different. Cut from a different cloth.

"Are you planning on being here long term?" he asks.

"There's nowhere else I'd rather be. Tyson's Creek has felt like home for the last few months," I admit, not sure if that's the correct response.

"I feel you on that one. There's something magical about this place. Seems like it gives everyone the one thing they've always been searching for."

"I hope that's true for me, too," I murmur, ensuring that Connor doesn't hear my words.

Sure, Tyson's Creek is a place that I can call home, but the only thing missing in that scenario is Bristol by my side.

"Anyway, we just got a big contract to revamp some villas a few towns over, so we could use the extra men. I'm not sure how long we can guarantee you work, but we would love to have you," he tells me.

"Thank you." I give him a genuine smile. "I plan on taking the civil service exam in a couple of weeks and hope to become a deputy soon after."

I lean back in my seat and rest my ankle on my knee. I may not have given him the answer he wanted, but it's the truth.

"The town would be lucky to have you," Connor answers as the door to the office flies open and someone walks in.

"Late as always, Vance," Connor says as I turn toward him.

Vance has a huge smile on his face as he comes strolling through the door. His red-and-black checkered flannel shirt is rolled up to the elbows and tucked into a pair of light blue jeans. He's about my height and has dark brown hair with a perfectly groomed beard that'd put any military man to shame. He has a muscular build, but leaner than Connor, but what would you expect from someone who lifts 2x4s every day?

"Hardy har." Vance reaches out his hand, and I stand slightly as I grasp it and give him a firm shake. "It's good to see you, man."

"It's good to see you, too. Thanks so much for the chance to work for Ace & Hammer."

"Enough of that. We told you before you deployed, you had a place here if you wanted it. All of this was just a formality, if you ask me," Vance tosses a bag onto Connor's desk and heads toward his own. "Seli wanted Chick-fil-A again."

"Thank goodness today isn't Sunday, or you would be up shit creek again," Connor laughs.

"Tell me about it. I love that woman to the end of the earth, but I can't make someone open their doors just to make her a crispy chicken sandwich with extra pickles because the baby wants it."

"You got your girl back, huh?" I question, my eyes locked on Vance as he takes a seat.

I knew Vance was still head over heels for his high school sweetheart, Selina. She left without saying goodbye to anyone and headed off to Juilliard and never looked back. When we were last in town, he was still waiting for her to come to her senses and come home. It seems a lot of things have changed for the better since Brady and I left on deployment.

"Yup," Vance responds smugly. "It wasn't easy, but she came to her senses and came home to me."

"Why do I have a feeling there's more to the story than that?"

"Because there is," Connor replies. "But none of that matters either way. Those two knuckleheads found their way back to each other. Making my girl and yours very happy."

"You're one to talk." Vance grabs something off his desk and throws it at Connor. "You were determined to remain a bachelor for the rest of your life, and now look at you. Blissfully in love with Audrey and my amazing niece, Love."

"Wait, Audrey?" I question, trying to piece everything together. "Leia and Bristol's friend?"

"The one and only. She moved here with her teenage daughter, Love, to help Bristol at Nurture Space. Business has picked up a lot since you shipped out, so she really needed the help." Vance shakes his head as he spins a picture on his desk around.

"And I took one look at her and knew they were the

piece Jade and I have been missing since her mom passed away," Connor says with a soft smile and a far-off look on his face.

I turn toward Vance's desk, leaning down to get a better look at the picture. I immediately pick out both Connor's and Vance's smiling faces, their arms wrapped around two gorgeous women. Beside Connor is a woman with warm brown skin and curly hair that lands just below her shoulder blades, with hints of gold and red shimmering in the sunlight. Her head is resting on Connor's shoulder, and her hand is resting on a girl's shoulder who looks just enough like Audrey to be her daughter. To her right is Jade, who I only recognize from all the pictures Connor showed me whenever I was in town. Standing directly behind her is another beautiful woman, her hand resting on her basketball-sized belly, dark hair hanging around her shoulders, and a soft smile on her face.

"Looks like a family photo." I laugh, yearning to have pictures like this of my own with Bristol standing beside me, maybe even a little girl with her bright hair and my brown eyes shining with happiness right back at me.

"It is," Vance answers with a blinding smile as he spins the photo back around.

"We may not all be blood, but we share a bond that's stronger than that. Being blood related doesn't make you family," Connor says with conviction, causing my heart to tug slightly in my chest.

His words settle around me like a warm blanket. I've spent so many years without a family and a place to belong that I was worried about what would happen once I got out of the military. The military gave me purpose and brotherhood, but maybe there is a chance I could have something more. It led me to Brady and his family—*our* family—but maybe my circle can grow even bigger.

"The family you chose."

"Exactly," Vance places a hand on my shoulder and squeezing it.

"I'll leave you to your lunch." I stand, gaining both men's attention. "I need to get back to the house and finish unpacking."

Vance quickly comes around his desk, stopping me from walking out the door. "How about we grab a beer down at Crawdaddy's tonight? We can catch up and fill you in on everything that's happened since you were last in town. We can also take the time to introduce you to a few of the guys. I'm sure hanging around with just Brady is getting on your nerves by now." He points over my shoulder toward Connor. "Besides, this one needs a night out."

"Oh, no. The last time you and I went out, I couldn't walk straight the next day." Connor grumbles as his eyebrows pinch together. Apparently, someone doesn't know how to pace himself.

"I was nursing a broken heart." Vance clutches at his chest as he takes a seat behind his desk. "Lucky for you, I got my girl back, or we would have had a few more nights just like that."

"Sure," I mumble. I don't want to be rude, but I have no desire to play nice with a bunch of people I don't know. "Brady will throw a fit if I don't bring him along. Apparently, I'm not allowed to have any other friends besides him."

"Fucking princess." Connor chuckles. "Bring him along. We haven't had a chance to catch up since he got back into town." He grabs a stack of papers from his desk, holding them out in my direction. "If you could fill these out and bring them back to the office tomorrow, we can get you started next week."

I take the papers from Connor before shaking his hand again.

"Welcome to the team," Vance says as I step around him and head for the door.

I have a feeling that life is about to get a lot more interesting with them in the picture. I spend the rest of the day filling out the paperwork Connor gave me this morning and trying *not* to call Bristol for the millionth time. After a few hours, I give up and go for a run, hoping to tire myself out before I have to head to the bar to meet Vance and the others.

* * *

"Let's get a move on!" Brady hollers down the hall as I pull up my jeans and button them.

That run did me a lot of good. Helped me clear my mind and come up with a plan for finding Bristol. I've decided to stop at the local coffee shop tomorrow morning, hoping I'll accidentally run into her as I walk past her studio. Pathetic, I know, but desperate times call for desperate measures.

"Hold your horses. They aren't going anywhere," I grumble as I grab a clean shirt out of the drawer and slam it shut.

Once I get it over my head, I stare at my reflection in the mirror and barely recognize myself.

Standing at a little over six feet tall, I'm not a small guy by any means, but a lot of the bulk in my muscles has disappeared. That's what happens when your plans consist of more than just lifting weights and patrol every day. A scruffy beard covers the bottom half of my face, but I can't say it bothers me. But there is a brightness in my eyes that wasn't there before. Maybe it's the excitement of having more to look forward to every day than I used to, or maybe it's something more. Instead of waking up every morning dreading the monotony that usually follows, I wake up even more excited about what the day holds or who I might run into as I familiarize myself with my new home.

"I need to get my ass back into the gym," I mumble as I continue to examine my body in the mirror.

At least that would give me something to do besides obsess over Bristol every day. Right. As if that could happen. Bristol is the only thing I think about every day. She even seems to occupy my dreams. She's the last person I think about before I go to bed and the first person who comes to mind when I wake up in the morning.

"If you're finished checking yourself out, I'm ready to grab some beers." Brady crosses his arms over his chest and leans against the door frame.

"Shut the fuck up, asshole."

"You're still God's gift to womankind, and you know it." He comes into the room and joins me in front of the mirror. "Almost as sexy as me." He rubs his hand down his face before smiling brightly at his reflection in the mirror.

I roll my eyes. "That's why you spend your evenings playing video games all alone."

"Everyone has their reasons, man," Brady growls at me before storming out of the room. Wow. Guess I touched a nerve, but damn if I know which one.

Not wanting to think too hard about the situation, I grab my wallet and keys off the top of my dresser and head toward the living room. "Let's go. I'll drive, since we both know you don't know the meaning of taking it easy."

He doesn't say a word as he follows me out the door, closing it tightly behind him, and we head right toward my truck. I click the unlock button on my key fob before opening my door.

Brady climbs in and pulls his phone out of his pocket. "Vance said they're already there and have grabbed some tables."

I nod and slowly back out of the driveway, heading for the center of town and stopping at the stop sign at the end of the street.

"Are you planning on driving?" he asks as he turns in my direction, a scowl on his face.

"If I knew where the hell I was going, I would," I snap back, not bothering to be nice about it. "I don't know what crawled up your ass, man, but figure it the fuck out."

"You've been there before, Seth."

"Over a year ago. Knowing where your best friend's bar is wasn't on my list of priorities."

"I bet you remember where Bristol's house is." He snickers, causing me to roll my eyes."Turn right and head toward the construction company. I can give you directions after that."

He's damn right, but there's no way I'm going to tell him that. Thankfully, I remember where I'm going, and with a little help, I get us to the bar.

I shake my head as I pull the truck into a spot, and we both hop out, striding right toward the front door.

Brady pulls it open and heads inside, holding it open long enough for me to grab it. Crawdaddy's looks just like any other bar I've been to in the States. A bar wrap runs the length of the back wall with some bar stools placed in front of it. Music blasts through the entire room from the dance floor off to the left of the entrance.

"What the hell?" I shout over the music as I smack into Brady's back.

He says nothing as he stares at the woman dancing on the edge of the dance floor with a small group of women. She moves seductively to the music, as if the beat is part of her, gaining the attention of almost every man in the room.

"You have got to be kidding me," Brady growls as he turns in the opposite direction.

"Seth! Brady! Over here!" I hear Vance call, bringing my attention to the small grouping of tables to the right of the entrance.

"Glad you guys could make it," Connor says as we both pull out a chair and have a seat. Vance gives me a mock salute before Connor continues.

"This is Tony, Lance, Ren, and Drew. They're four of the guys that will work on the crew with you and Brady. Jasper and Easton are working on another project right now with a few other guys, but you will more than likely see them around."

All four men are of average build and in their mid-twenties. Honestly, the four of them could be brothers, looking almost exactly alike. I stand and lean over the table, shaking each one of the men's hands. "Nice to meet you."

"Glad to have you on our team. Hopefully, you can keep that one in line," Lance says, and we all chuckle at Brady's expense.

I wait a few moments for his witty retort, but nothing comes.

"You guys want a drink?" Ren questions.

Brady and I nod in response as he lifts his hand to get the bartender's attention.

"Thanks for inviting me. It's nice to have someone else to hang around with except for this blockhead all day, every day." I motion over my shoulder at Brady, who's brooding in the chair beside me.

His eyes are locked on the lithe beauty on the dance floor, hands held high above her head as she sways her hips to the beat of the music.

I lean closer to him. "Take a picture. It'll last longer."

"Fuck you," he growls as the bartender stops at our table.

"Beckett, this is Seth. He's the newest addition to our crew." Vance gives me a hard slap on the back.

Beckett holds out his hand, and I give him a firm handshake.

"What can I get for you two?" he asks as he eyes Brady. "Eyes over here, asshole."

"Get us whatever dark beer you have on draft, and another round for my friends." I look over and notice Brady scowling at Beckett.

"Coming right up," Beckett responds, and the others send up a cheer at the free drinks coming shortly.

"What was that all about?" I ask Brady. Before he can answer, someone comes to a stop in front of us, grabbing his attention.

"Hey, Brady." The girl who's had his attention since we walked into the bar comes gliding to a halt in front of our table while the rest of her group continues to their table closer to the bar. Her eyes scan the table, and she gives us all a small smile. "Gentlemen."

"And what are you doing here, little lady?" Drew says as the other two men whistle softly below their breath.

"Just came to say hello to a friend," she turns her attention back toward Brady.

She's the same height as Audrey, but her attitude commands attention as every man at our table focuses on her. Her flawless, golden-brown skin twinkles as the lights hit the slight sheen of sweat covering it, while her honey-brown eyes focus directly on him as if there's no one else in the room.

"Emersyn," Brady replies tersely, not bothering to spare her another glance.

Emersyn doesn't bat an eyelash at his response but turns her attention to me instead.

"Who's your friend?" She flashes me a bright smile and leans down slightly, putting her body directly between us.

"Seth," I reply as Beckett places a beer in front of me. I don't break eye contact as I lift my beer and take a healthy swallow. "Nice to meet you."

"The pleasure is all mine," she purrs as her eyes shift to Brady before she stands back to her full height. "Can we get another round, big brother?"

"Sure thing, Em." He turns and heads back toward the bar.

Emersyn and Brady continue to stare at one another for a few moments. Neither one of them says a word, but you can see the silent conversation going on between them.

"Pull up a chair and have a seat. I'm sure any of us would be better company than that asshole." Tony smirks in her direction as he pulls out the chair between himself and Ren.

Brady's eyes narrow slightly, and annoyance at Tony's interference is written all over his face. "Run along, Emersyn. We have better things to do than play babysitter."

"Why are you such an asshole?" Her voice catches slightly as she places both hands on her hips.

"It comes naturally," he bites out, taking a sip of his

beer and cocking his head toward her table. "Your friends are waiting."

Emersyn turns, finally noticing her friends waving to get her attention.

"See you around, Brady," she murmurs before turning around and sauntering back toward her friends.

Once Emersyn is out of sight, the table erupts into laughter, and the conversations between everyone flow once again.

"Is there a particular reason you were such an asshole to her? Beckett damn near bit your head off for just speaking to her." I growl as I chuff my best friend on the back of the head.

Brady can be broody sometimes, but he has never been an outright asshole to *anyone* before, especially not to a lady.

"If your mama knew how you acted with that girl, she would tan your hide."

"Good thing she'll never know," he grumbles.

There is something more going on between Brady, Beckett, and Emersyn than I know, but one thing is for sure: My friend has a secret of his own.

six
bristol

"Come on, Rebekah. Mama just wants a few more minutes of sleep," I groan into my room, praying she will go back to sleep.

Rebekah turned seven months old a few days ago, and all the baby books say she should sleep through the night soon. I'm praying that they're right. Waking up three to four times a night for feeding, diaper changes, or just because she thinks I should be awake is for the birds, but I wouldn't trade her for anything in the world.

When her crying gets louder, I know there is no hope of me getting any more sleep. I swing my legs over the side of the bed and walk to the other side of the room, where her travel crib is. Yes, I know I should have her in her own room, but if I'm being honest with myself, I enjoy having her close.

"How's Mama's baby girl?" I coo at her.

She gives me a smile and giggles, and her hazel eyes —a pale green around the outer edges with a light brown center with flecks of gold—twinkle with mischief as she kicks her legs in glee. There's a softness to them that mine don't have. Something I can guarantee she got from her father.

"Let Mama grab you some clothes to wear, and I'll be right back."

I turn and head toward her closet, stuffed with clothes from her grandmother and aunts. I swear, this little girl is the best-dressed kid in this town. If she doesn't have it, it's because those five ladies haven't discovered it yet.

As I comb through her closet for the perfect outfit, I think over the last seventeen months of my life.

As I open the door, Leia's face pops around the corner.

"What are you blaming me for now?" she asks.

"Me getting pregnant," I deadpan as I slam the bathroom door in her face.

"Last I checked, I don't have a penis. So, I highly doubt it was my fault you got pregnant." She shoves her way into the bathroom and freezes. "Wait. You're what?"

I push past her as the timer on my phone goes off.

"You could've knocked. People close doors for a reason," I quip before picking up the test and looking at the two pink lines in the little window.

"Well, that's interesting," she mumbles as she takes a seat on the toilet beside me.

"Yeah, tell me about it."

"Is it Seth's?" she asks, even though she already knows.

Seth is the only person I have been with in years. Ever since Austin and I broke up, I haven't been interested in anyone.

I nod in response before taking a seat on the edge of the bathtub, burying my head in my hands.

"What am I going to do?" I question, already knowing the answer.

I'm going to have this baby.

"You should call him," Leia whispers as she moves to sit beside me and wraps her arm around my shoulder, pulling me into her side. "I know this isn't what you expected, but he should at least know he's going to be a dad."

"Are you kidding me?" I shriek as I stand and storm out the bathroom door. "He's off fighting a war! The last thing he needs is to know the girl he had a one-night stand with is knocked up."

My cell phone rings, but I don't even pick it up to see who's calling. I hit ignore before turning back to Leia.

"Who was it?"

"Does it matter? I have bigger things to worry about," I grumble as I throw the phone onto my bed and flop down, pulling a pillow over my face.

Maybe if I just lie here long enough, I can pretend none of this is happening.

After that day, Leia dubbed herself Rebekah's substitute dad. She was there for me through most of my pregnancy, but when her dad had another heart attack right after Audrey moved to Tyson's Creek, she needed to be at home with him. Walker does what he can, but he can only be so much help all the way in Rose Hill.

Thankfully, Audrey and Selina have taken to being aunties just as easily as Leia. The three of them take turns helping me take care of Rebekah, checking in on the two of us, and spoiling Rebekah rotten. The four of us can't get together as much as we used to, but we try to get together for a girls' day every few months. Selina is four months pregnant with her and Vance's first baby. Although they had a rocky start, I've never known two people more in love than them. Audrey and Connor have been together for months now, living together in Connor's house with their two teenage daughters. Everything differs from what I had imagined, but it's exactly how it should be at the same time. All my friends are happy and in love, except Leia, but that's her own fault.

A pang of jealousy flashes through me, but I push it down. I'm beyond happy for my friends, but there is a part of me that wishes that kind of happiness was in the cards for me. Now that I have Rebekah, it has become even harder to find someone to call my own. But it also might have something to do with my inability to forget about the man who gave me Rebekah—her father, Seth.

"Time to get dressed, little one." I plaster a smile on my face as I grab an outfit for her and place it on the bed.

"The girls will be here any minute," I mutter before lifting her out of her crib and placing her on my bed, then get to work changing her diaper and getting her dressed. I dress her in a special outfit to commemorate my first girls' day in months, so she's wearing one of my favorite outfits: a maroon jumper with ruffles along the bottom and a short-sleeved bodysuit with matching-colored roses underneath. I top her outfit off with a maroon headband with an enormous bow on the side of her head. Her small red curls peek out the sides.

"You are the cutest little girl in the world," I squeal as I lean to my right and grab my phone off the end table, snapping a quick photo.

"Where's my baby?" Leia's voice echoes through the house before she barges into my bedroom, still unable to respect closed doors.

Leia is about two inches taller than me, her blonde hair hanging in loose curls down her back over the pastel pink sweater that says *Favorite Auntie* scrolled in an elegant script across the front. She's wearing the gray Lululemon yoga pants we bought the last time we had a girls' day. Her wire-frame glasses are perched on the end of her nose, and thick black eyelashes frame her crystal blue eyes, which are shining with excitement.

"Knock much?" I question as I pick Rebekah up and hand her to Leia.

"If you wanted any of us to knock, you wouldn't have given us keys," Selina chimes in as she steals Rebekah right out of Leia's arms.

Selina is wearing the same sweatshirt as Leia, but instead of pink it's a lavender color—her favorite—stretched across the curve of her swollen belly. The sleeves are pushed to her elbows as her lightly tanned skin is accentuated by her chocolate brown hair, which is pulled back in a tight bun, the typical hairstyle for a ballerina even with it being at the nape of her neck. It's in drastic contrast to how she usually wears her hair, hanging loosely down her back.

Since Selina returned from New York because of her injury, we've been thick as thieves. Leia told me that she left to become a famous ballerina, but now that she's back, it's like we've been friends forever. with the addition of Leia and Audrey rounding out our friend group.

"Hey!" Leia shouts as she plops onto the bed to pout.

If I didn't know these two loved each other and my daughter to death, I would be afraid a fight would break out.

"I haven't seen this little one in almost a week. Damn morning sickness."

All three of us laugh as I grab a shirt, a pair of underwear, and yoga pants to change into before heading toward the bathroom.

"Hurry and get dressed. I need coffee," I hear Audrey grumble as she blows a piece of her unruly curly hair out of her face. She is also wearing a *Favorite Auntie* sweatshirt in green. I know her favorite color has been teal blue for most of her life, but it's changed to green recently. I have a very sneaking suspicion I know why.

All my friends have been incredible since Rebekah was born, and I'd be lost without them, but there is still one more person I need to tell about my little girl: her father.

"I'm going, I'm going." I shut the bathroom door and change.

I glimpse my reflection in the mirror. My red hair is dingy and slightly greasy, since I threw it on the top of my head in a messy bun after I took a quick shower in the middle of the night because Rebekah spit up all over me.

"I look like shit," I say loud enough for my friends to hear.

"No, you look like a single mother who's trying to do everything on her own!" Audrey shouts through the door.

I sigh. I wish I could let them help me more, but they all have other responsibilities. Audrey just moved in with Connor and is trying to get their combined families situated. Selina just got married to the man of her dreams and is now pregnant, and Leia is working on making sure her family business doesn't fail. I can't put any more on them than I already do.

Leia and Audrey both know about who Rebekah's father is, but I haven't told anyone else. I'm not ashamed of my daughter by any means, but it feels wrong to let people know who her father is before telling him myself. I know it's silly, especially since I have no idea when I'm going to see him again. I'm sure I could get his cell phone number or email address from Brady or his parents, but telling someone they have a daughter is something that should be done in person. It also requires a lot of explaining on my part, explaining that I'm not entirely sure how to do.

Someone knocks softly on the door and eases it open.

"Wash your face, pull down your hair, and put on some makeup. You're beautiful." Audrey flashes me a smile as she steps into the bathroom. "Oh, and your phone rang, but we let it go to voice mail."

I give her a tight smile in the mirror and sigh. If anyone understands what I'm going through, it's Audrey. Having had Love at eighteen and having hippies for parents, she has had to figure out this mom thing all on her own.

"You've got this, Mama," she whispers as she wraps her arms around my waist and squeezes. "Now, get a move on. I need coffee, stat. I barely got any sleep last night."

"Not my fault you and Connor can't keep your hands off each other."

We both giggle as I quickly undress and put on clean clothes. Most people are too embarrassed to change in front of others, but since I exposed myself to a room of strangers while giving birth to my daughter, all sense of modesty has gone out the window. Audrey and I work together to get my hair to behave, and I throw on some tinted moisturizer, mascara, and lip gloss and call it good before striding out of the bathroom.

"Hey, Bristol," Emersyn says as she bounces Rebekah on her lap.

She must have come while Audrey and I were having our heart-to-heart. When she isn't working, Emersyn is my go-to babysitter. She's in her early twenties, and I've known her almost her whole life, having gone to high school with her older brother, Beckett.

She also works for Selina at the dance studio as a receptionist as well as teaching some classes. It makes it extremely easy for me to work at the yoga studio and ensure Rebekah is close to me. Have I mentioned I have separation issues?

"Thanks for agreeing to watch her for me. I really need a day out," I retort with a smile.

"How are you feeling today, Emersyn?" Selina asks, a sly smile spreading across her face, which causes Audrey to laugh loudly.

Emersyn eyes them both skeptically as she answers. "I'm fine."

"We heard from a little birdy that you may have had a little run-in at Crawdaddy's last night with a certain someone?"

"Oh, really?" I take a seat next to Emersyn. "Do you have something to tell us, missy?"

"No." Emersyn's cheeks are pink as she stands. "I think this little one may be hungry. Is there a bottle in the fridge?"

I nod, and she scurries out of the bedroom.

"What's gotten into her?" Leia questions from beside Selina on the bed.

"I have a feeling Selina and Audrey might know something," I reply, narrowing my eyes at them. "Now spill."

"Our lips are sealed," Selina responds as she mimes, locking her lips and throwing away the key.

"For now. Let's get out of here before I change my mind." I grab my phone and check the missed call. "Hmm..."

Why do I keep getting calls from the same unknown number? It's been happening for almost a year, sporadically, but the person never leaves a voicemail. I try not to think too much about it, but I can't help wondering who it is.

"Anyone special?" Leia asks as she pushes off the bed to stand.

"No, just a wrong number," I reply as I head out of the room, my friends following closely behind me.

"Brady was at Crawdaddy's last night with a bunch of guys from the construction company. It seems he was paying a little too much attention to her," Audrey says, and I freeze.

"Oh, yeah. I ran into him and his hot-ass friend last night at Crawdaddy's," Emersyn chimes in from the kitchen as she pulls a bottle out of the warmer and gives it to Rebekah, who's cradled snuggly into her arms.

"Huh," Leia replies, her eyebrows pulled down as if she's deep in thought.

"That must have made your heart flutter," Selina threads her arm through Audrey's. "I've heard her talking to the girls about Brady coming home. I have a feeling there is something more than friendship between you two."

"Much like a relationship between two other people we know and love." Audrey jokes as Leia grabs a pillow off my bed and throws it at her, missing her entirely.

"I don't know what you're talking about," Leia mumbles, her cheeks turning a light share of pink.

"Brady was a complete jerk, but I wouldn't mind climbing his friend like a tree," Emersyn replies, turning her attention to Rebekah.

My eyes widen in shock as I try to process who could be in town that Emersyn doesn't know by name. I haven't had any contact with Seth since we parted ways the morning before he left for deployment, but now that Brady is home, it's only a matter of time before I run into him. I'm going to have a lot of explaining to do if he sees me with Rebekah. It won't take a rocket scientist to connect the dots and figure out who her father is.

"Did you catch his friend's name?" Audrey prods as she wraps her arm around my waist, giving me a squeeze in support, and Leia flanks my other side. Seems like my friends have come to the same conclusion as I have.

"His name was Seth," Emersyn replies, not paying any attention to any of us.

My knees give out slightly, but thankfully, Leia and Audrey were there to support my weight.

"That's great," Selina says, louder than necessary, as she releases Audrey's arm and walks toward Emersyn. "We better get going before we miss our appointments."

She heads for the door, holding it open as my other

two friends practically drag me outside. My mind is a swirl of conflicting emotions as I try to process that my daughter's father, a man I vowed to never see again, is in Tyson's Creek, of all places. What's going to happen now? Will he try to take Rebekah from me? What am I even going to say to him?

My body tingles at just the mention of his name. Memories of the night we spent together fill my mind, and my core clenches with need. Seth was the last man I've been with, ruining me for all others. Even if I had wanted to be with another man after Rebekah was born, I couldn't. I've compared every man I've met since then to him. The one man I wanted but knew I couldn't have. But with him being back in town, maybe things have changed. Maybe he still feels that magnetic pull toward me and has come back to Tyson's Creek, hoping to start over again with me.

"Yeah, right," I mumble, knowing there isn't a chance in hell a man like him gave me a second thought after we slept together.

"Are you all right?" Selina asks as my mind snaps back to the present.

I look around and notice we're in Selina's car and heading toward the center of town, probably to grab a coffee before our pedicure appointments. I was so out of it I didn't even notice my friends dumping me into the car and leaving my house.

"I didn't say goodbye," I reply as tears trickle down my cheeks. I know it's not a big deal that I didn't kiss Rebekah goodbye, but I'm still trying to process that Seth is back in town, and that, on top of my separation anxiety, is just too much.

"Are we going to talk about this?" Leia glances at me in the rearview mirror.

"Talk about what? I'm excited to be having a girls' day with all of you." I try to feign excitement, but my friends see through my shield easily.

"More like avoiding the subject." Audrey pulls me to her side, and I rest my head on her shoulder. "I get not wanting to talk about it, but you need to deal with this eventually."

"What are you talking about?" Selina asks. "Although I have a feeling I know the answer already."

Shame fills my heart as I look at Selina in the rearview mirror. She's the only one in the car who doesn't know about Seth being Rebekah's father. I didn't do it on purpose, but we weren't as close when she lived in New York, and then she was so worried about what would happen between her and Vance that I pushed it to the back burner.

"I'm sorry, Selina." I sniffle, tears filling my eyes.

"There's no need to apologize, Bristol. I'm just a little hurt that I was the only one who didn't know. I get it, I do, but that doesn't make it any easier to swallow."

I reach between the seats and place my hand on her

shoulder. "I need to apologize. I didn't keep it from you for so long on purpose. It's just..." My voice trails off, trying to find the right way to explain, but she answers for me.

"Life."

"Yeah, life." I sigh, leaning back in my seat, my eyes meeting Selina's stare in the rearview mirror before flicking them toward Leia as she turns around in her seat.

"What am I going to do? I can't let him take Rebekah from me."

I know in my heart that it was unfair not to let Seth know he was a father. While he was deployed, I could hide behind the fact that I didn't know where he was or how to get a hold of him, but now my excuse is invalid. I know nothing about Seth other than that he is a United States Marine and the last man I should want to be in a relationship with, but that doesn't seem to change the fact that just the mention of his name feels as if all the air in the room has been sucked out. My chest tightens, my heart yearning to be close to him once again. But that doesn't change the fact that we have a tiny human together.

"You're going to put on your big girl panties and tell that man he is a father. I know it won't be easy, but it needs to be done." Selina gives me a stern look in the mirror. "To be honest, you should have done it months ago."

Ouch. Nothing like a healthy dose of reality from your best friend.

"Seli, I haven't spoken to him since he left!" I pull out of Audrey's embrace. "It's not like I can just walk up to him holding Rebekah and say, 'Hey, Seth. This is your daughter.' Life doesn't work like that." I cross my arms over my chest and turn my attention out the window.

"I understand it's not that easy, but you need to tell him before someone else does. How long do you think it'll be before he comes looking for you?" Selina lowers her voice slightly. "I'm sorry, Bri. I know my mouth can get ahead of me sometimes."

I give her a tight smile and nod my head. I know she means well, but it still hurts. I know I should have done a lot of things differently, but I didn't, and no number of words can change that.

"I doubt I made that big of an impression," I mumble, hoping that he only feels a tenth of the pull I do toward him.

"You're fucking kidding me, right?" Leia screeches as Selina pulls into a parking space in front of our favorite coffee shop and shuts off the car. "Did you forget we all watched the two of you dance around each other for *months* before you *finally* got together?" She spins around in her seat, focusing all her attention on me.

I shake my head, hoping she will change the

subject. I don't want to think about the way his eyes scanned me from head to toe as if he was ready to devour me, body and soul, or how his voice would send a shiver of pleasure through me when all he said was my name.

Nope, no thinking about it. It will only get my hopes up. There is no way that things will be the same after not seeing each other for over a year. Not to mention, I don't look like that girl anymore.

"We were all placing bets on when it was going to happen," Leia mumbles. "To be honest, we were all surprised you guys weren't an item."

"We would have been if he wasn't leaving," I respond, dropping another bombshell on my friends.

How I wish that thing between Seth and I had turned out differently, but I refuse to subject my little girl to the same heartache I went through with my father. Now, if I could just get my heart on board, this would be a hell of a lot easier.

"Well, you don't need to decide today." Audrey gives my hand a squeeze and opens her car door. "And you promised me coffee for being awake at this ungodly hour. Let's get a move on."

We all giggle in response as we open our doors and climb out.

"No more worrying. Everything will turn out just fine." Leia throws her arm over my shoulder as we walk toward the entrance.

I take two steps before I freeze, my eyes widening in surprise. I was hoping to have more time before I ran into the root of all my problems. More time to come up with a plan on how to deal with all the warring emotions running through me. But fate had other plans.

"Seth."

seven
bristol

"Hello, Bristol." His gravelly voice sends a shiver down my spine. It should be illegal for this man to still have this kind of effect on me after all this time.

"How have you been?" Seth stares at me intensely, waiting for me to reply, but I honestly have no words.

I can see the question in his eyes, like he's trying to understand why I'm being so standoffish. I would love nothing more than to throw my arms around his neck and breathe in his scent, letting him know how much I've missed him, but the world doesn't work like that. People change. How do I know if he wants anything to do with me anymore?

My eyes roam his body, cataloging everything about him. Seth looks almost exactly like he did the last time I saw him. His skin is a little darker, but being in the desert sun will do that to you. The addition of a scruffy beard gives him a rugged "mountain man" look that makes him even more delicious than before. I clench my hands into fists, resisting the urge to brush the few strands resting on his forehead out of his face.

"Hey, Seth. How have you been?" Leia breaks the silence as she squeezes my shoulder.

Seth tears his eyes away from me to focus on her, giving us both a bright smile. "Hey, Leia. I've been good. Just got out of the Marines and decided Tyson's Creek was a good place to settle down."

His eyes shift slightly in my direction, leaving no room for confusion. Seth is back in Tyson's Creek for a reason: me. *Wait. He's staying here. For good?* My entire body stiffens as images of us taking Rebekah to the park or having someone to wake up with her in the middle of the night flash through my head. I open and close my mouth a few times, trying to come up with the correct response, but my brain doesn't want to cooperate.

Thankfully, Leia swoops in to save the day. "That's great."

"How have you been? Finally made an honest man out of Riggs?"

"I wouldn't be caught dead within ten feet of that man if my brother didn't force me to."

"Keep telling yourself that," Selina grumbles. "There is a very thin line between love and hate, my friend."

"That there is," Seth responds, his eyes shifting

back towards me as if he's waiting for me to say something.

The last thing I need is to give him the impression that he is getting to me or that I have something to hide. I do, but he doesn't need to know that yet. Right now, my main concern is getting out of this situation. I can worry about the rest later.

"Where are you staying?" Audrey chimes in, saving me once again from having to say anything to Seth.

I scowl in her direction. The point was to end this conversation as quickly as possible. However, having more information about where he is *will* make him easier to avoid.

"With the Thomases." He pauses, gripping the back of his neck. "Brady and I are staying in the apartment over the garage. It's nothing special, but all I need is a bed to sleep in."

Holy fucking shit! He's practically my neighbor. There is no way in hell I'm going to be able to keep Rebekah a secret for long, but I need to try. I doubt he'll take too kindly to seeing me walking down the street with a stroller when he is out for his morning jog. It would be practically impossible to pass her off as someone else's child.

"Isn't that a coincidence?" A sly smile crosses Selina's face. "Bri lives—"

I jab her in the side, stopping her from finishing that sentence.

"It was nice seeing you, Seth, but we have an appointment to get to. Trust me, you don't want to stand in the way of four women and their spa day." I laugh nervously as I rush past him toward the door of the coffee shop.

"Wait, Bristol."

I turn around slowly, keeping my eyes focused on the ground.

Please don't ask me out.

"I was wondering if you would like to get dinner together. I'd love to catch up with you."

Seth steps closer as he reaches out and lifts my chin, and his golden-brown eyes take my breath away. "I've missed you," he whispers before wrapping me in his arms.

I melt into his chest, feeling safe in a way I've never experienced before. As if I can lay all my burdens at his feet and no longer worry about them.

"She would love to," Selina chimes in, breaking the spell. "You can pick her up here around six. We should be finished by then."

My cheeks instantly heat with embarrassment as I step out of his embrace and turn toward the door.

"I'll be here," he says. "It was really great seeing you, Bristol."

I nod in response without bothering to turn around. If I take one more look into his eyes, I know I'll tell him everything, and I don't know if either of us is ready for that. I quickly pull the door open and step inside, not bothering to wait for my so-called friends to follow me. All three of them are on my shit list.

"Hey, Bri." Katie flashes me a bright smile as she steps around the counter. "What can I get for you?"

I look up at the board and try to decide what I want today. I used to have a regular order of an Americano and cheese Danish, but since I had Rebekah, I haven't been able to stomach either of them.

"She'll have a caramel macchiato and a brownie." Leia steps up next to me, and I scowl at her. "I'll have an Americano, please."

Katie types our order in, and I spin on my heels, passing Selina and Audrey on the way. If Leia is going to order for me, the least she can do is pay, too. My mind wanders as I search for a table, pondering how things could have turned out so differently if either of us were different people. I had everything I thought I wanted in life, and I was happy... until I laid eyes on Seth. I barely know anything about him, but there has always been this magnetic pull between us whenever we're in each other's general vicinity.

I tried to convince myself it was nothing more than me being lonely and wanting some company, but I knew in my heart it was something more. The moment our lips connected, I felt it in my soul. Seth was the man I was meant to be with. But there was one huge problem: He was shipping off to the sandbox for Lord only knew how long, with no promises he would return. He could have been hurt or, worse, killed. I didn't know if I'd be able to handle that, so I let him go. Not because I wanted to, but because I had to.

When my dad was in the military, I watched my mom pace the hallways every night and jump every time someone unexpectedly knocked on the door, and I knew I never wanted that for myself. Despite the connection I feel with Seth, I need someone who will always put me first before everything else. Someone who will be there whenever I need them and doesn't have to clear it with someone else first.

Don't get me wrong; my dad loves my mom, sister, and me with all his heart. But after so many missed birthdays, school plays, and other memorable events, I wondered if there was something more important to him than us. Being in the military was a huge part of who my dad was, and I was always proud of him, but I knew that wasn't the life I wanted for myself or my future children.

I find a quiet table in the corner and wait for my friends, and a few moments later, Leia places my order in front of me and takes a seat, followed closely by Audrey and Selina. I break off a piece of my brownie and pop it into my mouth, waiting for one of them to break the silence, but none of them do. My foot bounces under the table as the silence gets to me. I'm sure they can't wait to share their opinions on Seth's news.

"Why aren't you saying anything?" I screech, gaining everyone's attention.

"Loud much?" Selina grumbles.

I slouch down in my chair, hoping to hide from all the prying eyes. The last thing I need right now is more attention.

"I don't know why he's here," I mumble as I grab my cup and take a sip. The warm liquid travels down my throat, calming my nerves slightly. "I didn't even know he was getting out."

"I'm sure you had more important things to discuss the last time you saw each other," Selina snorts. "Besides, he said he was here for you."

"No, he didn't." I pop another piece of brownie into my mouth. "He said Tyson's Creek was a good place to settle down, and he's right. I couldn't imagine living anywhere else but here."

Getting my yoga studio up and running and settling down has been my main priority since I moved here after graduating from college. I wanted to find a place to settle down, to put down roots, something I didn't have growing up. I was always the new girl in school almost every fall because we moved around so much. New Orleans was the place we stayed the longest. I met Audrey, and everything was almost perfect, but then we had to move away. I had to start all over again from scratch. I promised myself that I'd find a place to call home. To make friends, maybe get married, and start a family. The first time I stepped foot in this small town, I knew this was the place I wanted to land. It felt like home.

"Pull your head out of your ass, Bri. You know damn well the only reason he came back here is for you," Leia chimes in.

"Did you not see the way he looked at you? He looked the same as Vance when he—" Selina starts to say.

"Enough! We do not need to know about you and your bedroom habits!" I shout, and all four of us break out into a fit of laughter.

I wish I had as much faith in whatever this thing is that I have with Seth as my friends do. It's been a year; he knew where I was the entire time, but I never heard a peep from him. Then again, I never gave him any inkling that I was interested in starting a relationship with him in the first place. Maybe I made more of an impression on him than I thought.

"You could do worse," Audrey says out of nowhere as she takes a sip of her drink. "Seth is here for you. He came back *for you*. You could do worse in terms of baby daddies. Maybe this is a sign."

"You and your signs, Audrey" I giggle, knowing how much her tarot cards mean to her.

I swallow the last bit of my drink and push back

from the table. "Enough with my drama. We're supposed to be relaxing."

I give them a forced smile as I grab my trash and head toward the exit. There is no way I'm going to let my run-in with Seth ruin my first girls' day since before Rebekah was born. We all have families and different responsibilities, and it's rare that we all can have the same day off.

"You're right! Besides, we need to make sure you have enough time to get ready for your date tonight." Audrey steps up beside me and shoves her garbage into the trash can.

"I'm wearing exactly what I have on. Besides, most of my clothes are covered in some form of bodily fluid."

Motherhood, bitches. It's hard to be sexy when you can guarantee you will end up with puke or urine on your clothes at some point during the day.

"Fine, but we *are* getting your hair and makeup done since we'll already be at the spa," A smug smile spreads across her face as Selina pushes through the door.

The cool air hits me in the face, and I inhale deeply, hoping to calm my nerves.

"Do I have a choice?" I quip, opening the passenger door and climbing in.

"And before you complain, I will watch Rebekah for the night. You can come get her in the morning," Audrey says as she slides into the back seat behind me.

"I don't plan on staying out all night," I mumble.

I hear Selina and Leia getting into the car, and Selina starts the engine and reverses out of the parking spot.

"Whether you plan on it or not, I'm taking her," Leia insists.

I catch a glimpse of her sticking her tongue out at me in the rearview mirror.

"I thought you were my friends. Shouldn't you be on my side, not his?" I roll my eyes at them before turning my attention out the window.

I know all they want is for me to be happy, but I don't know if this is the right thing. This isn't just about me. I have Rebekah to worry about and too many unanswered questions.

"We *are* on your side, Bri. We're doing this for your own good," Leia says as she turns around and squeezes my shoulder. "Now, let's figure out how we're going to do your hair."

Whether it's for my own good or not, I know spending any amount of time with Seth is going to be nothing but trouble.

eight

seth

"Brady!" I shout as I come barreling into our garage apartment, an ear-splitting grin on my face.

"What set your ass on fire?" he grumbles as he comes strolling out of his room. "Did you get the house?"

"Maybe. I put in an offer on it immediately," I respond robotically, my mind racing through everything that's happened over the last few hours.

Connor mentioned in passing one day that Audrey had moved out of her rental home a few blocks away from him and that I should look at if I was looking for some place to stay. I went to see one of the two realtors in town the same day, booking an appointment to view the house. It's a lot bigger than I'd need for myself, but it's the perfect place to live with a family. I had just left the realtor's office when I ran into Bristol and her friends in front of Just the Drip.

It was a lot easier to convince Bristol to have dinner

with me than I imagined, although I think that has more to do with her friends than her desire to see me. Either way, everything seems to be falling into place exactly how I imagined it would.

"That's good, man. Fingers crossed for you." Brady grins as he drops down on the couch.

"Thanks," I bark over my shoulder as I head for the kitchen. "But you need to get out now. Better yet, stay gone until tomorrow, just in case."

Bristol promised to spend time with me tonight, and I'll be damned if I have Brady or anyone else around to distract her. I have been dreaming of this night since we said goodbye to each other on my last morning in Tyson's Creek over a year ago. I need to ensure that everything is perfect.

"I don't want to go," I groan as I grab Bristol's hands and bring them to my mouth, brushing a gentle kiss on her knuckles. "I know this seems insane, Bristol, but I can see myself spending the rest of my life with you."

The sun is barely touching the horizon as Bristol and I stand at the end of her driveway. I continue to search for the right words to explain how spending last night with her changed my world. I gave her a part of myself that I've never given anyone else. I know it's fast, but I don't care. The idea of getting into my car and never seeing her again makes my heart ache. My mind races, searching for a way to prolong our time together, but I'm shipping out on deployment in two weeks.

I want more time to show her how good we are together. I want to take her on dates and be seen in public with our friends. I want to be with her, to be the one she comes home to after a long day of work. The person she shares her burdens with when she's having a rough time. At the moment, I'm none of those things. But I only need the chance to prove that she means everything to me.

"You have to go, or you'll end up in jail."

"I have two more weeks until I ship out. We could spend some time together for real this time. It will give us a chance to see..." I begin, but she places her fingertips on my lips, cutting me off.

"I told you this was a onetime thing. I can't be in a relationship with you, Seth. Tonight is all we can have."

I rest my forehead against hers. "I think I love you."

"Don't say that," she murmurs.

"Why not? It's true," I reply with conviction, trying to pour every emotion I'm feeling into my words.

"It can't be true. It can't." She tries to pull away from me, but I tug her hands slightly, causing her to lose her balance and fall into my chest.

"I can see spending the rest of my life with you, worshipping you." Tears spring to my eyes as I bury my nose in her neck, clinging to her body like it's an anchor holding both of us together.

"Seth, don't make this harder than it needs to be. Please." Her voice breaks slightly.

I wrap my arms around her and bury my nose in her hair, hoping to commit her smell to memory so I never forget this moment while I'm away. "I meant every word, Bristol. I understand how you feel about being with a man in the military, and I respect that, but why are you doing this to us? I know it has to be something more than the fact I'm in the military."

"I can't do this again, Seth. My dad..." Her voice cracks slightly. "He always made promises he couldn't keep. Hell, after a while, he stopped trying, and it broke me. I refuse to feel pain like that ever again."

"I'm not your father," I whisper.

A lone tear trickles down her cheek, and I release her waist and catch the next one as it falls, brushing my index finger under her eye.

"I just need you to hold on and believe in me. Believe that I'll come back to you."

I pull back slightly and stare into her eyes. Those emerald-green depths swirl with uncertainty and doubt, but also hope, and she sobs as she steps out of my embrace.

"You can't promise that, Seth. You're going to war. You could be killed, left behind, or taken by the enemy. There are so many things that can happen to you, things out of your control. You can't promise me you'll come home no matter how much both of us may want you to.

"Every time someone in uniform walked past our front yard, my sister and I would hold our breath, tears

filling our eyes as we waited to see if they'd turn and head up our driveway toward the front door. Thankfully, they never did, but then we'd feel sick to our stomachs for being glad that someone else was getting the news we were dreading. That he was knocking on someone else's door instead of ours, ruining their lives forever with the news their loved one wasn't coming home."

Bristol covers her mouth with both hands, trying to hold back the sobs wracking her body, her head swinging back and forth as she tries to regain some of her composure. "I can't live like that again, Seth. I won't."

Everything else fades into the background as she continues to back away from me, but I follow her movements. My mind races, trying to find some way to help her understand how badly this is hurting me, too, but she holds up her hand and freezes. I watch as she wraps her arms around her waist, as if trying to hold the pieces of her soul together. As if she's gathering the strength she needs to walk away from me. From us.

"You're right, I can't promise you that, but what I can do is tell you I'll do everything in my power to come back to you." I clench my fist at my side as my own eyes fill with tears. "This isn't the end, Bristol. Not by a long shot."

Bitterness courses through my veins that fate could be so cruel. That it'd allow this angel to light up my entire world before ripping us apart and plunging me back into darkness. I have a duty to my country. We both know that, but that isn't enough anymore. Why couldn't we have met when we were younger, when we had all the freedom in the world to be together? I don't doubt fate played a part in pushing us together, but I only wish it would have been sooner.

Bristol finally gets her emotions under control and steps closer to me, grasping my hand. She gently pries my fingers open on my right hand and presses a small piece of paper into my palm.

"Please be careful." She gives me a watery smile before closing my hand around the piece of paper, turning around, and walking toward the end of the driveway.

I clutch that piece of paper in my hand. "This isn't the end, Bristol. You and I are meant to be together," I call after her, but she doesn't turn around.

I'm glad she doesn't, or my entire world would crumble around me.

"Earth to Seth." Brady snaps his fingers in front of my face, bringing my mind back to the present. "Care to explain to me why I need to leave my own house?"

"Bristol." I don't even bother to explain further as I go back to rummaging in our fridge.

"Holy shit." Brady gasps as if someone has knocked the wind out of his sail. "Anything you need from me? Other than getting lost for the night?"

I give up on finding anything edible in this fridge besides beer and some protein shakes—the perks of having our own personal chef downstairs. Not that we force Mrs. Thomas to cook for us every night, but it *is* nice to have a home-cooked meal to come home to.

Now I can look forward to that with Bristol.

I shake my head and chastise my inner voice. She only agreed to have dinner with me. Really, *she* didn't even agree to it. Her friends accepted on her behalf. She could have come up with an excuse to refuse, but she didn't. I can't stop myself from hoping that she still feels the spark between us. I know that I'm going to have my work cut out for me trying to win her heart, but at least there's hope. All I need to do is make it through tonight.

"No, nothing that I can think of. I'm gonna head to the store and figure out what I can cook for her." I grab two beers out of the fridge before slamming the door shut and offering him one.

"Sounds like a plan. You know, you could always ask Mama for help. She would be over the moon." Brady pulls the beer out of my hand and leans up against the counter.

"I know she would, but I want to cook for her myself." I'm a little rusty, but I know the basics. I can come up with something.

"You've got this, man." Brady taps the neck of his bottle against mine before pushing off the counter. "Well, I guess I should shower and find something to do since you're kicking me out."

"You should call Emersyn and apologize for being a jerk last night."

Brady's entire demeanor changes. "Just leave it alone, man. Emersyn is a big girl. She's just fine. I don't need to run over there and apologize for being myself."

"What's going on, man?" I ask, taking a healthy pull from my beer before placing the bottle on the counter.

"Nothing," he growls as he tries to leave the kitchen, but I grab his arm.

"That doesn't sound like nothing, Brady."

"It's complicated, and to be honest, I don't even know what's going on myself." His shoulders slump in defeat.

This isn't my friend. I can tell that there's more to this story than he's willing to share, but I can't force him. Brady has always been such an easy-going guy. No one ever has a bad thing to say about him, and he damn sure never loses his temper, but there's something about Emersyn that pushes all his buttons.

"Just know I'm here if you need someone to talk to, all right?" I grumble.

I'm not the guy who usually discusses his emotions. Unless it's about Bristol. There's no way I could hide my feelings for her, even if I wanted to. When it comes to her, I'm an open book. But *this* is the last thing I want to be discussing right now. Brady needs to confide in someone, though, so I'm willing to listen if he needs me to.

"Thanks." He gives me a tight smile before continuing out of the kitchen. "I'll be out of your hair in thirty minutes." He turns and heads down the hallway, back to his room. A few moments later, I hear the shower turn on.

Reassured that he will be on his way out soon, I grab a piece of paper and a pencil out of a drawer to make a list. I don't have a huge repertoire of things I can cook, but I make a mean lasagna. I write all the ingredients down on the list, adding wine and beer, before shoving it into my pocket and walking out the door.

There's only one grocery store in Tyson's Creek, and thankfully, they have everything I need. After grabbing all the ingredients, I head right back to my apartment. As I pull into the driveway, I notice Brady's Jeep is gone.

Mrs. Thomas comes out of the front door, holding something. "I was just going to leave this in the apartment for you two. I know how much you love my apple pie."

I give her a bright smile before taking the dish from her hands. "We sure do. Thank you."

"Are you coming down for dinner tonight?" Mrs. Thomas asks.

I'm sure she knows someone is coming to visit me tonight. I just hope Brady didn't let on who it was.

"No, thank you, Mrs. Thomas. I'm going to be having a friend over for dinner."

"What did I tell you about calling me Mrs. Thomas?" she scolds as she pats my cheek. "Well, enjoy your evening. If you need anything, you know where to find us."

"Yes, Mrs.—" I cut myself off. "I mean, Mama."

"That's a good boy." She smiles in my direction before turning around and striding back inside.

Once I'm sure she is safely inside, I walk around the side of the garage and up the stairs, depositing the pie on the counter before walking back downstairs and grabbing the groceries. After a few trips, I get everything into the apartment and check the time. I have about three hours until I need to pick up Bristol. I'll probably be cutting it close, but I have just enough time to get everything prepped, in the oven, and take a shower before it's time to pick her up.

I scan the apartment, looking for anything out of place. Our apartment is small, but there's more than enough space for two bachelors. We have a decent-sized living room with a small sectional pushed up against the outer wall and a sixty-inch TV mounted on the wall across from it, separating the living room from the kitchen. There's a small table in the kitchen, enough space for Brady and me to eat, although we usually eat on the sofa if we even eat up here.

Once I'm sure there's nothing out of place, I head into the only bathroom and stick my head inside. Brady did a good job of picking up. Not that we make much of a mess anyway. Satisfied with the state of the bathroom, I turn around and head back into the kitchen to start preparing the ingredients for dinner. My body moves on autopilot as I assemble everything to create the perfect lasagna and turn on the oven to preheat.

"I should have made sauce," I grumble as I grab the jar of sauce and pour some along the bottom of the baking dish I found in the cabinet, before layering lasagna noodles, ricotta, and mozzarella cheese, the ground meat, and sauce on top of each other.

Once everything is arranged to perfection, I cover the dish with aluminum foil and shove it into the oven. Setting the time for forty minutes, I pace back and forth in front of the oven, willing the time to pass as quickly as possible. I'm getting antsy. All the nervous energy about being alone with Bristol comes bubbling to the surface, making it almost impossible for me to sit down.

"I need to get rid of some of this energy or it's only going to get worse," I mumble to myself as I turn toward the back of the apartment, heading directly into my bedroom.

Running has become second nature to me at this point. When I first joined the Marines, it was exercise. A way for me to remain in tip-top physical condition when I was on the battlefield. However, ever since I spent that one night with Bristol, it was my time alone. A time when I would let my mind remember what it was like to be with her and imagine what it would be like when I came back home to her as I promised.

Right now, it's neither. I need to quiet my brain, and maybe the 3k that Brady and I mapped out when we first arrived is just the thing to do about it. Either way, I'll have just enough time to shower, get the lasagna out of the oven, and head to pick up Bristol in town. After formulating my plan, I change into running shorts and a fresh shirt before walking back out the door.

Here's hoping everything works out the way I planned. My happiness depends on it.

nine

As luck would have it, I get everything done with time to spare. As I pull into a spot near Just the Drip, I notice Bristol standing in front of another store a few doors down. I turn off my car and wait for her to notice me, but her attention is focused elsewhere.

"I guess she's just as nervous as I am," I mumble to myself as my eyes wander down her body. Instead of letting her hair hang loosely around her shoulders, it's pulled back, with a few stray pieces framing her face. She's changed out of the clothes she had on when I saw her earlier, swapping her outfit for a knee-length forest green dress that hugs all her curves.

Bristol blows a stray piece of hair out of her face before checking her watch a second time. I'd love nothing more than to continue to watch her, cataloging every part of this moment in my mind, but something tells me she won't wait much longer.

"Time to put us both out of our misery," I say to

myself before climbing out of my car and jogging toward her. "Am I late?"

Bristol jumps slightly, her hand coming to her chest. "No."

I smile, running the back of my fingers across the apple of her cheek. Her eyes close slightly, her cheek relaxing against my touch as she sighs softly. "I'm sorry if I startled you."

"It's fine," Bristol responds, her eyes flying open as she takes a step back, putting some space between us.

"You ready for our date?"

"This isn't a date."

I smirk as I step closer to her. "Are you sure about that?"

"Yes," she whispers, her body leaning towards mine slightly. "This is just two old friends having dinner together."

"Whatever you say, darlin'." My hand slides down her arm before threading my fingers through hers and planting a kiss on her cheek. "You look beautiful."

"Oh, this? Nothing special, just a dress I had hanging in my closet." Bristol turns from side to side, as if she has no idea what that outfit is doing to me. "Did you have somewhere in mind for dinner? Crawdaddy's shouldn't be too busy this time of night."

"This is the first time I'm seeing you in over a year; the last place I want to take you for dinner is Crawdaddy's," I turn on my heels and pull her toward my car. "I wanted to have you all to myself, so I figured I could make you dinner."

Bristol's breath hitches slightly as she nods in response. "Sounds like fun."

She follows closely behind me as I lead her toward the passenger side door, holding it open for her.

"Your chariot awaits, milady."

She giggles softly as she steps into the cab. I quickly close the door behind her before jogging over to the driver's side of the truck, getting in, and pulling out of the spot. The cab fills with uncomfortable silence as I search for something safe to talk about. I doubt laying my heart on the line the second we're alone together is acceptable first-date behavior.

"How have you been?" I ask, hoping that's a safe topic to discuss.

"Busy," she responds as she turns slightly in my direction. "My yoga studio is finally doing well enough that I can hire some employees. My friend, Audrey—you met her this morning—and her daughter, Love, moved here a few months ago to help."

"That's great, but I hope you take time for yourself every once in a while," I tell her.

"I have Audrey, and that has been a tremendous help. But she has Love, and now Jade and Connor. I know she'd have a fit if she heard me say this, but I wish I could give her more time to spend with them."

"Why's that?"

"Connor and Audrey haven't been together for long. The first few months of a relationship are important. The last thing she should be doing is spending all her time teaching classes at the studio. I give her as much time off as I can, without working myself to the bone."

I reach over and grasp her hand. "I understand that. I guess you're in luck now that you have me to take care of you."

Bristol pulls her bottom lip between her teeth and shifts her attention back out the window. Noticing her discomfort, I change the subject. "It must be hard starting a business from scratch."

"Not so much hard as time-consuming, but it could be worse. Everyone was willing to lend a helping hand when I got started. It also helps that I'm the only yoga studio in town."

"Does that mean you're still single?" I ask as I turn onto my street, hoping she hasn't moved on to someone else in my absence.

I never told her about my decision to retire after meeting her. Honestly, I don't think I thought about it myself until a few months after I was deployed. Either way, it would be naïve of me to think she waited all this time for me to keep my promise, but deep down, I hope she has.

"Yeah, still single." She hesitates for a moment before asking her own question. "What about you?"

I wait until I'm ready to pull into the driveway before I reply. "The answer to that question depends on you."

"What do you mean?"

I reach over and take her hand in mine, pulling her closer to the center console before leaning over and resting my forehead against hers. "It's always been you, Bristol. I never stopped thinking about you when I was deployed. I know you didn't make me any promises beyond that one night, but I hoped that when I came back, you would still be here waiting for me."

"You know how to lay it on thick, Casanova."

"Only for you," I release her hand and climb out of my side of the car.

I know I should probably take things slower and try to ease her into wanting to be in a relationship, but I've spent the last year dreaming about the moment we could be together again, and I'm not about to waste another moment on games. Bristol needs to know that I'm all in.

I rush around the truck and open her door. "It's not much, but the Thomases are giving me somewhere to stay until I can find a place of my own."

"Oh, so you're here for the long haul." She takes my hand and steps out of the truck.

"Have you heard the saying, *Home is where the heart is*?" I look deeply into her eyes, bring her hand to my lips, and brush my fingers across her knuckles.

She nods her head slightly.

"Tyson's Creek is my home," I continue.

She must understand what I'm trying to say because I watch her cheeks flush a light shade of pink.

"Come on, I want to show you my place." I wink at her before turning and leading her up the stairs to the apartment.

"What do you think?" I ask, releasing her hand to hold the door open as Bristol steps inside and looks around, taking in our limited decorations.

"It's not what I expected. But also, exactly what I expected." She giggles as she points at the large television on the wall.

"You know, boys and their toys." I chuckle. "It's a little more 'frat boy' than we were hoping for, but this place is only temporary for both of us. Once we get started working at the construction company with Vance and Connor, we can make some changes."

"Somehow, I can picture you doing construction." She takes a seat, tucking one of her legs underneath her before arranging her dress around her.

"It's not my goal, but it'll do for now until I can take my civil service exam," I say as I turn toward the kitchen and turn the oven on to preheat. "Would you like a glass of wine? I figured red would go best with dinner."

She hesitates slightly. "Sure. One glass won't do too much harm."

I quickly grab the bottle and pour her a glass, then pull a beer out of the fridge for myself.

"Oh, fancy," she giggles as I hand the glass to her and take a seat.

"To be honest, you can thank Mrs. Thomas for that. I asked her for one after I bought the wine."

Bristol stiffens, placing the glass on the table in front of her before shifting over slightly to put more space between us.

"Sorry. I didn't mean to make you uncomfortable." I sigh, getting up to move to the other portion of the sectional. I'm a lot farther away from her than I want to be, but making sure she's comfortable is more important.

"I'm sorry," she mumbles as she relaxes back onto the couch. "This is all just a little much for me."

She reaches forward, grabs her glass, and takes a drink, then moans softly. The tip of her tongue peeks between her lips and swipes the leftover wine off them. I adjust my position on the couch slightly as my cock hardens down my leg.

We sit in uncomfortable silence, our eyes looking around at everything but each other. I knew things might be awkward between us, but this is more than I anticipated. I open and close my mouth a few times, searching for something to say before choosing an easy out.

"Hope you're hungry." I smile, pushing to my feet.

"I made lasagna for dinner, and Mrs. Thomas baked a pie for desert."

"Lasagna?" She sounds completely surprised that I'm cooking anything at all.

"What did you expect? A DiGiorno's pizza?" I question as I head toward the kitchen and grab the lasagna off the counter. "It's one of the few things I know how to cook. Italian food always reminds me of my parents. My mother used to make a full Italian dinner every Saturday for our family. It was always just the three of us together, but it was amazing."

I give her a sad smile as I push the lasagna back into the open to warm and turn on the timer.

"I'm sorry," she mutters as she comes up behind me and tugs my shoulder. I turn around slowly, my eyes locking with hers. "I'm sure you miss them terribly."

"I do." I sigh, wanting to share more of myself with Bristol. "My parents died when I was young. I didn't have any other family, so I was put into the foster care system."

Over the few months I knew her before deployment, I didn't go into too much detail about my past. Instead, I wanted to focus on her, drawing out every bit of information from her I could. I told her things about me, but they were only surface level because I was afraid of what would happen if she knew.

I didn't want her to think any less of me because I didn't grow up the same way she did. It wouldn't be the first time someone thought less of me because I was a part of the foster care system. To most people, it meant that I was unwanted by my parents or that I was the stereotypical drug addict's son. No one bothered to ask me what happened to my parents or why I was in foster care until I was in high school, and by then, I learned to keep that information to myself. It was safer for my heart that way.

"Oh, no," she whispers, her eyes instantly filling with tears.

"It wasn't bad." I turn around, not wanting to see the look of pity in her eyes everyone gets when I tell them my story. "I had great foster parents. I moved around a lot, but not as much as most kids."

"Is that why you joined the military?"

I continue moving around the kitchen, grabbing dishes from the cabinet and setting the small table. I try to think of the right answer that will keep her from running out of here screaming, never to return. Bristol has an aversion to the military; I've known that since the day we met, but that part of my life is over. However, I can't deny that being a Marine is a big part of the man I am today.

"Partially, but mostly it was because I wanted a place to belong. I wanted to be a part of a family." I turn and notice Bristol staring at me, her eyes shining with unshed tears as she wraps her arms around my waist.

"Once a Marine, always a Marine," she murmurs, planting a kiss over my heart before taking a step away from me.

"No, it's a little more than that." I chuckle as the timer sounds, signaling that dinner is ready. "Being a Marine gave me a place to work through my anger while learning to trust others again. To trust that there were people out there in the world that would have my back no matter what."

I bend down and open the oven, pulling out the lasagna and placing it to cool on the stove. Carefully, I remove the aluminum foil. The smell of cheese and seasonings fills the air. "But it wasn't until I met Brady that I felt like I was part of a family again. Spending time with him and his parents made me feel safe and loved in a way that I haven't since my parents died."

"I'm glad you found them." She smiles brightly in my direction, as if I'm the only person in the world, and my heart swells.

"I am, too, for no other reason than because they led me to you."

Everything I have gone through in my life has led me to this moment: the moment I lay my heart on the line for the woman I love. Sure, this might seem fast, but nothing about our relationship has ever been conventional. If I've learned one thing from being in the Marines, it's that we don't have time to wait. We have to take what we want when we're given the opportunity or take the chance of losing out on it forever.

"A lot of things can change in a year, but deep down, you're still the girl who stole my heart before I left on my last deployment. The only woman I'll ever love."

Electricity sizzles between us. She leans toward me as if she's being pulled by an invisible string in my direction. I scan her face, trying to commit every detail to memory: the color of her eyes, the way a few strands of her hair fall into her face. But neither of us makes a move. It's as if we're in our own world, and nothing else exists but the two of us.

"You don't need to lay it on so thick tonight. I don't need your fancy words and pickup lines," she whispers as she attempts to put some space between us, but I grip her hand.

"You don't need to run away from me, Bristol."

"I'm not running away, Seth. I'm protecting myself. There are things going on in my life that you don't know about. I'm afraid that once you learn what they are, you'll leave me heartbroken and alone. Again."

"I don't want to ever leave you again." I lean forward, brushing my lips lightly against hers a few times.

Bristol relaxes, running her hand up my chest and around my neck. Her nails scratch across the sensitive skin at the base of my neck, and I groan.

"I'm going to kiss you again," I warn her, giving her a chance to pull away or give me a signal that this isn't what she wants.

"Please," she moans, just like before, and she pulls me closer to her.

I run my tongue against the seam of her mouth, and she opens for me, sweeping her tongue into my mouth. I let her take control of this kiss as she tentatively massages my tongue with her own. I can taste the red wine and something else that is entirely her, and I'm lost in her... until her stomach growls loudly.

"Well, that's embarrassing." She snickers as she pulls back, our foreheads resting against each other as we wait for our breathing to calm.

"I guess I should feed you." I stand and head back toward the couch to grab my beer and her wine.

She smiles. "I think that's probably a good idea."

I lead her to the tiny table in the kitchen, placing our drinks on the table and pulling out one of the chairs for her. "Sorry it isn't much, but I tried to make this a little special."

The table is set to perfection with a small vase of wildflowers in the center that I picked while on my run earlier. I also scored two small votive candles from Mrs. Thomas that I placed on either side of the vase. It's nothing fancy, but I wanted Bristol to know that I put some thought into tonight, wanting to make it special for both of us.

"More help from Mrs. Thomas." She giggles as she sits down. "This is perfect."

I press a gentle kiss to her cheek before turning to check the lasagna. I cut us both a piece and set a plate in front of Bristol.

"More wine?" I ask.

She nods, so I grab the open bottle of wine off the counter, topping off her glass before grabbing my plate and taking my seat.

"All right, if it's gross, I do, in fact, have a frozen pizza I can make in a jiffy," I tease.

Her tinkling laughter fills the kitchen. "I'm sure it's delicious."

She takes a small bite, and I wait impatiently. After a few seconds, she hums in delight. Relieved that she is enjoying her dinner, I dig in.

Bristol and I spend most of dinner catching up on what has been going on in our lives, laughing and talking about the time we spent apart. She tells me all about the shenanigans she has gone through with Leia, Selina, and Audrey over the last year, but you can tell she is unbelievably happy for her friends. In turn, I tell her about all the hijinks and pranks that Brady and I got into in the middle of the desert.

However, both of us are dancing around the inevitable conversation as we get up from the table and head back toward the couch. Neither one of us wants to go there, I can tell, but it's an important conversation, and we have to have it if we want to see where our relationship is headed. I take a deep breath, deciding now is as good of a time as any.

"Are you ready to talk about us?" I ask, taking a seat close to her on the couch.

"There isn't really anything for us to talk about. We spent an amazing night together over a year ago before you left to serve our country."

I ball my hand into a tight fist on my leg. "I told you I was coming back for you, and I meant it."

"I know, and you kept your word. I broke my own heart that day when I walked away from you, not knowing whether you'd make it back in one piece. I spent weeks worrying about you, begging for a sign from the universe that you were okay, but after a while, I had to stop waiting." She swipes angrily at her cheek before turning her face away from me.

"I meant every word I said in the driveway that morning. If there is one thing you can be certain of, it's that I'm a man of my word." My voice scratches against my throat from all the emotions clogging it. "Please give me a chance to prove how much you mean to me."

Bristol sighs softly as she turns toward me. Her eyes scan my face, looking for any sign that I might be lying, but she won't find one. We stare at each other for a few moments as I lean forward and brush my lips against hers. My eyes remain locked with hers as I press my lips against hers a second time, trying to put all my feelings into that simple touch, to let her know that I never stopped thinking about her.

"Seth," she replies breathlessly before gripping the back of my neck and pulling me in for a deep kiss.

I'm caught by surprise at first, but soon lean my body into hers. She drags her lips up the left side of my face and whispers in my ear. "Make me forget. I want to forget any of this ever happened. That we've spent more than a year apart, that this probably won't work between us. Everything."

I pull back and search her eyes, looking for any signs that her judgment is clouded. Finding none, I kiss down her neck as I place both my feet firmly on the ground and stand, knocking her bag to the floor.

"Leave it," she mumbles around my lips before wrapping her legs around my waist, grinding her core against my cock.

Taking that as my sign to continue, I make my way down the hallway toward my room. I kick the door open and spin her around, slamming her back into it.

"Are you sure?" I ask one last time.

"I want you," she moans.

My last thread of control unravels as I capture her lips with my own in a heated kiss, trapping her with my body. We moan in unison as my hand slides between our bodies. My fingers brush against her soft skin as I trail them up her thigh, grasping the bottom of her dress. We break apart long enough for me to drag it up and over her head before I toss it over my shoulder. My teeth scrape down her neck, nibbling and sucking my way across her collarbone before pulling one of her nipples into my mouth through her bra.

"Are you wet for me, baby?" I ask, slipping my hand into her panties. My fingers run along her slit before sinking two fingers into her.

"Please," she begs, rocking her hips into my palm.

"Your pussy is hungry for me," I growl into her ear, finding that magic spot and curling my fingers. "So beautiful."

I pull my fingers from her and shove them into my mouth, licking them clean before gripping her ass tightly in both my hands and lifting her into the air. Bristol squeals in surprise, and she wraps her legs around my waist, grinding her pussy down on my cock.

"Patience, darlin'," I mumble against the skin of her neck as I stumble into the room.

I don't turn on the light before stalking toward my bed and dropping her onto it with a bounce. Soft moonlight filters through my window, casting just enough light into the room to allow me to look at Bristol. Really look at her for the first time in over a year. Her body looks pretty much the same. Her breasts are slightly fuller than I remember, and she has more pronounced hips than before. Her body is still toned from yoga, but my mouth waters at the idea of nipping at the soft swell of her stomach.

Bristol's eyes fill with worry as she lifts her arms to cover herself, but I rush forward, grabbing both of her hands and pinning them to the bed above her head.

"Don't hide from me," I whisper, pulling her ear between my teeth before nibbling gently on it. "You're even more beautiful than I remember."

Bristol moans softly, her back arching off the bed as I unclasp her bra with one hand and slide the straps from her body. Her rosy nipples call to me as I discard her bra to the side and feast on her once again. Her skin is like nothing else I have ever tasted: slightly sweet, but something that is entirely its own. I take my time worshiping her breast before sliding down her body.

I nip and suck at the exposed skin of her stomach, circling her belly button with my tongue. My eyes lock with hers as I reach for the waistband of her panties. Seeing nothing but desire in her eyes, I bite down on the band and pull. Bristol lifts her hips and helps lower them before kicking them off onto the floor.

Without a word, I stand and strip off my clothes, pulling my shirt over my head quickly and taking a condom from my pocket. I place the foil packet on the bed, then shove my jeans and boxers to the floor. Her eyes travel down my body, locking on my cock as I unbuckle my pants and pull it out. Her pupils dilate, and she licks her lips, desire written all over her face.

"Do you want my cock, baby?"

"Yes," she moans breathlessly as I lower myself onto the bed between her legs.

My tongue drags along the seam of her pussy before I suck her clit deep into my mouth and ease my middle finger into her folds. We both groan in pleasure as her walls tighten around me.

"Nothing will ever taste as good as you for as long as I live," I mumble, burying my face deeper and lapping at her juices as they drip from inside her.

"More. I need more." Bristol grips the end of my hair tightly and pulls, causing ripples of pain mixed with pleasure to run down my spine.

I grind my hips into the bed, searching for some relief, and nip at the inside of her left leg as I insert another finger, continuing to pump them in and out. Bristol arches her back, screaming my name as I find that bundle of nerves and bring her closer to the edge.

"Are you ready for me, baby? Do you need me inside you, fucking you until you scream?" I growl, then attack her clit and suck hard.

Her screams of pleasure fill the room as I drag my fingers from her center. I sit back on my heels and shove them into my mouth, licking them clean. Bristol leans forward and grabs the foil wrapper, quickly ripping the package open and sheathing my cock, before threading her fingers through mine and lying back.

"Make me yours again," she breathes.

I slide my cock against her soft skin before plunging my tongue into her mouth. Her hands make their way around my shoulders, and she tugs on my neck, pulling me toward her. I'm pouring all my feelings into this one kiss, hoping I convey my feelings to her without using words.

I love you.

I missed you.

Please be mine.

I rock back and forth, rubbing my cock between her folds and not-so-accidentally hitting her engorged clit.

"You going to have your wicked way with me?" she asks with a smile.

"I plan to do much more than that," I say as I line my cock up with her center. "I plan to keep you forever."

I hoist her up by her ass cheeks and thrust into her core, both of us moaning. Her juices drip down my balls as I pump in and out of her at a punishing pace. Bristol bumps her head against the wall, meeting me thrust for thrust. "I don't know if I can be gentle, baby. I need you too much."

Bristol's eyes meet mine as she releases one of her arms from around my neck, snaking her hand down to rub her clit, first slowly and then faster and faster. Her inner walls clench around my cock, signaling her pending release.

"I love you," I whisper in reverence as I piston my

hips in and out, feeling her juices dripping down my balls.

"Yes! Yes! Seth!" Bristol's head thrashes from side to side as my pace quickens, and I pound harder into her core.

"I'm close, baby." I grit my teeth together, trying to hold off my impending release. "Come for me, Bristol,"

My hips slap against hers until she shouts my name, and both of us tumble over the edge into oblivion. I slow my pace, pumping in and out of her as both of us come down from our high, not wanting to lose the connection we have finally made. Then I roll over to the side, dragging her body along with me and pulling her tightly to my chest.

I don't care about the past anymore. After tonight, there is only the future. And I'm going to do everything I can to make sure that Bristol is part of it.

ten

bristol

Sunlight filters in from the window of the room, waking me up. *Did Rebekah let me sleep?* I can't remember the last time her crying didn't wake me up because she was hungry or needed a diaper change. Then I feel it: the wet patches on my shirt from not nursing last night.

What in the actual fuck *have I done?* I chastise myself as Seth wraps his arm around my waist and pulls me tightly to his chest. I bite back a groan as pain shoots through my body. This is one of the many drawbacks of spending a single night away from your nursing infant. Leakage.

My mind filters through last night, trying to remember if Seth said or did anything to indicate he knows about our daughter. The taste of breast milk isn't something the average man would know for sure, but you never know. Of all the ways to discover he is a father, finding me leaking breast milk all over his bed was not my choice.

I need to get out of here, and fast. As gently as possible, I lift Seth's hand and try to shimmy out from underneath him without waking him up. It takes me a few minutes, but I disentangle myself from his embrace without incident. I send up a silent prayer of thanks as I throw my legs over the side of the bed and begin searching for my clothes.

I quickly find my panties at the edge of the bed and pull them on but decide to forego the bra. Just the thought of putting it on right now brings tears to my eyes. I tiptoe toward his bedroom door in search of my dress as I feel Seth grab my hand.

"Morning, beautiful." He spins me around and pulls me into his bare chest. "What the hell is that?"

I bite my lip to stifle a groan of pain as he pulls away from me and looks down at my chest. My arms fly up to cover my breast, pretty sure milk is now leaking from my nipples, and I try to search for a reasonable explanation.

"I drool a lot. Sorry." I pull out of his embrace and scurry straight into the bathroom, slamming the door shut behind me. What have I done... again? I knew going on a date with Seth would lead to disaster, but sleeping with him was even worse.

A soft knock on the door causes me to jump. I open the door a few inches and poke my head out. Seth is standing in front of me in a pair of low-hanging sweat-pants and no shirt.

"I grabbed your dress, but I have one of my shirts and some sweats to change into if you'd like."

I nod before realizing he can't hear me. "Sweats and a shirt would be great," I respond as I stick my arm out the door and take the clothes from his hands.

"You can take a shower if you want. There are towels under the sink."

"Thank you," I whisper as he kisses my forehead gently.

"Anything for you, love." He turns on his heels and heads toward the front of the apartment, and I shut the door quietly behind me.

There he goes, throwing that word around again. *Love.* How can he be so sure how he feels about me? Yeah, we spent months circling around each other before he left on deployment, but that was over a year ago. Can we really go right back to how things were before? We haven't even spent a whole twenty-four hours together since he came back to Tyson's Creek. Not to mention he has a daughter that he doesn't know about. I have a feeling he's going to look at me differently once I tell him about Rebekah.

I shake those thoughts from my mind as I turn the shower on, allowing the water some time to warm up before turning to place the shirt and sweats from Seth, along with the rest of my clothes, on the counter. I spin around and shove my arm into the shower, feeling the warm water running down my hand before peeling my panties off and climbing in.

I let the warm water hit my engorged breasts and sigh in relief as I feel the creamy liquid drip from my nipples. There's one crisis averted. It doesn't take long for the pressure to diminish, and I wash, squirting soap into my hands and lathering myself up.

I take my time in the shower, hoping the repetitive task will stop my mind from wandering, but as usual, I have no such luck. I need to find a way to make sense of my feelings and figure out how to handle telling Seth about Rebekah before it's too late.

The connection I feel toward Seth is undeniable and so much more than I ever could have imagined, but how will he react when I find the courage to tell him about our daughter? I told him I had secrets that I was afraid to tell him, and that's an understatement. Couple that with the worry that he wouldn't understand why I wanted to keep her existence from him, and I have more than enough on my plate. The one thing I know for certain is the longer I wait to tell him about her, the harder it's going to become.

I know a lot about Seth, but the one thing we never discussed was if either of us wanted children. I don't regret Rebekah by any means, but maybe Seth will. He lost his parents at an early age and grew up in the foster care system. That must have left a mark on him. He laid his heart out to me last night, letting me know that his plans for the future include me. But a baby is an enormous responsibility, one that I'm not sure he wants or is ready for right now. He just got out of the Marines and is trying to build a life for himself. He doesn't even have a permanent place to live yet. Adding a baby to the mix will only complicate things for both of us. We aren't even in a relationship. Although it seems to be headed that way, things will change when he finds out about Rebekah. Will he still feel the same way about me as he does right now? Will he be able to love Rebekah? There are so many unanswered questions that my mind feels as if it's spinning out of control.

A knock on the door startles me from my thoughts.

"Yes?" I squeak.

"Wanted to make sure you didn't need anything else. I made coffee." I can hear the nerves in his voice.

"I'm almost finished," I say as I rinse off one more time and shut off the water.

"I'll be in the kitchen."

"I'll see you in a minute," I reply without thinking as I climb out of the shower and grab a towel.

Grabbing the shirt Seth gave me off the counter, I slip it over my head, pulling my hair out of the collar and letting it hang loosely around my shoulders. I then quickly throw on my panties and the sweats before grabbing my dirty shirt off the floor and striding out of the bathroom.

Seth is standing at the kitchen sink, staring out the

window and giving me the perfect view of his muscular form. As my eyes scan his body, I catalog every delicious detail, from the large Marine Corps symbol tattooed on his back along his left shoulder blade, to his rippling arm muscles as he clenches the counter in front of him.

I glance at the door, wondering if I can make my escape without him noticing and turn toward the living room to grab my bag. I make it all the way to the couch and thread my arm through the strap when the floor creaks loudly.

"Trying to sneak out, are we?"

My eyes shoot in his direction and find him leaning against the counter, his muscular arms crossed over his chest.

"No. I was checking to see if I had any missed calls."

"You don't."

"What?" I try to stay calm, but in reality, I'm freaking out.

"I shoved everything back into your bag after it fell off the couch last night, your phone included," he says as he brings a cup of coffee over and sets it on the table.

My phone chimes, and I rummage through my bag before pulling it out. A text from an unknown number appears on my phone. "Let me guess? Your..." My voice trails off as I remember that night before he left for deployment.

I should have just let him leave, cutting him off and forgetting what happened between us, but instead, I slipped a piece of paper with my number on it into his hand. After he left, I waited for him to call. To tell me how much he missed me and couldn't wait to come home to me, but after about a month of nothing, I gave up hope.

Then I found out I was pregnant with Rebekah shortly after, and everything changed. I didn't have time to daydream about the man who stole my heart. My only focus was taking care of her. Every time an unknown call came through on my phone, I'd pick it up and pray to hear his gravelly voice on the other line, but it was always someone trying to sell me something or contact me about my car's extended warranty, and I stopped answering them.

He raises his phone and shakes it from side to side, staring directly into my eyes. "You gave me your number. Hopefully, you answer the phone when I call this time."

Call? Nope. No way. He can't call me. I can't risk the chance of him hearing a crying baby in the background and asking even more questions. No, thank you.

"Text," I grab my bag off the table and back away toward the door. "I prefer text. No one ever calls me unless it's an emergency."

"Got it." Seth stands and stalks toward me, and I back right into the door.

"Running away again," he mutters in my ear, sending a shiver down my spine, before wrapping me in his arms and pulling me against his chest.

I step into his embrace, wishing that this moment would never end. Wishing that the two of us could remain here together, without a care in the world. I nuzzle into his chest, breathing in his scent, until my phone rings.

I sigh softly as I reach into my bag and silence it quickly. No doubt it's Audrey or one of the girls trying to figure out why I haven't come to pick up Rebekah yet. I'm sure they're all champing at the bit to find out exactly what happened last night.

"Well, I'm just gonna go..." My sentence trails off as I reach for the door handle, turning it and pulling the door open slightly.

Seth steps forward and rests his hand on the door right above my head, pushing it closed with a click.

"Look, Bristol." He tucks my hair behind my ears before cupping my cheeks with his hands. "Give me a chance. Let's chalk the last year up to bad timing. I wish things could've been different, or that we met at another point in our lives, but we can't go back in time."

"I can't do this right now," I whisper, shifting my head to the side and pulling my face from his grasp as tears pool in my eyes. "This is too much."

I need time to think, to figure out exactly how to explain to this amazing man that I stole the first seven months of his daughter's life from him. I know he needs to know, but I can't bring myself to say the words right now.

"Please, Seth. Not now. Please," I beg.

Seth stares into my eyes, pleading with me to give him an answer and put us both out of our misery, but I can't. I drop my head to his shoulder. "Let me grab my keys, and I can drive you home."

"No need," I say flatly, lifting my head off his shoulder. "I live a few blocks down the street."

"I won't keep you, then." He kisses my forehead and takes a step back, giving me space.

I open the door, but before leaving, I turn back. I want to tell him everything, to admit that I still feel the connection between us and want to see where things go. That I wish all the same things, but I just need more time. Time to figure out how to explain. But I can't right now. There are only two words that come to mind.

"I'm sorry," I whisper as I slide out the door, not even bothering to shut it behind me.

With tears streaming down my cheeks, I turn right at the end of the driveway. I don't dare look back. I know he's watching me walk away. I can feel his eyes on my back, begging me to come back to him, but I can't.

I hope he understands I need time to think. To understand how he can be so sure about me, about us.

He told me that he came to Tyson's Creek looking for me, but I just can't wrap my mind around it. What's going to happen if things don't work out between us? What is he going to do then? Pick up and move somewhere else? Or worse, find someone new? On top of all that, he has no idea that the enormous secret I'm keeping from him could change the way he feels about me entirely. Either way, I can't say a thing about Rebekah until I know how long he plans on staying in town. That he won't pick up and leave if things don't work out between us, and I can't even think about introducing him to Rebekah until then.

I make it back home in no time, heading up the driveway and hopping into the car.

"I need to see my baby girl," I mumble into my empty car as I pull out and head a few blocks over to Connor's house.

Although Audrey and Connor hadn't been together for very long, they were eager to start their life together. Thankfully, Audrey was only renting and could get out of the lease without too much hassle. It also helps that Connor will do anything to make sure he can come home to his girls every night. Last I heard, the owner put the place up for sale instead of searching for new tenants.

I pull into the driveway and take a deep breath. Just as I thought, all the girls are here, almost certainly waiting to get all the dirty details about my date with Seth last night. Trying to put off having this conversation, I recline my seat slightly and close my eyes.

I haven't even had time to process everything that went on last night. Seth told me he had been in love with me for over a year. That in itself is a lot to handle, but the fact that I think I might feel the same way should make me feel giddy with joy. However, what I'm feeling now is the exact opposite. Seth has retired from the military and uprooted his entire life to move closer to me, removing every obstacle that I listed for why we can't be together. He's everything I could ever imagine wanting in a partner and a father for our daughter, but I have no idea how he is going to react when I tell him. Until I do, there's no way I can let him anywhere near her.

"Hey! Don't think you can get out of talking to us."

I bolt up from my seat and spin toward the window. Selina's face is practically plastered to the glass, a bright smile covering her face.

"What the fuck, girl?" I open the car door, bumping her lightly on the stomach. "You could have given me a heart attack."

"I know, but I didn't." She smiles, wrapping her arm around my shoulder. "Besides, I drew the short straw to come and get you. Audrey and Leia were tired of waiting for you to come inside and spill the beans."

"I kind of figured that, hence my hiding in the car,"

I respond as I rub the top of her belly and head toward the front door.

"No rubbing the belly without permission," she grumbles as she follows quickly, reaching the door a few moments after I pull it open.

We both push through the door and head right to the kitchen. Everyone but Leia is seated around the large island in the kitchen; a pitcher of mimosas is sitting in the center, and everyone has a full glass. Leia is sitting at the table with Rebekah in the Moby wrap strapped to her chest, fast asleep.

"Look what the cat dragged in," Selina announces as I slide into the kitchen, heading directly for Rebekah.

"You need to lay her down. I don't want her to get used to being held while she's sleeping," I murmur to Leia before gently kissing the top of my daughter's head.

"Chill out, Mama Bear. She just fell asleep a few minutes ago." Leia pushes back from the table. "I was just about to lay her down in the playpen in the family room. Jade and Love are in there watching TV. They can keep an eye on her so we can talk." She throws a wink over her shoulder before brushing past me and striding toward the family room.

Jade is Connor's daughter from his marriage to Lydia. Lydia died during childbirth, but I hear from everyone that Jade looks just like her, with long dark hair and sparkling green eyes like her father's. She's the sweetest girl you'll ever meet, but I may be a little biased.

Love is Audrey's daughter and my favorite niece, but don't tell Jade I said that. I've known Love for most of her life, and she will always hold a special place in my heart. She has wavy black hair, the same color as her mother's, that she always has in a messy bun on the top of her head. Love was my entire world until I got pregnant with Rebekah, but she's a close second. Jade and Love are both fifteen and gorgeous. I feel sorry for Connor when those two start dating.

I take a seat at one of the empty stools at the island and reach for the pitcher of mimosas, pouring myself a glass and drinking it down with one gulp. "Did she give you any problems?" I'm going to need to pump and dump after drinking, but I need it.

Audrey smiles. "She was a gem. Nothing I couldn't handle."

No one else says a word. They just look at me expectantly, clearly waiting for me to tell them everything about my date. Just as I open my mouth to make more small talk, my phone chimes in my bag. I reach in and pull it out, and Seth's name is flashing across the screen.

"Are you going to answer that?" Selina asks as she leans over, trying to catch a glimpse over my shoulder. "It must be important if he's calling less than an hour after you left his place."

"Seth is calling you?" Leia chimes in as she comes back into the kitchen.

"Yes, but he can wait."

"That man has been waiting over a year for you already." Audrey giggles as she fills three glasses with the champagne and orange juice mixture, before grabbing mine and refilling it.

"Exactly. What is another few minutes going to hurt?" I snap before turning the volume off and shoving the phone back into my bag. The last thing I need is them asking a million questions every time my phone rings.

"Now that we have your full attention, are you going to tell us what happened last night?" Leia questions as she takes a seat at the opposite end of the bar.

I look around the room, trying not to make eye contact with any of them. They will know as soon as I look into their eyes how things have changed. "I can't tell him about Rebekah yet."

"You can't hide her forever, Bri." Leia reaches around Selina and squeezes my shoulder to get my attention.

"I can, and I will," I snap.

I clench my eyes shut tightly and inhale deeply. I need to get control of the fear and anger by taking a large gulp of my mimosa. I know my friends want what's best for me, but there are so many unanswered questions. I need to figure out how serious Seth is about all of this before I can even think about introducing him to our daughter. "I'm sorry, but I need to protect her. He said he came back to town for me. That he retired from the military for me so that we could be together. But he might change his mind once he finds out about her."

"Do you really think that's the type of man he is?" Audrey questions, as she hands Leia a glass.

"No. Yeah. I don't know." I sigh, throwing back the rest of my drink. "I just wish I had a crystal ball to tell me how he will react to the news. I've taken time with his daughter away from him. What if he hates us and leaves?"

"I doubt there is anything you can do to make that man hate you." Leia reaches over and gives my hand a squeeze. "Besides, Seth wouldn't have had those few months with Rebecca either way.

"Seli is right. He was on the other side of the world, fighting a war, for Christ's sake." Audrey chimes in as she takes a seat at the island on the stool beside me.

"We can all see how much he means to you." Leia smiles softly at me over her glass as she takes a sip.

"The same way we all know how you are secretly in love with Riggs Monroe but refuse to admit it to yourself?"

"We aren't talking about me, missy." Leia's cheeks turn pink as we all have a laugh at her expense.

"I know, but you're one to talk about having

someone who means so much to you right in front of your face."

"Touché. Let me worry about whatever is between Riggs and me. Right now, we are trying to help you figure out how to tell Seth. Either way, it needs to happen sooner rather than later because someone is going to slip and say something about Rebekah. It's inevitable."

"Don't you think he deserves to know he has a daughter?" Audrey murmurs, asking the one question I'm sure everyone has been wondering since yesterday.

"Of course, he does. He'll make an amazing father, and now that he's in town for good, there is no reason to keep them apart," I say without even thinking.

"Okay, then what is keeping you from telling him?"

Tears immediately well in my eyes and trickle down my face. "I don't know." I cover my face with my hands and sob. This secret was mine to keep, and I'll do anything to protect myself and my little girl from heartbreak. But now that secret is the only thing standing between me and the man I love.

"What does your heart say?" Audrey whispers into my ear as she lays her head on my shoulder. All the girls wrap me in a protective cocoon, giving me the support I need as my world crumbles around me.

"What happens if he doesn't want us?" I hiccup, attempting to stop the tears from streaming down my cheeks.

I've finally voiced my biggest fear. I've known in my heart since I laid eyes on Seth over a year ago that he was it for me. That he was the man I could see everything with. There were times when we were together that I could see it all playing out in front of my eyes like a movie, but loving someone with all your heart isn't always enough. I knew in my soul that if we ever saw each other again, there was no doubt we'd have ended up together. But that nagging voice in the back of my mind would whisper words of doubt to me, sparking the fires of my fear that I tried to keep buried deep in my soul.

When Seth never contacted me after deploying, I believed that was it. That the distance between us had squandered all the feelings of love and devotion he had before deployment, but it seems I was wrong. Knowing Seth changed everything in his life for a chance to be with me makes my heart flutter, reigniting the kindling of the love I was feeling for him before he left. I'm sure if I closed my eyes, those same images of our perfect life together would still be there. But that was before Rebekah was born, before I had this tiny human to protect from the heartbreak and evils in the world. I'd do anything to ensure Rebekah never has to feel the pain of losing Seth, even if that means losing my heart.

I should keep my heart locked away from Seth, protecting Rebekah and me from potential heartache. It would be so much easier to protect both of us if he wasn't slowly weaving his way into our everyday life. If he was still halfway around the world and thoughts of what it felt like to have his arms wrapped tightly around me or the press of his full lips against my cheek were nothing more than a dream, then I wouldn't have anything to worry about because the pain of not having him in our lives was minimal.

But after spending last night with him, my heart yearns for all those things and more. It doesn't help that soon, there will be reminders of Seth and how things could be between us popping up around every corner here in town. It's the blessing and a curse of living in a small town. He's slowly beginning to become a major part of my life without even knowing it. I doubt he's doing it on purpose, but we are all one big family here in Tyson's Creek. Seth lives within walking distance of my house. He works for two of my best friends' significant others' construction company. We are bound to run into each other, no matter how things play out between us, and I don't know if my heart can take it.

"If he doesn't want you, then fuck him, but we all know that man is madly in love with you." Selina flashes me a smile before pushing back from the island and sliding off the chair. "Now that that's settled, I'm going to sit here and drink my virgin mimosa while you three get day drunk and try to convince me to tell you if I'm having a boy or a girl."

eleven

bristol

"Is Seth coming by for lunch again today?" Audrey teases as she leans over the front desk.

"Maybe." My cheeks pink slightly, causing Audrey to giggle. "He said something about having to head to Ace & Hammer this morning, so he might not have time to stop by."

It's been about two months since Seth came back into my life and to say that things have changed would be an understatement. My normal schedule usually involved lunch with the girls, work, and taking care of Rebekah, but ever since Seth and I reconnected, I've had to add him to my routine. Between the sweet text messages that have not turned into phone calls, I talk to him more than my best friends, and that's saying something. Recently, he has taken to stopping by Nurture Space at least once a week for lunch.

"I have an in over there, so if you want me to make a call so your man can come to visit this afternoon..."

Her voice trails off just as my phone chimes on the desk. "Why do I have the feeling that's him?"

I roll my eyes at her before grabbing my phone and heading to the break room in the back to read my text message in peace.

SETH

Hey beautiful. I got done earlier than expected. Still want to have lunch with me?

BRISTOL

Aren't you lucky? I still have one more class this afternoon.

SETH

Aww, I was hoping you could play hooky, but I'll settle for lunch. You in?

BRISTOL

Of course!

SETH

Thank goodness! I thought I was going to have to beg. I'll grab some sandwiches from Just the Drip and be there in about an hour.

BRISTOL

Sounds good! See you soon. X

"Why in the hell did I add that?" I mumble to the empty room, instantly wanting to unsend the message.

Seth and I have been getting to know each other more and more with each passing day, but I still haven't worked up the courage to tell him about our little girl. I know most people would think I'm being heartless, but I never believed I would see Seth again, and now that he's back in town, I honestly don't know what to say to him. *"Hey, you have a daughter,"* would seem like an obvious choice, but it's not that easy.

"Because you're gone for this man but aren't ready to admit it to yourself." The sound of Leia's voice causes me to jump in my seat, dropping my phone on the floor.

Why the hell does she have to be so perceptive? I want to snap back at Leia and tell her she has it all wrong, but that'd be a lie. I want Seth Williams. I want him just as much, if not more than I did when I met him over a year ago, but that scares the shit out of me. I have a huge life-altering secret that I need to tell him on top of trying to figure out whatever this is between us without causing us both a world of hurt. And I've been hurt enough to last a lifetime. I'm not about to put myself in that kind of situation again.

"Jesus, woman. I swear you need a bell tied around your neck or something." I groan, leaning over to grab my phone.

"I made more than enough noise coming in here. You were so focused on your phone that a bomb could've gone off in here and you wouldn't have heard a thing." Leia snickers, giving me a one-armed hug before dropping into the seat beside me.

"It wasn't that bad."

"I wasn't even in here and I can say with certainty it was," Audrey comes strolling into the breakroom, Selina right on her heels. "Now, what am I agreeing to?"

"That Bristol is gone for Seth." Leia raises her eyebrow in my direction, daring me to disagree with her.

"Yeah, that's a given," Selina replies, walking around the table and taking the seat across from me.

"I agree, too," Audrey says as she takes a seat on my other side.

"Thanks. I'm glad to know that you all have an opinion on my relationship."

Leia leans back in her chair, wiggling her eyebrows. "A relationship, huh?"

"OMG! We aren't teenagers anymore." I reach up and pinch the bridge of my nose, quickly losing my patience with my friends.

"Maybe, but I live with two of them. I have an excuse." Audrey holds her hands up in surrender. "But seriously, if you aren't in a relationship with Seth, then what do you call it?"

"Friends. We. Are. Friends," I respond, punctuating each word with a nod of my head.

I'd be lying if I said that I wasn't attracted to Seth. Attracted might not be the correct word to use, but I'm going to roll with it. I had expected that we'd have dinner that first night. I'd tell him about our daughter, and we'd find some way to co-exist with each other, but that's not what happened at all. The idea of there possibly being something more between us never crossed my mind. But when his lips pressed against mine that first night, all rational thought went out the window. I reach up and touch my lips, remembering his against mine. The way his body pressed against mine reignited the fire burning deep inside me.

"With benefits," Selina snickers, causing me to roll my eyes, just as the sound of the bell above the door sounds. "Speak of the devil."

"Will you three behave for once?" I grumble, pushing back from the table and heading toward the front of the studio.

"What would be the fun in that?" Leia shouts loud enough for me to hear, followed by peals of laughter.

"Hello, ladies," Seth says loud enough for them to hear.

"Hello, Seth," they all respond in unison, causing me to roll my eyes.

"What are you? Charlie's Angels?" I grumble before walking past him and out the door. "I thought you said you'd be an hour?"

Seth smiles sheepishly at me, his eyes darting between my friends. "I really wanted to see you, so I asked Vance if I could head out a little early."

"He's so adorable," Audrey squeals, clutching her hands to her chest.

"Why don't we eat outside? It's a nice day.

"Sounds good to me." Seth smiles as he places a hand on the small of my back, leading me toward Just the Drip. "I'm sure they won't mind us stealing a table."

I smile up at him before motioning toward the bag in his left hand with my chin. "It's still pretty early, and you did already buy us sandwiches."

"Thanks for having lunch with me today." The deep baritone in his voice soothes the ache in my heart as he steps beside me, bumping my shoulder. "I missed you."

"Thanks," I say awkwardly and wince.

Of all the ways I could've said, I chose that one? I don't know what it is about Seth that fries my brain. I'm usually more articulate and have my wits about me. I have to, especially with a little girl to take care of. But with Seth, all my responsibilities fade into the background and so do most of my brain cells.

"I mean it, you know." He sighs, tipping his head up toward the sky. "I don't say things I don't mean. If I tell you that instead of lunch, I'd love nothing more than to throw you over my shoulder, carry you back to your house like a caveman, and show you how much I want you to belong to me, I mean it."

I freeze, and my eyes widen in surprise as he takes a step closer to me, his scent enveloping me and drawing me closer to him. I would love nothing more than to give in to the urge to raise up on my toes and allow him to wrap me in his warm embrace and bury my nose in his chest.

"But I won't, because I need you to trust me. I need you to know that I want so much more from you than just a quick fuck. I want everything."

"How do you know I don't trust you?" I try to act nonchalant about it, but I know deep in my soul he's right.

If I trusted him, I would've already told him about our daughter. I wouldn't still be keeping this secret from him. I also would know exactly how I feel about him, no longer allowing my fears to have a vise grip around my heart that tightens every time he tells me how he feels. I want to believe him; I do, but there's a piece of me that wonders if he truly means it.

"It's your eyes," Seth cups my cheek in this palm. "I can see that you're holding something back from me. A piece of yourself you want to protect from being hurt. I can see it in the way you move around me, the way your smile doesn't always reach your eyes, but I'm not giving up on you or us. I have faith that someday soon you'll understand the depth of my feelings for you."

Fuck me. No one besides my mom can read me that well, especially someone I barely know, but he sees it all just by looking into my eyes. His words have stripped me bare, showing the deepest parts of my soul to a stranger, and that's terrifying.

"Don't be scared, Bri." Seth leans forward, running

his hand along my arm and threading his fingers through mine.

"Okay." My breath hitches slightly as he leans forward and brushes his lips against mine.

I'm lost in his eyes as we stare at each other. The magnetic pull between us grows stronger as my gaze flicks back and forth between his lips and eyes.

"You're a dangerous creature, Seth." I groan as he steps away from me and pulls me toward an empty table.

He pulls a chair out for me, and I take a seat, my eyes locked on him as he makes his way around the table and sits. I peer at him, discreetly checking him out. Seth looks pretty much the same as he did when we first met. His eyes are still the same warm chocolate brown color, although he's slightly more muscular than he was. His smile still makes my insides melt just a little when it's directed at me. His voice still wraps around me like a warm blanket, making me feel safe and protected.

And still the exact opposite of me. On the outside, I hope I portray the picture of calm, cool, and collected, but inside, I'm a jumble of nerves, barely hanging on by a thread. I need to keep my wits about me when I'm around him. But that nagging voice in the back of my head keeps reminding me I'm keeping a secret from him. A secret that could ruin everything.

"Are you listening to me?" Seth chuckles, leaning forward and pressing a kiss on the tip of my nose.

A shiver runs down my spine as our lips connect, his hand sliding down my arm, before he winks at me and places a sandwich on the table in front of me.

"Since you weren't listening, you get the turkey and cheese."

"Okay." My cheeks heat as I drop my head, not wanting to see the smug look on his face as I unwrap my sandwich and take a bite.

"How many more classes do you have today?"

"One. Today is Audrey's half day at the studio."

"So, you schedule a lighter class load so you can get out earlier?"

"Yes, we have one day a week with only a few classes. Audrey and I take turns on who teaches the afternoon class. Today is my turn."

"Interesting. I love how you two balance each other. I can't imagine how much you worked before Audrey moved here," he responds, taking a bite of his sandwich. "I'm sure Audrey enjoys having some free time to spend with Connor and the girls."

There it is. The perfect chance to tell him why Audrey moved to Tyson's Creek. To tell him how much help she has been since I had our daughter, giving me a chance to be the best mother I can to our little girl, but I don't. It's like the words are clogging my throat, so I swallow them down and plaster a fake smile on my face, hoping he doesn't notice the change in my mood.

"Why are you asking so many questions?"

"Because, to me, you're the most fascinating person in the world. I want to know everything about you."

My mouth drops open as my brain seems to short-circuit for a few moments. For the first time in years, I'm speechless. This is an odd feeling because I always have a snarky retort or sarcastic comment for someone, but right now, my mind is completely blank.

If this was anyone else, I'd give him a hard time for trying so hard. That his poetic and flowery words are useless. That he's trying way too hard for another chance to get into my pants, but instead, they give me butterflies in my stomach. I can feel deep in my bones that he means everything he's saying to me with his heart and soul. And that is terrifying.

I clear my throat loudly, pointing toward the empty wrapper sitting in front of him. "Are you finished with that?"

"I sure am," he winks at me, trying to put me at ease. "Let me grab yours, and we can head back to the studio, unless you want to take a walk with me?"

"A walk sounds good, actually." I force a smile onto my face as he pushes back from the table and heads toward the trash can.

I can't keep doing this to either of us. I need to figure out a way to let him know about Rebekah. I can't keep lying to him. I can't continue to be afraid that he will reject her. I would love to think he wouldn't, but we barely know each other. Even though he seems like the same person I met over a year and a half ago, I could be wrong. And I can't take that chance because my little girl's happiness is at stake.

"Ready to go?"

I nod my head before gripping Seth's hand and allowing him to pull me down Main Street, away from Nurture Space.

There are a few mom-and-pop stores lining this side of the street, but not many. There's a park at the end where my mom and the girls take Rebekah if I'm teaching a class. Thankfully, I know she's almost three hours away at my parents' house. I usually leave her with Emersyn during the week, but she has a test to study for. When I was talking to my mom over the weekend, she insisted on spending some quality time with her favorite granddaughter. I didn't want to point out that Rebekah is her only granddaughter, but I gave in. I hated the idea of being away from Rebekah for so long, but with Seth back in town, maybe putting some space between him and our daughter is a good thing.

"What made you decide to move to Tyson's Creek?" Seth asks, his eyes focused in front of him as our arms swing slightly between us.

"I've always wanted to live in a small town. Being a military brat, we almost always lived in big cities with thousands of people. It never felt like a community, a place where everyone supported and cared for each other." I smile softly as we reach the entrance to the park. "That's what I felt the first time I came here to visit with Leia. Everyone asked her how she was doing, with warm smiles on their faces. Almost everyone knew each other, and they welcomed me with open arms. I've never had that before."

"I know exactly what you mean," he mutters, resting his forehead against mine. "That's exactly how I felt the first time I laid eyes on you."

A shiver runs down my spine as his nose runs along the shell of my ear before he inhales deeply.

"You don't mean that," I duck my head slightly.

A soft moan escapes my lips as he bites down on my earlobe, nibbling lightly, threading his fingers into my hair, and angling my neck to the side, trailing light kisses down my neck.

"What did I tell you?" he whispers as my eyes flick up to see if anyone is watching before focusing back on his face.

"That you never say anything you don't mean."

Releasing my hair, Seth tugs my body towards him. "That's right." He groans, brushing his lips against mine.

Unable to control the feelings swirling in my body, I lean forward, pressing my lips softly against his. Both of us moan as he grips the back of my neck, pulling me tighter into his body. He dominates our kiss, nipping and sucking my lip between his before thrusting his tongue into my mouth. I wrap my arms around his neck and pull him closer to me. Nothing but pure, unadulterated desire courses through my veins.

But as quickly as it starts, it's over, and we break apart with a gasp.

"Why don't we head back to the studio before I take you right here in front of everyone?" Seth chuckles softly before planting a kiss on my forehead.

"Yeah. That's a good idea." I unwrap my arms from around his neck and put a little more space between us. "I have a class to teach, after all."

twelve

bristol

"Do you have time to stay for dinner?" my mom asks as I strap my daughter into her car seat. "I feel like we never get to spend time with you anymore. If I couldn't convince you to let me keep my granddaughter occasionally, I'd never see either of you."

A few months after I found the nerve to tell my mom I was pregnant with her first granddaughter, my father was transferred to Naval Personnel Command in Millington, TN. It's a little over a three-hour drive from Tyson's Creek to my parents' front door, making it easier for us to see each other whenever we find the time, not that I find the time very often. Between raising Rebekah and the dance studio, I don't have much free time to do anything besides sleep.

My mom comes to visit Tyson's Creek often, sometimes spending the entire weekend spoiling both of us, but my dad is usually tied up with something at work, which suits me just fine, although my relationship with my father has gotten better over the last few years, and even more so since Rebekah was born. He's a much better grandfather than father. He may not have a lot of time away from work to spend with her, but he makes a point of seeing her as often as he can.

I roll my eyes at my mom, then walk over and kiss her cheek before leaning down and giving my dad a peck on the forehead. "I love you both, but I really have to go." I check my watch and move a little quicker. "We can have dinner together when you come down this weekend, okay?"

"And I can have Rebekah while you're at class?" my mom questions as she follows me toward the door, pushing it open and holding it long enough for Rebekah and me to walk out.

"Yeah, sure. But if I get any lip from Leia, I'm blaming you."

"Fine. Leia gets to see you both whenever she wants because you live so close to each other." My mom pouts as she leans down to plant a kiss on Rebekah's forehead.

"Nothing is stopping you from moving closer to Tyson's Creek, Mom. I'm sure they're gonna kick Dad out of the service soon." I giggle, trying to hide the yearning in my voice.

I'd love nothing more than my mom to live closer to us, but my dad is still in the military. He promised my mom he was going to retire a few times, but something always comes up at the last minute. I've never asked if it was his decision or the government's that he wasn't allowed to retire, and if I'm being honest, I don't know if I'd believe whatever answer he gave me. I gave up years ago on the hope he'd put my mom, Melissa, and me ahead of his career.

"I don't know what the future holds for your father. He has a very important position at Command, but he promised he'd find more time to spend with us."

I highly doubt that. I plaster on the same fake smile I give her every time she mentions spending time with my father. It's not that I don't love my father, but there's still a part of me that doesn't know if I can trust him with my heart. Some people are better to love from a distance, and my father is one of them. I won't be hurt or disappointed that way.

"Both of you are welcome to come visit us in Tyson's Creek whenever you want."

"You know your father is busy with work." My mom grimaces before plastering another bright smile on her face. "But I'll get with him so we can make plans for us to come and visit together soon."

"Sure thing, Ma." I give her one last smile, then head toward my car and quickly lock Rebekah's seat into the holder.

"All right, baby girl. Let's get you home." I glance in the rearview mirror at her smiling face before pulling out of the driveway and heading home.

I have exactly four hours to get home and in the house and make sure Rebekah is occupied before Seth calls me. He should be getting his dinner break in a few hours. Ever since they started their construction on Seaside Heights a few days ago, he's been working nonstop. Hopefully, once he passes the civil service exam and begins working as a county deputy, the hours will be a little more regular. Who could've imagined that I'd worry about someone else's schedule? I shake my head and smile as I pull my car out of my parents' driveway and head for the freeway.

Seth and I have been spending more and more time together recently, making it even harder to continue keeping Rebekah a secret from him. At first, I told myself that it wasn't the right time to tell him and that I needed to find the perfect opportunity, but the longer I wait, the harder it becomes to tell him. My excuses are sounding less and less plausible, even to me, and I know in my heart that the longer I wait, the more devastated Seth will be because I've been lying to him.

I would like to believe that this is nothing more than a mother's instinct to protect her child from pain, but I can't keep lying to myself, either. I'm afraid. Afraid of his reaction to finding out he has a child. Afraid of his anger at me for keeping it from him. But most of all, I'm afraid that he won't want to have anything to do with either of us because that'll shatter my soul into a million tiny pieces.

"I need to tell him, and soon," I whisper into the quiet car as I try to think of anything else besides Seth, but fail miserably. I spend the next few hours imagining every probable outcome to tell him about our daughter —the good, the bad, and the indifferent. Each one plays in full color through my mind as I make my way back home.

Although I can't think of anything besides Seth on the drive, I make it back to Tyson's Creek in no time. As I turn left onto my street, my phone suddenly rings.

"Shit," I mutter, worrying about Rebekah hearing me.

I thought I'd have enough time to get her into the house and be occupied with some toys before he called. Ignoring the call, I hop out of the car and unbuckle our daughter before grabbing the diaper bag. Just as I'm shutting the door, my phone rings again.

"Your daddy is persistent today," I coo at the baby as I scurry toward the house and let myself inside.

I set Rebekah and her car seat on the coffee table, then dig through my purse for a few minutes before locating my phone. Sure enough, my screen is illuminated, notifying me of two missed calls from Seth. My phone rings for a third time, and Rebekah fusses in her seat.

"Can't he just give me a few minutes to get situated?" I mumble to myself as I reject the call, then shoot him a text.

BRISTOL

Hey, I'm on the phone with my mom. Can I call you back?

SETH

Hey, beautiful. Sorry for the repeated calls, but I have news to share.

I inhale deeply, attempting to calm the thoughts running rampant through my mind. No one calls someone three times in a row if it's not important to them. My mind races as I imagine what he could want to tell me. My guesses range from him dying of an incurable disease to him getting recalled to the Marines. The probability of either of these options happening is practically nonexistent, but there's no telling my brain that.

SETH

I passed.

I sigh in relief as I flop down on the couch, dropping my phone beside me.

"Your daddy is trying to put me into an early grave," I say to Rebekah, who gives me a blank stare, as if asking who or what I'm speaking about. "Let's get you out of that seat."

I lean forward and unbuckle the many restraints keeping her safe before pulling her out.

"You are the most beautiful girl in the world," I say as I kiss both her cheeks and nuzzle my nose into her neck, blowing warm air across her skin, which makes her laugh.

SETH

There's no getting rid of me now.

I read the text and smile. "As if I wanted to get rid of you."

If it were up to me, Seth and I'd never be apart again. He has kept every promise he has ever made to me, but there is still the fear that at some point, we won't be enough for him. That he'll find something more important to him than being here with Rebekah and me. Not wanting to go down that rabbit hole again, I fire off a response text before shoving the phone into my pocket and striding into the kitchen with Rebekah in my arms.

BRISTOL

That's amazing. Congratulations! I should be finished with my mom soon. Can I call you in an hour?

I check the time as I put Rebekah into her highchair, grab a jar of chicken and carrots from the cabinet, and empty the contents into a kid-safe bowl. As I pull a chair in front of her, my phone vibrates in my pocket. Not wanting to ignore him again, I set the bowl on the highchair tray and pull out my phone.

SETH

I need to get back to work, but I'll call you on my way back to the house.

That'll give me enough time to feed Rebekah, give her a bath, and maybe even put her to bed if everything goes as planned. Just as I'm about to lock my phone, another text comes through.

SETH

I miss you.

My heart melts for the millionth time. This man is the personification of what every woman wants in a partner. However, the nagging voice in the back of my head chooses this moment to remind me that everything can change at the drop of a hat, igniting the flames of my fear again, reminding me for the millionth time since I left my parents' place that I need to figure out how to tell Seth about our daughter before it's too late.

BRISTOL

I miss you, too.

I add a heart emoji and a winking face before hitting send on the text and giving Rebekah my full, undivided attention. Just as I'm turning around to grab the bowl off the tray, I feel something splatter against the side of my face.

"Are we not hungry?" I smile as I turn toward my

little girl and find her hands covered in what was supposed to be her dinner.

Apparently, we are now in the playing-with-our-food stage. Rebekah giggles before shoving one of her hands almost completely into her mouth and licking it.

"How about we use a spoon like a big girl, shall we?" I quickly grab a towel out of the drawer and clean her hands before getting back to feeding her dinner.

Things seem to go smoothly for the rest of the evening, although she doesn't eat much. She does her evening workout in the umpire while I reheat some spaghetti from dinner the night before and shove it down my throat. Thankfully, I even get to eat it while it's still warm tonight. That's not always the case.

After I finish eating, we share a lavender-scented bath before I get her ready for bed and give her a nightly bottle. I'm just laying her down in the travel crib in my room when my phone rings. After checking to ensure the baby monitor is on, I leave the door cracked and answer the call.

"Hey, stranger," I chirp into the phone, my southern drawl coming out a little more than I would like.

Seth chuckles, which sends a shiver of pleasure through my body. Who could have imagined that the sound of one person's voice would affect me this much?

"Hey, beautiful."

"Trust me, I'm far from beautiful right now," I mumble as I look down at my oversized sweatshirt.

"You're always beautiful."

I swoon internally as I drop onto the couch. "You don't have to lay it on so thick. You've already got the girl."

"Do I?" he questions.

Seth and I haven't exactly tried to label what we're doing. Yes, we've had one date and have lunch together often, but I haven't given him any hint about how much his being here in Tyson's Creek means to me.

"Yes, you do," I whisper, holding my breath.

I've laid almost everything on the line by uttering those three simple words. Seth has shown me time and time again that he'll do anything to ensure things work out between us. It's time that I put in a little effort, too.

"What questions do you have for me today?" I ask as I get a little more comfortable and turn the television on low, not wanting to put too much focus on my response.

"Favorite food," Seth responds.

I hear something rustling in the background. Ever since he came back to town, he's been asking me random questions about myself every time we see each other. We spend hours talking about nothing at all, and it means everything to me.

"Don't laugh. Culver's. I love the sourdough melt

with extra pickles. If I'm having a particularly bad day, I get a chocolate milkshake to dip my fries in."

"I had Culver's for dinner tonight. Brady grabbed us some burgers, but I drew the line at dipping my fries in my milkshake. Potatoes and chocolate are two things that just do not go together," Seth snickers.

"You'll be eating your words after you try it once," I mumble into the phone as I pick up the remote and begin flicking through the channels, landing on reruns of *Golden Girls*. "How about you?"

He pauses for a moment. "You."

The deep timbre of his voice sends a shiver down my spine, making my cheeks heat with embarrassment.

"Be serious." I whimper as I rub my thighs together, attempting to gain some relief.

Seth and I haven't spent much time alone together since the night he cooked me dinner, but not for lack of trying. We meet for lunch and get coffee before I open the studio whenever our schedules line up, but anything besides that has been hard. Between his schedule at the construction site and my work at the studio, it's been next to impossible. But then I also have Rebekah to worry about. The girls have told me numerous that times they'd watch her whenever I asked, but they have lives and families of their own.

This would all be easier if you just told him about her.

Shut up, brain. No one asked you.

I'd love nothing more than to go back to the woman I was before our daughter was born. To be desired by someone as a woman, not as a source of nourishment and comfort. Now that Seth is back in my life, he has awakened a need I forgot I possessed.

"I am," he insists.

"Real food," I scold him as I push off the couch and head toward the kitchen. I need a cold drink of water and to steer the conversation back toward safer territory.

"I'm a sucker for Mrs. Thomas's fish fry, but I do have a soft spot for Mexican food," he replies.

"Well, you're in luck. I make a mean chicken enchilada. Maybe if you're a good boy, I'll make them for you someday." I instantly regret my word choice as Seth's boisterous laugh rings through the phone.

"Do you really want me to be a good boy?"

"It depends on your definition of a good boy." I fill my glass with water and gulp it down. I need to redirect this conversation. Now.

"What's your favorite TV show?" I blurt out.

I plop back down on the couch as another episode of *Golden Girls* begins on the television. Memories of all the nights when Selina and I would discuss which Golden Girl we were in our teens fill my mind.

"I didn't watch television much." He lowers his voice slightly. "Being bounced around between foster homes didn't leave much room for fun. I went to school, then to work when I was old enough, and then home to do my homework."

I pull my bottom lip into my mouth and begin nibbling on it. Seth has told me about his life growing up in foster care after his parents died. My heart aches for him, realizing all the things I had in life and took for granted. I spent most of my teens angry at my dad for always being gone, resenting the time the military kept us apart, but mostly I missed him. I can't imagine what it would be like if my parents were gone and I knew they were never coming back.

"I can hear the wheels turning in your head, Bri," Seth chuckles.

"Sorry. Sometimes my mind wanders when I'm tired," I retort quickly, not wanting to bring up anything too heavy.

We continue to ask each other questions like this for a while longer. Nothing too heavy or personal, but the usual "getting to know you" first-date questions, even though we both know we've progressed so much further than that.

"What's your favorite flower?" he asks, breaking a short silence.

"Are you planning on screwing up sometime soon?" I joke, but the idea of Seth bringing me a bouquet of daisies and sunflowers on my birthday, or even for no reason at all, sounds appealing.

"No, but you never know. I need to be prepared just in case." He laughs nervously.

"Sunflowers and daisies are my favorite. Roses are useless. Never bring me those unless you plan on being in the doghouse for a few months. They're beyond pretentious."

"Duly noted."

"Can I ask you a personal question?" he asks as I turn off the television. Something in his tone tells me this is going to be a serious question.

"Shoot."

"Do you want kids?"

I gasp in shock. Who would have thought Seth would touch on the one subject I've been trying to find the right time to bring up since he came back to town? This will be the perfect opportunity to have some of my questions answered. If Seth tells me he doesn't want a family or children of his own, I may have to rethink how our relationship will look moving forward, but I still need to tell him about our daughter. He has a right to know, and this might be the perfect chance for me to tell him.

However, instead of blurting out that he already has a daughter, I settle for telling him the truth, or at least part of it. "Sure. I always saw myself having children and settling down. I mean, I live in a small town. The white picket fence and two-point-five kids with a dog were drilled into my mind from birth." I giggle nervously before asking the one question I need to know the answer to more than anything. "Do you?"

"Do I what?" Seth clears his throat. "I mean, my parents died when I was eight. I spent the next ten years in foster care, bouncing around from house to house, until I joined the Marines. Most people would say children were out of the question, but I could imagine having little copies of you running around the house."

My cheeks instantly heat as I think of our daughter, who's lying in a crib down the hall. Her bright red hair and hazel eyes are a little combination of both of us. The doctor swore her eyes would darken to more of a brown color, but they were wrong. Although her red hair and her hazel-colored eyes were uncommon, I knew deep down that they'd stay the same. A one-of-a-kind creation from a one-of-a-kind relationship like ours.

"So, you imagine having kids with me?" he mumbles nervously.

It seems like we're both stepping into unfamiliar territory now. I open and close my mouth a few times, searching for the right words. Trying to figure out how to tell him we don't have to imagine having kids together because we already have a beautiful baby girl.

"Seth..." I begin.

I'm cut off by the sound of Rebekah's loud wails

coming through the baby monitor beside me on the end table.

"Shit!" I exclaim as I rush down the hallway, my heart in my throat.

Rebekah hardly ever cries. A few whimpers here and there when she's hungry, but nothing like this.

"Wow. You need to turn the television down," he teases.

Thank the Lord he came to his own conclusion about the crying baby, because that isn't the way I planned on telling him about our little girl.

"Yeah," I breathe as I tuck the phone under my ear with my shoulder and reach in to pick up Rebekah.

She is hot to the touch, her chubby little cheeks pink from the heat, and fat tears are rolling down her face as she cries louder. Panic begins to well in my chest at the idea of my little one being sick. Rebekah is hardly ever sick, but when she is, it's usually something that involves a visit to the doctor and some antibiotics.

"Is everything okay?" Seth asks, his voice filled with concern.

My heart squeezes in my chest, wanting nothing more than to tell Seth what is going on, but I can't, not right now. If I tell Seth about Rebekah right now, he could want to meet her and demand an answer that I don't know how to give him. Right now, I need to focus on my baby girl and do everything I can to ensure she gets better.

"Yeah, but I really should get going. I hate to end our call, but I have an early day at the studio tomorrow."

Seth yawns loudly, causing both of us to laugh. "I think you have the right idea. I'll talk to you tomorrow, beautiful. Good night."

"Good night, Seth," I respond before ending the call and throwing my phone on the bed. I rush into the bathroom and grab the baby thermometer, running it across her forehead to her temple. It takes me a few passes before I'm able to get a clear reading: 101 degrees.

"Fuck!" I wail, as tears stream down my face.

Now is not the time to lose it, Bristol. You need to be there for your daughter, since no one else is. But there could be someone else.

"I know. I know," I mutter into the room, suddenly regretting my decision even more to keep Rebekah from her father.

I'll figure out a way to tell Seth about Rebekah soon. He deserves to be here for her, for us, to experience the good, bad, and hard parts of having a little one. Like right now, I would love nothing more than to snap my fingers and take whatever is wrong with her away, but I can't, and it breaks my heart.

"Shhhhh, baby girl," I whisper against the top of her head as I grab the infant's Tylenol and a syringe out of the medicine cabinet and shove it into my pants pocket before running a washcloth under cool water. I squeeze it tightly in my right hand, hoping to get most of the water out before walking back into the room.

I lay her down on my bed as gently as possible and open her pajamas, pulling her tiny arms out of the sleeves before running the cool rag over her forehead and stomach. Now that she is lying down, I pull the medicine out of my pocket and draw out the right dosage.

I rub my finger on Rebekah's chin, hoping to coax her into opening her mouth. "Come on, sweetheart. Mama has something that will make you feel better."

After coaxing her for a little longer, she finally opens her mouth just enough for me to shoot the medicine inside. She coughs a little but keeps it down.

"All right, sweetie. Hopefully, you'll feel better soon."

For the next hour, I rock her back and forth, trying everything I can to soothe her, but it's all to no avail. Tears roll down both of our cheeks as I wrack my brain, trying to come up with something else to make her feel better.

I text Audrey, asking her for advice, but get no response. She's probably already asleep or busy with her family. I stare at my phone for a few moments, weighing the pros and cons of texting Seth, but decide against it. He won't know any more than I do about this, but I'm sure we could figure it out together.

"Let's check your temperature again," I mumble as I lay Rebekah down and check her temperature again. The light flashes her temperature: 100.4. I sigh in relief. At least the medicine is helping a little.

"Do I need to call the doctor?" I ask my little girl, as if she could answer me.

Rebekah has never had any type of fever before. She even took to teething like a champ. No crying fits or issues sleeping since she started. All I have to do is make sure we have teething rings available for her to chew on, and we're set.

This is a different story altogether. It's completely uncharted territory for me as a first-time mom. I grab my phone off the bed, searching through my contacts for someone to call and ask for advice, but quickly change my mind.

"It's just the two of us." I sniffle as I bury my nose in my little girl's hair.

Rebekah coughs and gags loudly before throwing up all over me and herself. "It's okay, it's okay, it's okay," I repeat like a mantra as I gently set her on the bed and rip my shirt over my head.

I should be worried about getting her spit-up all over my hair and other parts of my body, but I'm too tired to care. I pull her pajamas off her legs and wrap her in a blanket. No sense in putting her in a clean onesie if she's just going to be spitting up for the remainder of the night.

I take a seat in the rocking chair in the opposite corner of my room and slowly rock back and forth. The rocking seems to do the trick, and she calms slightly, sniffling softly as she tries to calm down.

Fat tears roll down my cheeks as the exhaustion consumes me. The last time I looked at the clock, it was almost one in the morning. What I wouldn't give for someone, anyone, who knows more about taking care of a child than me to appear, but there is no one I can turn to. Everyone has their own lives, and I can't keep bothering them as I try to learn how to take care of my daughter.

I was ready to tell Seth about Rebekah earlier, but now I don't have another choice. He should be here for the good and the bad. Her first stomachache and her first steps. I shouldn't have taken this away from him, no matter what my reasons. I could have done any number of things to get a hold of him, but I let my fear get the best of me.

I need to do the right thing, for both mine and Rebekah's sake. At times like this, when I'm at my wit's end with no one to turn to, it would be nice to have someone else to rely on. Someone else that loves and cares for Rebekah as much if not more than I do, and there's no better person to do that than her father.

And Rebekah? Well, every little girl needs her daddy.

thirteen

seth

"Trouble in paradise?" Brady asks as he flops down on the other side of the couch and puts his feet on the coffee table.

"You could say that. Bristol hasn't been answering my calls or texts for the last few days," I grumble, trying to think of anything I could have done to turn her off.

"Maybe she's just busy," he responds absentmindedly as he turns our PlayStation on.

It's been about a few weeks since our date, and things were going well. We haven't had much time to spend alone together. I try to drop lunch off to her at the studio once or twice a week, but I haven't been able to as much since things picked up with the new construction project Vance and Connor hired me to work on.

Now, most days I'm exhausted when I get home, leaving no room for more dates with Bristol, but I haven't left her hanging. Usually, I call her every night when I get home or shortly after dinnertime, depending on what her class schedule is for that week. Thankfully, being the owner of her own business, she understands being tired at the end of the day and just needing time to hang out and relax, so instead of dates, we settle for phone calls and text messages.

We usually text back and forth during the day and, if time permits, have long talks into the night. We talk about everything and nothing at the same time. She asks me questions about being in the military and about the places I've visited over the years, which I answer easily. I ask her all the mundane questions about herself, like her favorite color and food, her favorite hobby—other than yoga, of course. I want to know everything about her, even the small stuff.

We even briefly touched on the future. I told her about taking the civil service exam in hopes of becoming a deputy and how that might affect our spending time together. Bristol was clear about her fears that something would happen to me overseas, and she could very well have the same fears about me becoming a deputy. Bristol hasn't said anything specific, but she has hinted that there's always a possibility of something happening, even if Tyson's Creek is a quiet town where nothing ever really happens.

Instead of blowing off her fears, I confronted them head-on, explaining to her that although I understand there's just as much of a threat of me getting hit by a car crossing the street as there is of something happening while I was on the job, I'd do everything in my power to ensure I came home safely to her. That seemed to ease her worries, but Bristol promised to talk to me about her fears and concerns if they arise, and I promised to always listen to what she had to say. I understand her fears are valid no matter how unlikely anything happening to me is.

I hoped that conversation had brought us closer, and it seemed we were heading in that direction the last time we talked, but something's changed, and I have no idea what it is. Either way, I need to ensure she knows I have no intention of leaving Tyson's Creek or her.

With every conversation, the connection and love I feel for her grows more and more. I know people will ask how I can love someone I've only spent a few weeks with, but when your heart knows, it knows. Besides, Bristol and I aren't just meeting each other for the first time. Yes, we went more than a year without speaking to each other while I was on deployment, but that wasn't for a lack of trying.

But out of nowhere, she's stopped answering to my messages and has been sending my phone calls to voicemail. The sudden cold shoulder has me second-guessing everything.

"Too busy to respond to a text?" I huff as I push off the couch.

Once Brady gets into gaming mode, there is no talking to him.

"Yeah, you're probably right. People are attached to their phones."

I cuff him on the back of the head. "Thanks for the vote of confidence, man."

"Anytime." He winks at me as I head past him toward my bedroom.

As soon as I walk into the room, images of the night I spent with Bristol filter through my mind. I never believed in love at first sight, but meeting Bristol has changed the way I view the world. I'm no longer going through my days on edge and waiting for the other shoe to drop. Instead, I'm thinking about the future. More specifically, a future with Bristol in it.

I believed that after we spent more time together, she'd understand where I was coming from. I thought if I just showed her how much I cared for her, even after all this time, I could convince her to open herself up to me a little more. But instead, things have just gotten more complicated.

Something has scared her off, and I need to find out who or what it was and fast, or I could lose her. The one time I spoke to her via text a few days ago, she said things were busy for her right now, but I can't shake this feeling that there's something else going on. Bristol told me there were things she wasn't ready to share with me just yet, and I understood, not wanting to push her away. But I was hoping after spending all this time reconnecting and getting to know each other again that she'd trust me enough to share those parts of her, even if only a little bit. Instead, I feel like I'm back to square one.

My phone rings, breaking me from my thoughts. "Hello?"

"Seth Williams?" an unknown voice asks.

"Speaking," I reply gruffly, wanting to know the meaning of this call as quickly as possible.

"Hello. This is Amie from Pointe Realtors. This call is to inform you that the owners of the home accepted your offer."

I sigh in relief; things may just be looking up. Now, not only is Connor my boss, but he's my neighbor, too. If he wasn't such a decent guy, I would have reservations about it, but it seems to have made us better friends.

"That's great. Thanks. Is there anything else you need from me to finish the process?"

"Not at the moment, but we'll let you know. Thank you for choosing Pointe Realtors, and congratulations."

"Thank you." I hang up the phone quickly and head back out of my room, stepping right in front of the television to ensure that I have Brady's full, undivided attention.

"What the fuck? I was in the middle of a game!" Brady shouts, leaning from side to side and trying to glimpse the screen around my imposing form before pausing the game.

"No, you aren't. I got the house." I smile down at my friend as he pulls his headset off and drops the control, his game now forgotten.

"That's amazing, man." Brady stands and gives me a manly hug. "One step closer to sealing the deal with your girl."

"I'm going to need to have a lot more than a house to convince her I'm not going anywhere, but this is a step in the right direction."

Don't get me wrong, I love that Brady and his family opened their home up to me when I needed a place to stay, but it's time for me to have space of my own. Having spent the last twenty-plus years sharing a room with two or three other men, it will be nice to not have to worry about anyone but myself.

"We need to celebrate. I'm sure Connor and Vance are busy with their ladies, but Walker and Riggs are in town. I bet they'd be down to grab a few beers at Crawdaddy's."

Leave it to Brady to find any excuse to head to Crawdaddy's. He suggests we go there every chance he gets, whether it's grabbing a beer with the crew from Ace & Hammer after work or a bite to eat. Yeah, it's one of the few bars in the area, but there is something that keeps drawing him back there... or I should say, some*one*.

Ever since his run-in with Emersyn a few months ago he's been moody. He claims it's nothing more than stress and adjusting to civilian life, but I know better. Nothing sets my friend on edge more than a beautiful woman. I always thought he had someone back here in Tyson's Creek who had his heart, but he always denied it. Now I have a feeling I finally figured out who his mystery woman is.

"Is Emersyn going to be there?" I question, already knowing the answer.

It's the weekend, and Crawdaddy's is the place to be. Especially for a twenty-something-year-old girl wanting to blow off steam.

"I have no idea," he grumbles before dropping back down in his seat. "If you don't want to celebrate, I get it. But could you kindly get out of my way so I can finish my game?"

I step out of the way. "When are you going to tell me the story behind you two? Look, I'm not stupid. I know there's more to the story between you two than her just being your friend's baby sister."

Brady stares into my eyes, and I know that look. He's fighting demons of his own, ones that no one can help him overcome.

"Soon," is the only answer he gives me before turning back toward the television, signaling the end of our conversation.

"I'll text Walker and ask if they can meet us there at six. Sound good?"

Brady nods his head in response. Hopefully, he'll work through his issues before we head out tonight.

I head toward the front door, deciding to leave and give him some space for a little while.

"Where you headed?" Brady calls as I turn the knob.

"To see Bristol. She can't ignore me if I'm right in front of her face," I say over my shoulder, pulling the door shut behind me.

As I make my way down the stairs toward my truck, I glance at my watch. It's lunchtime, and what better way to show someone that you're thinking about them than bringing them food? Remembering from our conversation how much she loves the sourdough melt from Culver's, I stop there and grab us both some food, then head toward the center of town.

Since it's a Saturday afternoon, I know Bristol shouldn't have too many classes today, but she has been working since early this morning. Instead of having a relaxing Saturday to herself, she's helping everyone else to relax instead. If my memory serves me right, she and the girls should be at the yoga or dance studio, since they're all between classes. Here's hoping she's happy to see me.

I pull into a parking spot between the two studios and play a quick game of eeny-meeny-miny-moe before deciding to try the yoga studio first. I grab both our meals, then decide against bringing mine inside. I have no idea how busy she is today. The point of bringing her lunch is to let her know I'm thinking about her, not to get another date out of it. I mean, if it happens in the process, I won't complain, but that's not why I'm here.

I stride toward the door, pulling it open and stepping inside. The lobby of the yoga studio's walls are painted a muted green and are covered in different pictures of women in different poses and one of Bristol smiling brightly at the camera surrounded by her students. Relaxing music playing softly filters through the door of the studio that's propped open. But instead of being greeted with a hello as I come in the door, I'm met with complete silence.

Audrey, Selina, and Bristol all stare in my direction, no one moving or saying a word. I have no idea what these three were discussing before I came in, but it doesn't take a genius to figure out that it has something to do with me.

My eyes zero in on Bristol, noticing the dark circles under her eyes, and her hair is piled high in a messy bun on the top of her head. She has on a baggy T-shirt that engulfs her body, hanging past her butt, and another pair of those tempting yoga pants complete the outfit.

"Hey, beautiful," I say, waving to the other ladies as I stride toward Bristol.

"Hey yourself," she replies, her eyes looking everywhere but at me, and takes a step to the side, putting the small welcome desk between us.

I try to give her a reassuring smile as I come closer, but she wraps her arms around her waist, her shoulders pulling inward like she's closing herself off to me. Something is definitely off with her, but what is it? I try to think of anything I could've said or done during our last conversation to make her react this way to me when the realization hits me.

I asked her about our relationship status. I promised her I would give her time to sort out her feelings for me, but instead, I pushed her to decide what we were without even knowing what I was doing. It seemed like a natural enough question to ask, but I guess I was wrong, and now she's pulling away from me.

I give her a reassuring smile as I come to a stop right in front of her, holding the bag of food out in front of me like a peace offering. "I figured you would be ready for some lunch."

I wait a few moments for her to respond, but she says nothing, and she doesn't take the food from me. I set the bag on the counter before walking around and giving her a hug.

"Sorry to barge in like this, but I missed you."

Audrey and Selina sigh softly, but Bristol's entire body stiffens as I wrap my arms around her before she steps away from me.

"I missed you, too," she whispers, grabbing the bag off the counter and peaking inside. "You remembered."

"Of course, I did. I remember everything you've told me about you."

Tears stream down her cheeks as she clutches the bag tightly in her hands and pushes past me, rushing toward the back of the studio.

I rub the back of my neck, looking over at the other two ladies for some help. "What did I do wrong?"

"She's just having a hard time right now," Audrey says, leaning forward and resting her arms on the reception desk.

"Is that code for I just made things worse without knowing?" I shake my head as I take a seat in a chair under the large glass windows in the front of the studio. "I just wanted to let her know I was thinking about her."

"Trust me, she knows." Selina takes a seat beside me, resting her hand on my shoulder. "I'm sure you know Bristol isn't the best at telling people how she feels. Sometimes it's like pulling teeth to get her to admit when she's worried about something."

I nod my head in understanding, remembering how hard it was to get Bristol to warm up to me after we first met. At first, I thought it was because of her statement about not liking men in the military, and she hated me on principle, but the more I talked to her, I discovered it was something more. Bristol has always had to keep her heart guarded against new people, a product of being a military brat and being the new kid more often than any child would like. People always wanted to poke fun at the new kid and see how far they could push her before she snapped. After a while, she built a wall around her heart, making people prove to her they were genuine before she let them in. But once you worm your way into Bristol's heart, you're there forever. You're part of her family.

I thought I had gotten past the walls to her gooey center, but I guess I was wrong. By pushing her, I was asking for something more than she was ready to give me. And I broke the promise I made to her, which is an unforgivable offense to Bristol. It's the same thing she told me her father used to do. He'd make promises she knew he couldn't keep for any number of reasons, but she always hoped that he'd come through for her. But he never did, leaving her devastated.

"Thanks for trying to make me feel better, but I know she's pissed at me." I sigh, running my hand along the back of my neck. "I just wish I knew how to apologize to her."

"Wait a second. What?"

"Why would she be pissed at you?" Audrey questions, as if the answer wasn't staring her right in the face.

"I pushed her. Just like I promised I wouldn't, and now she's pulling away from me."

Audrey and Selina share a knowing glance before Audrey takes a seat on the other side of me. "Okay, slow down and tell us exactly what happened."

"Maybe we can help you come up with the perfect plan to get back into her good graces." Selina giggles softly, resting her hand on top of the little bump of her belly.

"Congratulations, by the way," I say with a smile, motioning toward her belly. "Vance hasn't shut up about how he's going to be a father since we met. Don't tell him I told you, but we have a pool going about whether you're having a boy or a girl."

"That sounds just like him," Audrey replies as she and Selina both laugh loudly. "We do, too, because someone won't tell us what she's having."

"And what would be the fun in that? Surprises keep us young, don't they?"

"Speak for yourself. I may have a fifteen-year-old, but I'm far from being old," Audrey retorts before turning her attention back to me. "Way to change the subject, but you aren't getting out of explaining yourself."

"I should've known nothing would get past you two." I chuckle, looking for the right words to explain what happened. "Bristol and I have been getting closer since we had the date a few weeks ago. Talking on the phone and getting to know each other better, but about a week ago, I asked her something, and I don't think she was ready to answer."

"What did you ask her?" Selina asks, cocking her head to the side.

"Where she saw things going with us." I push to my feet and pace back and forth across the room. "I know I messed up, but it just kind of came out. I promised her I wouldn't push her, but I broke that promise. I've gone on and on about how I'm not like her father, that she can count on me to keep my promises, and I did the exact opposite."

"I doubt you messed up that badly. Bristol isn't one to hold grudges against anyone," Audrey says, gripping my shoulder tightly, causing me to stop pacing and look at her. "She's trying to work through some things right now. When she's ready to talk, I'm sure you'll be the first person she talks to."

"This is honestly a case of *it's her and not you*, trust us. She'll get things figured out soon," Selina chimes in, pushing to her feet and coming toward us, gripping both of my hands in hers and squeezing them tightly. "Just keep reminding her you aren't the enemy. We all know how stubborn she can be. If being with Bristol is what you really want, then don't give up on her."

I turn toward the door for the studio, willing Bristol to appear again and give me a chance to apologize to her for pushing. For breaking my promise to give her the time she needed to decide how she felt about me.

For being just like her father and breaking my promise. I stand there for a few moments before pulling my hands from Selina's grasp and sighing.

"I hope you ladies have a good day."

I stand and head toward the back of the studio but pause. Bristol obviously doesn't want to see me, but it still feels wrong to just leave without saying goodbye.

"Talk to you later, Bristol," I call out before turning on my heels and heading out the door.

Neither Audrey nor Selina say anything as I leave. Hopefully, they can at least tell her how sorry I am and that it wasn't my intention to push her. Bristol looks exhausted—probably working herself to the bone again. Maybe those two can convince her to take it easy for a few days. I'm sure she needs it.

My visit didn't turn out how I planned, but I should have known she wouldn't want to see me. I open the truck door and am immediately hit with the delicious smell of my food. My stomach rumbles loudly as I climb into the truck and shut the door behind me.

She can be as stubborn as she wants, but like Selina said, I need to make sure she understands that I'm not going anywhere. If she believes that this slight hiccup is going to scare me off, then she has another thing coming.

fourteen

bristol

My phone chimes from its place beside me in the break room, but I don't even bother to pick it up. I know it's Seth asking what's wrong with me.

I've been ignoring him for the better part of the week. I'd love to blame everything on Rebekah being so sick, but that'd be a lie. I need to tell him about our daughter. I just can't figure out how. I've written letters and speeches and even thought about just bringing Rebekah to see him at his place one night. But every time I decide on a specific course of action, I change my mind, allowing my fear to get the better of me for the millionth time. I know the next time I talk to him, there will be no escaping the fact I need to tell him about Rebekah, so I've been ignoring him.

"You could have been nicer to him," Audrey says as she comes into the room, taking a seat beside me at the table and reaching toward the bag of uneaten food.

"Hands off," I grumble, and grab the bag from her

reach and open it. The scent of my favorite sandwich fills the room, making my stomach growl. "I guess I've gotten my appetite back."

"Good. You need to take better care of yourself, Bri. We're worried about you."

"I know," I whisper, reaching into the bag and grabbing a few fries before shoving them into my mouth.

I couldn't stop the tears from falling when Seth handed me the bag of food with my favorite sandwich, which I only mentioned once a few days ago. He has been asking me anything and everything he can think of, and this tells me he's been paying attention to my answers.

"Are you still planning to tell him about Rebekah?" Audrey's voice brings me back to the present.

"I don't know." I sigh as I reach into the bag and pull out my sandwich. I unwrap it and moan as I take a huge bite. I didn't even realize how hungry I was until this moment. "I'll be surprised if I didn't already send him running for the hills with my hot and cold behavior. He'll probably never speak to me again."

She shakes her head. "Yeah, like your tears could scare that man away. Besides, I consider sleep deprivation a valid reason for any erratic or emotional behavior."

Rebekah's awful night a few nights ago was just the beginning. She's slowly getting better, but between her needing to be held most of the night in order to sleep and my having to run the studio, to say I've been in a bad mood is an understatement. I've barely slept over three hours a night since then.

"I've also been ignoring his calls. Honestly, I'm surprised he showed up here today. Most men would have written me off as a tease and moved on to the next person."

"You and I know both know Seth isn't like most men."

"That we do." Leia comes strolling into the room, a stern look on her face. "Why else would he come all the way over here to check on you?"

"I thought your dad had a doctor's appointment in Nashville today?" I mumble, suddenly more interested in my food than looking any of my friends in the eye.

"He does, but Walker called and said Riggs was on his way to pick him up. Apparently, Seth texted and asked him to go out and celebrate."

"Riggs?" Selina says, as she comes into the room and reaches into my bag, grabbing a handful of fries before winking at me. "Why isn't Walker coming?"

"Walker has a shift at the station today." Leia's cheeks pink slightly as she walks around the table and plops into the only empty seat. "I guess Walker said something to Riggs about Dad's appointment, and he offered to take him for me."

Selina rolls her eyes, plopping down into the seat on my other side. "I think Riggs is trying to suck up to a certain someone. What better way to do that than to help take a few things off your plate?"

"There's nothing going on between Riggs and me."

"You keep telling yourself that, Leia. Maybe if you say it enough, you'll believe it, too." Selina pats her softly on the hand as we break out in fits of laughter at Leia's expense.

I wrap my arms around my side as I try to control my laughter before I suddenly remember what Leia said. "Wait. Did you say Seth is celebrating something?"

My eyebrows pull down in confusion as I try to figure out what Seth would be celebrating. The last time we spoke, he told me about passing the civil service exam and his plans to become a deputy, but that's the only thing I know of. I'm sure he'd have celebrated that before now, wouldn't he? Or are the guys coming to take him out for another reason? A reason I don't want to know about.

"I can see the wheels turning in your head, Bri." Leia giggles. "There are no nefarious plans. Walker just said Seth got some good news, and Brady needed an excuse to stalk Emersyn."

"He didn't say anything when he was here," I mumble, rubbing the spot on my chest over my heart.

Just the idea of Seth having something to celebrate and not being included sends my world into another tailspin. I want to know everything about him. I want to be the first person he calls when he has good news, the shoulder to cry on when someone upsets him. I want to be the first person he thinks about in the morning and the last person he sees when he goes to bed at night. It all hits me like a ton of bricks. What a fool I've been. I've been so worried about protecting my heart that I may have sabotaged my only chance at being happy.

Unimaginable pain shoots through my body at the idea of seeing Seth around town, knowing that I had my chance to be with him, but I let my own fears get in the way. My fear that he wouldn't want Rebekah, but what I was worried about most was that he wouldn't want me. The frayed edges of my heart rip open for the second time today.

"I just..." Tears pool in my eyes as all the emotions I've been trying desperately to keep in check come bubbling to the surface. "I'm so scared."

Audrey, Leia, and Selina surround me, their arms wrapping around me in a warm hug as I let all my emotions free. Tears stream down my cheeks as I sob, wishing I could find some way out of this situation. A solution that will allow all three of us to have a happy ending where Seth, Rebekah, and I are a family. The way it all should've been from the start.

"I've ruined everything and don't know how to fix it. He's going to hate me."

I clutch my friends tightly, biting down on my bottom lip, hoping to quiet the sobs bubbling from my throat. My heart feels as if it's breaking in two. I want nothing more than to rush out of here and find Seth, to tell him everything, and then it will all be okay, but this is the real world. There's no way Seth is going to easily forgive me for hiding his daughter from him. I should have told him the first night I saw him. Hell, I've had a million chances to tell him the truth, but I chose to keep it a secret. And that secret is going to ruin everything.

I'm just praying that I can hold on for just a little longer until the pain subsides. I yearn for numbness to cut me off from all these feelings that I'm so desperate to forget. "Tell me what to do," I whine, wrapping my arms around my waist in an attempt to hold myself together.

"I'm going to go turn the closed sign on and call to cancel your classes this afternoon," Audrey murmurs, pushing to her feet and heading back into the studio.

"Thank you for doing that," I grumble, grabbing her hand as she walks by and giving it a squeeze.

"We know it kills you to cancel class and let people down." Leia reaches across the table and grasps both of my hands, squeezing them slightly.

"I'm going to call your mom. We need to come up with a plan, and you need a break," Selina says as she dials my mom's number.

My mom showed up on my doorstep this morning, demanding to spend time with her granddaughter. I'm sure she knew how hard the last few days have been with Rebekah being sick, but I never expected her to show up on my doorstep. I figured she could spend the day with Rebekah, and I could get a home-cooked meal and maybe a few hours of sleep after work. However, now I have a feeling her arrival wasn't such a coincidence.

"You called my mom and told her to come down today, didn't you?"

"We did no such thing," Audrey responds as she comes back into the room and retakes her seat.

Her eyes look everywhere but at me. Bingo. Audrey is a terrible liar, and I should be livid with them for interfering, but I'm not. I know these ladies are just looking out for me. "But even if we did, you need the rest, and your mom is the only person you will listen to."

I open my mouth to protest but slam it shut almost immediately. I know she's right. I haven't had a decent night's sleep in days, and it's showing.

"Hey, Mrs. Reid." Selina narrows her eyes at me, daring me to say something, but I raise my hands in surrender. "Would you like to hang out with all of your granddaughters for a few hours? Bristol has been burning the candle at both ends. She needs some rest."

Granddaughters? As in plural?

"Love and Jade have been wanting to spend some time with your mom. We're killing two birds with one stone," Audrey whispers. "I already called Connor to let him know she was coming over with Rebekah."

"You guys are too good to me."

Selina listens intently to what my mom has to say before smiling. "You bet. Connor is expecting you and has already ordered pizza, so don't you dare try to cook."

My mom grumbles something on the other end of the line, and Selina snickers. "You're spending time with your granddaughters, not taking care of all of us. Bristol will be there around seven. See you later."

"Rebekah is taken care of, and so are your classes," Audrey says with a smile.

"You need to remember you aren't alone," Selina insists, which causes tears to well in my eyes.

"I know I'm not alone, but you guys have families to take care of." I place my hand on her baby bump. "Or babies to grow. I can't ask you guys to keep helping me as much as I do. It's not fair."

"First, you never ask. That's the problem." Audrey throws her arm over my shoulder and pulls me into her. "We're here to help you. Seth is here to help you. Damn, he was more worried about you not eating than the fact that you've been ignoring his phone calls and texts. All you have to do is let us help you."

"You're not alone, Bristol. You never have been and never will be," Leia adds.

"Fine. I can take a hint." I pull away from Audrey

and raise my hands in surrender. "Now, how are we going to get me out of this mess?"

I've been trying to figure a way out of this on my own, but maybe I need to rely on my friends a little more. Yes, I got myself into this situation by keeping Rebekah a secret for so long, but I don't have to find a solution on my own.

"There's no perfect way to let someone know they have a seven-month-old daughter," Leia huffs. "But what we need is to figure out how to explain it to him. We need to make sure he understands why you kept her a secret."

What if it's not a good reason? I think to myself, once again afraid to give voice to my innermost thoughts. At first, I wanted to be sure that Seth was staying in town, that he was going to be a permanent part of Rebekah's life, but *I was afraid* doesn't seem like a good enough explanation, but it's the only one I have. I was afraid of what his reaction would be to me keeping such a tremendous secret from him. He might understand why I didn't get in contact with him during deployment, but he's been in Tyson's Creek for months.

Honestly, I'm surprised no one has said anything to him about me having a child. We live in a small town where everyone knows everyone. Hell, Mrs. Thomas delivered Rebekah, and there's no way she doesn't know that Seth and I have been seeing each other. I know there are some types of laws that don't allow her to say things about patients, but still.

"You also need a place where you feel safe. This is going to be just as hard for you as it is for him," Audrey says, stopping my thoughts from spiraling out of control.

"You know," Selina begins, "we're having a BBQ to let everyone know the sex of the baby next weekend. Why don't you invite Seth?"

"Sure, that's an amazing idea." I scoff.

"Just think about it, Bri."

"What's there to think about? I won't ruin your gender announcement just so I can have a buffer in case Seth loses his shit when he finds out about Rebekah."

With every conversation we have, I feel more and more guilty about keeping Rebekah from him. Especially after our conversation about children and the future. After learning more about Seth, I'm convinced he wouldn't do anything to purposely hurt either of us. If anyone has the power to ruin everything, it's me. This secret has been eating me alive, and if I want this relationship to go any further, I have to fess up.

"Are you sure he is going to lose it?" Audrey questions, pulling out her phone and typing something before shoving it back into her pocket.

I cock my head to the side and eye her skeptically, trying to make sense of her question. "Of course, he will. I've been lying to him ever since he came back into town. I never tried to get a hold of him to tell him he had a daughter."

"But he didn't contact you either, Bri," Leia responds with conviction. "You said you gave him your number the last time you saw each other. He could've called you, too."

"I know. I know, but I've had more than enough chances to tell him since he came back, and I didn't."

"And he'll understand that, Bri," Selina mumbles, pushing to her feet and placing a hand on my shoulder. "I was so afraid to tell Vance what I thought I saw; I spent fourteen years separated from the man that I loved because I was afraid of getting my heart broken."

I've heard Selina and Vance's story more times than I can count. Although it's not the same, Selina let her fear of being hurt keep her away from Vance and Tyson's Creek for years. She assumed Vance had moved on while she was at Juilliard but never once asked him. They could have spent all those years together, but instead, they spent them trying to mend the broken pieces of their hearts. Thankfully, they found their way back to each other and are married with a little one on the way, but can the same happen between Seth and me?

"Just think about it, okay? The BBQ would be the best place to tell him. We will all be there to support both of you."

I glance at the clock on the wall. My mom has probably already packed up Rebekah and is on the way to Connor and Audrey's. I may as well head out of here and get some rest. I have a lot to think about before the next time I talk to Seth.

"I'll think about it." I push back from the table and stand, turning to my right to grab the broom and basket of cleaning supplies near the door.

"Oh, no, you don't." Selina grabs the items from my hands and turns toward Audrey, handing them to her. "Audrey's got this. It's what you pay her for." She grips my shoulder and marches me out of the break room toward the front door, stopping by the desk so I can grab my bag and keys. "You are heading straight home. Get some sleep and relax."

"Okay, you win," I groan as Leia hands me my keys and bag and shoves me toward the door.

"Get some rest. I'll see you at the house later," Audrey says from the break room doorway. "Love you!"

"I love you guys, and thank you," I say, pushing the door open and walking toward my car.

If there's one thing I know, it's that my three best friends won't let me slide on getting some rest. If I dare show my face at Audrey's house before seven and interrupt my mom's granddaughter time, she'll have my head. And so will the three of them.

My eyes droop as I pull into my driveway. "I guess I was tireder than I thought. Wait. Is that even a word?"

I shut off my car and head for the door. It takes a few tries, but I unlock my front door and stumble to the couch before falling into a deep sleep. "What the heck!" I shout as I tumble off the couch onto the floor.

I look around in confusion as I hear the doorbell echoing through the room. I push to my feet and stumble toward the door and open it. My mom is standing on the other side, holding Rebecca's car seat in one hand and a larger bag thrown over her shoulder.

"Hey, Mom," I say groggily as I rub my eyes. "I thought I was meeting you at Audrey's at seven."

"You were, but it's almost nine," she responds, handing over the car seat and coming inside. "We didn't want to call and wake you, so I gave Rebekah a bath at Audrey's before bringing her home. I also cooked a few things to stock your fridge."

"I thought you were under a no-cooking restriction." I snicker as I shut the door behind her.

"I spent time with my granddaughters, as promised. They just helped me cook."

"And Rebekah. How was my baby girl?"

"A perfect angel, as always." She places the bag down on the table before coming back to the couch and taking a seat. "I think she's feeling better, too. She was a little fussy when I gave her a bath, but other than that, there weren't any problems."

No one would know that Jade and Love aren't really my mother's granddaughters. I have a feeling she'll feel the same about Selina and Vance's baby when they're born, as well. My mom always wanted grandbabies and doesn't care that they aren't hers by blood. Audrey, Leia, and Selina are just as much of my sisters as Melissa is. And by extension, she has adopted their significant others, as well.

"Her mood changed for the better after we talked to your sister on FaceTime after dinner."

"How is Mel doing, anyway?"

Melissa moved to Tennessee a few months ago, and we haven't spoken since Seth got back to town. Although we aren't close in age, she chose to come live here for a few months after college to help me take care of the studio and Rebekah, but I knew her heart wasn't here. Every day, she was going on and on about her best friend from college and her family. It took some doing, but my mom and I finally convinced her to move there with them, since she missed them so much. Now, she's the happiest I've ever seen her.

"She's great. Although she seems to have her panties in a twist about some guy she met. Apparently, he's the bane of her existence at the moment." My mom giggles.

"Sounds a lot like Leia and Riggs."

"Oh, dear. When is that girl going to stop putting Riggs through the ringer? We all know he's crazy about her."

"I know, Momma. I know," I grumble, remembering my conversation with Seth earlier.

"You just have to find the right one. That's probably why she's having such a hard time. Melissa is all about doing things in order and wants to have her business up and running before she thinks about love," she gripes.

Melissa has always had a written plan for her life that must be followed to the letter. If this guy is getting her this worked up, he must mean more to her than she is letting on.

"Sometimes the best surprises in life are the ones we least expect," I whisper. I never planned on getting pregnant with Rebekah, but I wouldn't change having her for the world.

"I'm glad Rebekah was there to see Mel. Those two were thick as thieves before she left. It doesn't hurt that she and I look exactly alike. I bet if Mel hadn't left, Rebekah would call her 'Mama', too."

"I highly doubt that. There's only one other person in this world she could love more than her mother..." My mom's voice trails off.

"Mom," I grumble as I reach for my cell to check the time, noticing the text from Seth that I ignored earlier.

SETH

I'm sorry if I ruined your day. I just wanted to let you know I was thinking about you. Hope you enjoyed your sandwich.

"Fuck," I murmur

As if I needed another reason to feel like a shitty human being. Not only have I been keeping this enormous secret, but then he felt the need to apologize to me because I was too tired to act like a decent person.

"Language, young lady." She clicks her tongue. "Now, what's gotten you so upset?"

"I've been a mess for the last few days, and I made someone feel bad because of my mood. They didn't deserve it," I mumble as I lean back on the couch.

"Okay, nothing out of the ordinary."

"Mom," I gripe as I pull my right leg up, resting my heel on the edge of the couch. "What am I going to do now?"

"Well, the tried-and-true response of apologizing always seems to do the trick."

"Can you be serious for a minute?" I shake my head. Here I am, trying to get advice from my mother, and she has jokes.

"I am! If this person is worth your time, apologizing will fix everything," she insists.

"Thanks for coming all this way so I could get some sleep. I'm sure you had other plans for the evening." I push up from the couch and head toward my bedroom, quickly glancing at the clock in the kitchen before I pass by. "Are you staying or heading home tonight?"

"I'm staying. I want to be here to help take the load off you for a few days."

"Thanks, Mom." I reach over and wrap her in a tight hug. "I don't know how I'd survive without you and the girls to help me."

"If you told Seth..." my mom says, her voice trailing off without ending the sentence.

My parents have been nothing but supportive of me since I let them know I was pregnant. They never once pushed me to tell them who her father was, but I finally broke down and told them after she was born. We don't see eye to eye on the issue of Seth, but they respect my decision to not tell him... mostly. But it's at times like this she tries to push the subject.

"I heard from Mrs. Thomas that he was living in the apartment above their garage," she huffs as she unbuckles Rebekah from her seat, her annoyance at my reluctance to tell him about our daughter clear in her voice.

Another negative of living in a small town: everyone knows everyone. My parents and the Thomases became fast friends when I moved to Tyson's Creek, meaning my mom now has someone who will check in on me and tell her everything she wants to know. I don't doubt for a second that Mrs.

Thomas has probably been pumping my mom for information, as well. Maybe her friendship with my mom is why she hasn't said anything to Seth about our daughter.

"Mom..." My voice trails off, trying to find the words to explain what's going on between Seth and me.

"He came back from war, and of all the places he could go, he moved to the same town you lived in."

"It's complicated." I try to keep my voice calm as I head into the bathroom. I need time to think, to get some space from my mom and all her questions, so I turn on the water and push the stopper in on the tub. A relaxing bath sounds like just what I need right now.

This isn't the first time I've had this conversation with my mom, and I doubt it'll be my last, especially now that Seth is back in town. I've told my mom all my reservations about even thinking about starting a relationship with Seth while he was in the military. I've watched what my mother went through and refuse to have that kind of life, for myself or Rebekah.

"Your father loves you, Bristol," she mutters as she comes into the bathroom, knowing how hurt I still am about all the events my father missed because he was off fighting a war or protecting the world from evil.

"But he always loved the military more," I argue.

I know she means well, but there's a part of me that resents my father's service to the country. Choosing to serve your country is a noble decision, one that no one should take lightly. A part of me knows that, but there's another part of me that resents all the important dates my father missed and promises he made and knew he'd never be able to keep. I don't know how to rectify those two parts of my father.

She sighs and places a soft hand on my shoulder. "Okay. I understand what you're saying, but Seth's retired now. And from what I hear, he's not planning on going anywhere. You should at least give him a chance to get to know his daughter."

"That's the plan, Mom, but I'm scared."

"If you weren't afraid, I would call you a liar. This is a big secret that you've kept from him, but if everything you told me about this young man is true, he'll forgive you for it."

"And how long might that take?" I ask her as I bend down and shut off the water.

"That depends on how much longer you wait, sweetie."

I hate to admit it, but my mother is right. The longer I wait to tell Seth about Rebekah, the more hurt and confused he will be. I need to put on my big girl panties and get it over with, but that's easier said than done.

After a few moments of silence, I sigh and turn around. "I love you, Mom."

"I love you, too, Bristol. Go enjoy your bath. I'll

make sure Rebekah gets her bottle, and I'll heat up some dinner for us."

"Thanks, Mom." I smile, reaching over and giving her hand a squeeze. "For everything."

"You're welcome." My mom smiles at me before placing my cell phone on the edge of the sink. I wait for her to close the door behind her before I strip out of my clothes and climb into the tub. I sink down into the warm water and groan as I let it loosen the muscles in my body.

I know everyone is right. I need to come clean with Seth before it's too late. Things between us have seemed like they're moving at warp speed, which to the outsider would seem impossible, but after spending all this time pining for each other, now is finally our time. The last thing I want to do is ruin everything by continuing to keep secrets from him. If this relationship, or whatever this is between us, is going to last long term, I can't let it all start on a lie.

"First, apologize," I say, giving myself a mini pep talk as I lift slightly out of the water and lean over toward the counter.

It takes me a few tries, but I knock my cell phone onto the floor without breaking it and slide it closer to the tub. I quickly unlock it and dial Seth's number, stopping before I hit *call.* A text would probably be better. Less confrontational.

BRISTOL

Sorry I was such a mess earlier. I've been dealing with some stuff the last few days and haven't been sleeping much. Forgive me.

I hit *send*, but then remember I forgot something.

BRISTOL

P.S. Thanks for the sandwich. It was delicious. Unfortunately, I had to sacrifice some of my fries to Selina. Apparently, the baby was hungry. Lol.

My phone immediately chimes with an incoming text.

SETH

No problem. Everyone is allowed to have a bad day occasionally. I'm glad you enjoyed your sandwich, but I'm sorry about your fries. We can't let Selina get too hungry. I've heard Vance's stories. It's not a good thing.

I laugh slightly at memories of a very hangry Selina ordering Vance to get her Chick-fil-A on a Sunday. It was not a good day to be Vance. I set the phone on the floor beside the tub, feeling better for apologizing, and sink back down into the water.

After a few minutes, my phone vibrates across the floor, and I freeze. I reach over and grab my phone, turning it over to see Seth's name flashing across my screen.

"Shit," I whisper as I unlock it. "Hello?"

I phrase that more like a question than a statement, but I'm nervous. I figured after I sent that text, that would be the end of it, but it looks like I was wrong.

"Hello, beautiful."

I can't help but smile at being able to hear his voice.

"I didn't disturb you, did I?"

"Not exactly. The girls ordered me home shortly after you left. I just woke up from a nap and am now taking a bath before having a late dinner."

A guttural groan comes through the phone. "You can't say things like that, Bri. I'm trying to be a gentleman."

"Sorry," I squeak as images of the dirty things I would rather have him doing to me right now flood my mind. If only I wasn't keeping the fact that we have a daughter together from him... Wait. This could be the perfect chance. My mom is here to watch Rebekah for me while I make plans to meet with Seth. Leia said something about meeting up with the guys for drinks, but I'm sure I could talk him into meeting at Just the Drip for a cup of coffee so we can talk.

"Anyway, I'm glad you could get some rest."

"Thanks. I needed it for sure."

An awkward silence stretches between us. Neither of us knows exactly what to say at this moment, and for good reason. Seth isn't blind. He has to know there's something going on with me, but he has no idea what it is. I need to come clean before it's too late. Just as I'm about to say something, Seth beats me to it.

"All right, I don't want to keep you. Enjoy your bath." He pauses for a few moments. "I miss you."

"Do you want to come to Vance and Selina's with me next weekend?" I blurt out, startling us both.

I've missed my chance to suggest we meet up and talk tonight, but Selina offered her party. The last thing I want to do is take the focus off their news, but I need my friends. We'll both need our friends after I drop the news of our daughter into Seth's lap. There was probably a better way of going about asking Seth to hang out with me, but if I hadn't said it right now, I know I would have chickened out.

"I would love to."

"Great. Awesome. I'll talk to you later. Bye, Seth." I trip over my words, getting them out in one breath. I quickly hang up the phone, not even bothering to give him a chance to say goodbye.

"Could you be any more of a spaz, Bristol?" I groan as I drop the phone onto the floor and sink back down into the water.

If I'm going to tell Seth the biggest secret of my life, I think I need a little more practice. If the awkwardness of this conversation is any sign of how it's going to go, it won't be easy.

fifteen

seth

Things with Bristol and I have gone relatively back to normal since our talk last weekend. I guess she really was just having a bad couple of days. I'm glad I could help her feel a little better. We exchanged a few texts and phone calls, but she surprised me out of the blue on Wednesday, coming to the construction site I was working at and bringing lunch.

It's the little things like that that make me fall even more in love with her. I've learned more about Bristol in these last few weeks than I know about people I've known for a major chunk of my life, and I'm desperate to discover more. She's slowly opening her heart to me, and I couldn't be happier, but I can tell she's still holding something back.

Shaking the dark thoughts from my mind, I pull on a white T-shirt and some socks, shove my feet into my boots, and slip my wallet into my back pocket before striding toward the front of the house.

"You ready to head out soon?" Brady asks as he pulls a jacket on over his long-sleeved flannel shirt and puts a backward baseball cap on his head.

"Yeah. I just need to text Bristol and let her know we are running a little early." I pull my phone out of my pocket and unlock the screen, my thumb hovering over her name.

"Did you already tell her we would be there at three? What's it going to matter if we arrive ten minutes early?"

Vance invited the whole crew to celebrate with him and Selina today. He hasn't shut up about this party since he came in to work on Monday. I have no idea what a gender reveal party is, but I guess finding out the sex of your child is a big deal. One I can't wait to have the chance to do with Bristol.

I'd be lying if I said I haven't been thinking about having children with Bristol since we touched on the subject. Sometimes I catch myself dreaming about what our child would look like. Would they have a complexion closer to mine or Bristol's? Would they have my brown eyes or her piercing green ones? Would they have midnight black hair like my parents or a more auburn color? A perfect mixture of the two of us, or would they favor one of us more? Not that it matters. If Bristol and I are ever blessed with a child, I'll love him or her with my whole heart. They'll become the center of my universe, just like their mother already is.

"Earth to Seth?" Brady waves his hand in front of my face. "Where'd you go? Are you that nervous about tonight?"

I'm nervous about my plans with Bristol for tonight. I had wanted to meet Bristol at her house and ride to the BBQ together, but she said something about needing to help Selina get ready. I was hoping we'd have a chance to be alone, and she'd finally tell me what she's been hiding from me.

"Not even a little." I chuckle, shoving my phone back into my pocket. "I wish Bristol would trust me."

"Bristol trusts you, Seth."

"How do you know that?"

"I just do," he responds with conviction, patting me on the back. "Don't forget my mom is dropping a pie off at your place around dinner time."

Everything is falling into place. Since I already had a pre-approved VA loan, it only took a few weeks for me to close on the house. The moment I had the keys in hand, I went right to work on getting everything in my new home ready for tonight. The guys and I spent the last few days after work doing some minor repairs, painting, and changing out appliances. There wasn't much that needed to be done, and since Audrey moved in with Connor, I was able to buy a few pieces of furniture from her to make the place feel a little more like home.

I nod my head, grabbing my keys off the hook

beside the door. "Thanks, man. I don't think I would have been able to pull any of this off without your help."

"No thanks needed. Just remember, you owe me." He winks in my direction, then opens the door and heads down the stairs.

As I pull our front door shut and lock it, my mind runs down a list of everything that has changed in the last week. Not only have Bristol and I gotten even closer, but I'm finally ready to tell her how I feel. I've been in love with her since I first saw her over a year ago, and my feelings have only grown since having her back in my life. I've told her I love her before, but tonight, I'm going to make sure she really hears it.

"Are you sure you want to do this tonight?" Brady questions, opening the passenger side of my truck and climbing in.

I roll my eyes at him as I open my door. "Yes, I'm sure. More time won't change how I feel about Bristol. I need her to know that I'm here for the long haul. Showing her my place and telling her how I really feel is the first step in that direction."

I slam my door shut a little more forcefully than intended, then turn my truck on and pull out of the driveway. I rub the spot over my chest at the thought of things not working out between Bristol and me. We've had a rocky start and many obstacles in the way of us being together, but buying this house should make things a lot easier. I'm putting down roots, showing her with my actions that I'm not going anywhere. My life in the military is over, and now I can spend the rest of my life making her happy. I've told her a million times, but now is my chance to show her. Words can only get me so far. I need to show her with my actions that I am serious about the two of us.

"But you can only do this once, man. You said yourself that she's been holding something back from you. What happens if it's something bigger than you can imagine?"

My grip on the steering wheel tightens as his words play over in my head. Brady has a point. I've always known that Bristol was hiding something from me, and I hope that once I tell her how I feel, she will know that nothing could scare me away from her. That she no longer has to hold herself back from me because I'm someone she can depend on.

"I know, man, but I need to do this. For both our sakes," I say with conviction.

No matter what she's keeping from me, I know I love Bristol with my entire being. Everything else is just background noise. If we can find our way back to each other with everything life has put in our way since our first meeting, we can overcome anything. Even Bristol's secret.

"All right, man. Whatever you need, I'm here for you," he replies, before turning his attention toward the window. "I didn't mean to let my shit rain on your parade."

Ever since our run-in with Emersyn at Crawdaddy's when I first got back into town, Brady has been more like me than himself, which says a lot about what is going on in his head, but he has yet to tell me what's going on.

"I've been so wrapped up in my own shit, I haven't been there for you," I say as I turn onto Vance and Selina's street.

Their house is a little further out from town, being closer to the river, but it's worth the drive. Most people are knocking these older houses down to make room for cookie-cutter housing developments, but these two had a different idea. Vance and Connor renovated this entire house, turning it into the home of Selina's dreams.

"I wish I had it all figured out like you." Brady sighs. "Everything has changed since I came home. Everyone moved on with their lives, like my being gone meant nothing. Everyone except her."

I remain silent, giving him the time to sort through his thoughts.

"It seems like Emersyn has spent the last year of her life waiting for me to come back, but everything is different. I'm different."

Brady hasn't told me much about his relationship with Emersyn since I met her for the first time at Crawdaddy's, but I know enough. Beckett is one of Brady's oldest friends, but he happens to also be Emersyn's half-brother and her biggest protector. At some point during their friendship, Brady began to see her as something more than his best friend's baby sister. And Emersyn felt the same way about him. It all came to a head at his going away party for deployment when Beckett saw them kissing in the backyard and threatened to beat Brady's ass if he came near his sister again. Whatever he said convinced Brady to stay away from her, no matter how much she wrote to him. He had hoped she'd move on to someone else, but that wasn't the case.

At first, I was hurt that he didn't share any of this with me, but after thinking about it, I wouldn't have been any help. I was so wrapped up in what was or wasn't going on between Bristol and me that I didn't have the capacity to help with his problems. Now I can be there for my friend, the same way he was for me when we were deployed.

"You're still the same person you were before we went over to the sandbox. The same person she fell in love with. But something's holding you back."

Brady scoffs. "I never said she was in love with me."

"A girl doesn't look at a man the way she did that night if they aren't in love with them."

Brady chuckles humorously. "She's barely lived life

yet. She's not old enough to know about anything, especially love."

"Any woman who's still waiting around for your ass after this long is in love with you," I respond sternly. "Besides, her age has nothing to do with this, and you know it."

I pull into Vance and Selina's driveway, shut off my truck, and turn toward my friend. Brady's shoulders slump forward in defeat, as if his dream has been shattered into a million pieces.

He says nothing as he opens the door and climbs out. I watch him as he walks around the front of the truck, his shoulders rolled forward as if he's carrying the weight of the world. I hate seeing my friend like this, but he isn't ready yet.

I throw my door open and step out, and Brady smiles and wraps his arm around my shoulder.

"What is it you said to me about Bristol?" I tap my chin, pretending to think. "Everyone knows that girl loves you. Now you just need to prove to her you're worthy of her love."

Brady's eyes widen in surprise, a plethora of emotions rolling across his face as he processes what I just said to him. I could keep poking at him, trying to convince him to fight for whatever this is between him and Emersyn, but I won't. Brady has his own demons to fight—just like I did—before he's able to be the man

Emersyn deserves, and he knows that. Hopefully, our conversation gives him the courage to do so.

"Enough about me. It's time for you to go claim your girl."

I smile back at him as we both head toward the front door. I don't know what the future holds for me, but as long as Bristol is in it, I'm content.

Brady knocks hard on the door, and we wait patiently for someone to answer. It only takes a moment before Vance opens the door.

"Come on in, guys. We just started the grill."

Brady and I walk through the door.

"Through there is the kitchen, where the ladies have congregated." Vance points to the right and then turns in the opposite direction. "This way to the beer."

"Lead the way, man," Brady grumbles before turning and following Vance.

Instead of following my friends, I turn to the right and head directly into the kitchen, eager to see Bristol for the first time in almost a week. I can hear muffled voices float out of the kitchen; each voice becomes clearer as I get closer.

"How's my girl feeling today? Any better?" Leia says. I notice her walking across the room and sitting down at what seems to be a large island in the middle of the kitchen. "I hate it when my baby is sick."

Baby? I didn't know Leia had a baby. Not that

there's anything wrong with being a single mother, but she never struck me as the maternal type.

As I get closer to the kitchen entrance, I catch a glimpse of Bristol. Her bright red hair shines in the light as it filters through the large windows lining the wall behind her. A bright smile covers her face as she takes a sip of her drink. Every time I look at her, she takes my breath away, and it's like seeing her for the first time all over again.

"Yes, thankfully. My mom is watching Rebekah tonight so I can have some time alone with Seth."

Her words make me freeze.

I must have heard her wrong.

Bristol has a daughter.

A swirl of emotion fills my body, the most prominent emotion being anger. Anger at myself for not being here for her. Anger that I couldn't protect her from all the pain and heartache she must have felt being left alone when she brought a life into the world. Despair at the thought that she was once again made to feel like she wasn't good enough to stick around for, that whatever life the baby's father had planned for himself was more important than their child together. Anger at whatever asshole walked away from her when she needed him the most.

My heart aches for Bristol, knowing that she has always wanted children, but the family she yearned for doesn't exist. Bristol has told me several times she wanted a family, a husband, someone to help her raise her children and share her life. But now she has me.

I stop just outside the kitchen entrance and out of sight of all the ladies, waiting for the perfect time to make my presence known. Bristol has been keeping this secret for weeks, and it seems to have taken its toll on her. I would be lying if I said I wasn't hurt that she couldn't trust me with this, but in a way, I understand. We've only just begun getting to know each other again, and although I know my love for her will never change, she had to be sure of my feelings before letting me into her daughter's life.

"You're going to tell him tonight?" Selina questions as she places a plate of fruit on the island directly in front of Bristol.

My future with Bristol rests on how I react to this news. No matter what, I need to ensure that Bristol knows how much I love her and that this changes nothing. I will be there for her and Rebekah if they'll have me. My only desire in life is to make sure that Bristol is happy, and by extension, that includes Rebekah, too.

"Yes, it's about time he knows the truth," Bristol says with conviction.

"Truth about what?" I ask, not wanting to let anyone in the room know I've been standing there eavesdropping on them.

"You're early," she gasps softly. Her eyes widen in

horror as I step into the room. "How long have you been standing there?"

I'm sure this isn't easy for her, finding the perfect time and way to tell me about her daughter, but I need her to know that it's okay. That I'll still be here for her and her daughter, no matter what.

I don't hesitate as I stride toward her, pulling her tightly into my chest. "Long enough to know you have something to tell me." I kiss the top of her head and notice the ladies inching toward the doorway, hovering just out of sight, but not leaving the room. "I love you, Bristol. I've loved you since the first day I laid eyes on you, and it has grown every day since then."

"You don't understand, Seth." Bristol hiccups as she threads her fingers through mine. "Let's go into the other room and talk."

I allow her to pull me down the hallway toward what looks like a small office in the front of the house. The moment we step into the room, I notice it's not an office, but a dance studio. Vance said something about building a custom dance studio for Selina in their home, but I assumed he was exaggerating.

Bristol's eyes fill with tears as looks around the room, looking anywhere but at me. I reach up, cupping her cheek in my hand. Her eyes drift shut as a single tear trickles down her cheek. "I understand how hard this is for you to share with me, but it changes nothing. I will love you both with all my heart if you let me."

"No, Seth. You. Don't. Understand," she insists, taking a step back and putting space between us.

"What is it, Bristol?" I ask as I try to sort through everything I've heard in the last few minutes.

"It's not that simple," she croaks, her entire body trembling.

"I understand you not wanting to tell me immediately." I take a step closer to her, but she continues inching away from me. Bristol wraps her arms around her waist as if trying to hold herself together. She opens her mouth to answer but closes it again. "You were scared that I'd leave you again, weren't you?"

Bristol freezes the moment those words leave my mouth, allowing me to get closer to her. I wrap my arms tightly around her waist. "Have you been raising her on your own?" I press, running the tips of my fingers along her spine.

"Yes, but it's not what you think," she croaks, trying to wiggle out of my grasp, but I tighten my hold.

"It doesn't matter, Bristol. None of it does." I lean back, cupping her cheeks in my palms. "I plan on spending the rest of my life loving the both of you." I kiss the tip of her nose. "She will be as much mine as she is yours."

"I've wanted to hear you say that for so long." She nuzzles her cheek against my palm, clenching her eyes shut. "But you don't know everything yet, Seth."

Bristol covers her mouth with both hands,

attempting to stop the sob from ripping out of her throat as she backs away from me.

"I don't understand." My eyes lock on her as I search her face for any answer, any sign of what I'm missing, but the only thing I see is fear.

"She's yours."

I stumble backward as if she punched me right in the chest. The walls of the room feel as if they are closing in around me as my mind attempts to process what she's telling me. "We have a daughter?"

Bristol nods her head yes as she reaches toward me, tears streaming down her face. I want nothing more than to run to her, scoop her into my arms, and promise never to make her feel this type of pain again, but I can't. I need to know what she was thinking. Why she kept our daughter's existence from me for months.

The room goes completely silent as my mind reels, trying to search for the perfect explanation for her keeping my daughter away from me. On the one hand, I can understand her need to protect her—I mean *our* daughter—from the pain of losing a father. I was on the other side of the world, and we didn't have any communication with each other. She had no way of knowing when I was coming back or if I even wanted a family of my own.

Bristol swipes angrily at her cheeks before she inches toward me. "Our daughter's name is Rebekah. She's eight months old. She has curly red hair and the most gorgeous hazel-green eyes with a golden-brown circle in the center. It always feels as if she's looking right into my soul, the same feeling I get whenever you look at me. I always look into her eyes and imagine what it would be like for us to be together as a family. But I had no idea when or if you were coming back, and then you showed up out of the blue. What was I supposed to do?"

Bristol grips my shirt tightly in her hand, her eyes filled with pain and regret. "I never meant to hurt you, Seth. Please understand that I love our daughter more than life itself. I needed to protect her from getting hurt by all of this. To make sure that you wanted to be a part of her life as much as I wanted you to be, but you need to decide if that's enough."

"Please make this make sense to me, Bri. I understand wanting to protect the two of you from being hurt, but I've been in town for over a month. You've had plenty of chances to tell me about her, and you've said nothing." I bite my lip to hold back a cry of pain as my heart shatters.

"I know." Bristol hiccups as she buries her face into my chest, trying to regain her composure. She doesn't touch me or wrap her arms around my waist. She's giving me some space to process what's happening. "It was unfair of me to keep her from you, but you weren't here."

"That's bullshit Bristol, and you know it." My hand

clenches tightly into a fist at my side as I tilt my head back, searching for the words to explain what I'm feeling. "You were scared. Scared that someone might love you the way you've always wanted. That you couldn't keep your heart locked behind a wall so no one could hurt you."

"That wasn't it at all," Bristol says as she spins on her heels, trying to escape the truth of my words, but I grab her hand.

"No. You know the real reason you're scared? It's because you love me just as much as I love you. Not some superficial love, but the soul-deep, burning love that consumes you. The kind of love that will rip you to shreds when and if you lose it. The type of love your soul will never recover from. The same way I know you love our daughter."

"You're wrong, Seth."

"Then tell me why. Why have I been in town for weeks, fucking weeks, and you haven't said a goddamn thing?"

"I didn't know how to tell you. I hadn't seen or talked to you in over a year! You never once called me or even sent me a text. Heck, I would've settled for a smoke signal. I didn't know if you were coming back. If you even wanted to be with me, and then you show up one day, ready to pick up where things left off."

"You are all I ever wanted from the moment I laid eyes on you, Bristol Reid," I bite out, emotions clogging my throat. "I called you every fucking chance I got. All I did the entire time I was over in the sandbox was think about finding a way back to you and dream about starting my life with you when I came back."

"You called me?"

I nod my head and move toward her, unable to resist the pull I feel in case this is the last time I set eyes on her. "I'll love you always."

"Please, don't go, Seth," she sobs, her entire body trembling.

I plant a kiss on the top of her head before turning on my heels and leaving the room. I can vaguely hear someone shouting my name, but I don't stop as I fling the front door open and stride through it.

I don't know where I can go to escape the pain that radiates through my body. I should've stayed, given her more time to explain to me why she did this. But I can't. Not right now. I don't look back as I climb into my truck and pull out of the driveway, leaving my heart right there, shattered into a million pieces.

sixteen

bristol

"This can't be happening," I sob into my hands as someone comes into the room.

"Everything is going to be okay," Leia whispers into my ear as she wraps her arms around me, and my knees give out.

It's as if the weight of everything that has happened hits me all at once. Seth is gone, probably for good, and it's all my fault.

"You don't know that," I sob, burying my nose into her shoulder and letting all my emotions go free. Searing pain flows through my entire body as waves of agony pull me under. I'm just praying that I can hold on for just a little longer until the pain subsides. I yearn for numbness to cut me off from all these feelings that I'm so desperate to forget. I don't know how long I sit there wrapped in Leia's arms as she mutters soothing words into my ear, but at some point, my tears slow.

"Do you feel better now?" Leia asks, smoothing my hair back from my face.

"No," I croak, leaning back and looking around the room, hoping that Seth with reappear at any moment but come up empty. "He really left."

"He did, honey," Audrey comes into the room, Selina right on her heels. "But he'll be back."

The shrill ring of someone's phone fills the room for a few moments before it stops and starts right up again. And again. And again.

"Will someone answer that, please?" I ask, not wanting to keep any of them from something important.

Audrey, Selina, and Leia all pull out their phones to check whose it is as Leia's phone rings in her hand, but she quickly silences it.

"You should answer that."

"It's just Riggs, probably calling to annoy me about something." Leia rolls her eyes as her phone rings again.

"Just answer it." Audrey smiles, nodding toward her phone. "If someone is calling you multiple times in a row, it's important."

"Go on, answer it," I mumble, moving out of Leia's arms and pushing to my feet.

"I'll only be a second." She kisses me on the cheek before moving towards the other side of the room to answer the phone.

My eyes remain locked on her as I speak to my other two friends. I watch all the color drain out of her face, and her phone goes clattering to the floor. All three of us rush toward her and wrap her in a protective embrace.

"My dad is on his way to the hospital. One of our employees found him passed out in the hallway a few minutes ago. Walker and Riggs are on their way. I need to meet them there."

"Go." Audrey kisses her cheek before running toward the kitchen, probably to grab Leia's things.

"We got this and her." Selina motions toward me, threading her fingers through mine and squeezing. "Call us when you know more."

"I love you, guys." Leia's voice crackles slightly as she wraps us in her arms.

"We love you, too," Selina and I reply in unison as Audrey comes around the corner holding Leia's things. She murmurs something softly to Leia, and she shakes her head no before rushing out the door.

My eyes remain locked on the window facing the front of the house as I watch Leia disappear down the driveway, sending up a silent prayer that everything with her dad is okay.

We stand there for a few moments before I break the silence. "How much of that did you hear?"

"Enough to know he needs time, but he'll be back," Selina pulls me out of the room, down the hall, and into the kitchen.

Everything is the same as it was when I left the room with Seth what feels like a million years ago. A nice spread of different appetizers, baked beans, pasta salad, and corn on the cob is placed strategically around the table with white balloons tied on either end, with black question marks written on each one.

"I'm sorry I ruined your party," I whisper as I run my fingers along the string of one of the balloons before taking a seat at the table.

"Hush now, you didn't ruin anything," Selina murmurs, as she takes a seat beside me.

There's no one else in the room. The boys ran to hide the moment the tears started. My friends talk softly around me as my mind conjures up all the ways I had expected today to go, but this wasn't one of them. My emotions keep fluctuating between wanting to give in to the soul-crushing pain radiating through my entire body and numbness. Every time I hear something odd, my head snaps toward the door, waiting for Seth to reappear, but he doesn't.

When I woke up this morning, I truly believed that everything would work out, and I'd finally get the happily ever after I always dreamed of, but that was nothing but a dream. Seth left me standing in the middle of Selina's studio to pick up the pieces of my broken heart, and I deserved it.

I knew he wouldn't take finding out about our daughter well. I expected him to be angry, if not furious, at me for keeping this from him, but instead, he was understanding and compassionate. He said I was afraid, and he was right. Rebekah was an excuse that I clung to, a way for my mind to allow me to push him away before he could hurt me, and it worked, but now I'm an empty husk of the person I was before Seth came back into my life. I never really listened when he spoke to me, the promises he made, and how he spent every moment we were together showing me how much he truly loved me. I've been hurt before, but the way I felt about them was nothing compared to what I feel for Seth Williams.

"I broke both our hearts." Tears pour down my face as I lean into Selina's side, close my eyes, and try to think of anything but the devastated look on Seth's face. "If I'd have said something sooner, been honest with him from the start, none of this would have happened." I bury my face in my hands and sob, trying to make sense of the last few hours of my life.

Everything was perfect. I was wrapped in Seth's arms, feeling safe. Loved. Protected. And in blissful ignorance of the pain I was about to cause the two of us. If I learned one thing from all of this, it's that I was denying my feelings for Seth. Self-sabotaging the first real love I've ever had in my life because I didn't want to get hurt. If I didn't love him, I'd have stayed away from him when he came back into town. I don't think I'd have told him right away about Rebekah, but I damn sure wouldn't have waited this long because our daughter deserves her father.

I wasn't truly afraid of her being hurt or him mistreating her in any way. What I was afraid of was the chance that he wouldn't want me, too. I've seen it happen many times before. Co-parenting is possible and is a healthy way for two people to remain in their children's lives, even if a relationship doesn't work out between them. But that isn't what I wanted. My heart knew the moment I laid eyes on him that it had found its other half, and I wouldn't take the chance of giving that up for anything.

I tried to be careful and protect my heart from Seth, but he broke down all my defenses, worming his way into my heart and becoming a part of me. A part that will remain broken until the day I die. He promised to give me everything I ever wanted, but I was too afraid to take that leap of faith. If I can't fix things between us, Seth will be there for our daughter. Even before this moment, I knew Seth had always wanted a family, a place to feel like he belonged, and he'd get that with our daughter. I'll make sure of it, even if it means we can't be together.

"I was so selfish," I mumble softly, not expecting anyone to answer me.

"I'm glad you finally figured that part out." My head snaps toward the door as I glimpse Brady leaning against the doorframe.

"Not helping, Brady." Audrey scowls at him as the rest of the guys come filing into the room, each one going directly for their partner. "We can't change the past, but we can change the future."

I stare at him for a few minutes, waiting for him to say something useful, but he doesn't say a word. Brady can't be much taller than me, if at all. His skin is tanned darker than usual, probably because of all the time he spends outside at the construction site. His muscular build is covered in a flannel shirt, rolled to the elbows with a pair of dark-washed jeans. My eyes flick back to his, a soft, reassuring smile plastered on my face, but I don't get the same in return. Instead, he narrows his forest green eyes as he crosses his arms over his chest, glaring at the four of us.

"What are you even still doing here?" Selina questions as she throws her arm over my shoulder and pulls me into her chest.

"My ride left." Brady sighs, coming further into the room and dropping into one of the empty chairs at the table. "Why didn't you tell him sooner? Hell, why didn't *any* of you say anything?"

"They didn't know. At least the guys didn't," I respond, looking all my friends in the eyes and begging them to understand. "By the time I found out I was pregnant, enough time had passed that no one put two and two together. Then Audrey moved here, and Selina came home, and well, life happened.

"I told Audrey and Leia because I was scared. Leia was there when I found out I was pregnant, and

Audrey was a single mother for fifteen years. I needed someone to talk to."

Connor plants a kiss on the top of Audrey's head before he wraps his arms around her waist and pulls her toward him. My heart aches for that. I want more than anything to have someone stand behind me and support me when I feel as if my entire world is falling apart. Too bad the only person I want right now may never want to speak to me again.

"I convinced myself that keeping this a secret was protecting Rebekah from getting hurt. I didn't know when or if Seth was going to be coming back."

"I get that, but you could've called, written him a letter, anything," Brady says as he pulls his ball cap off his head before running his hand through his dark blonde hair. "You knew we were in the same unit, and you didn't even try to get in contact with him."

"You're right, but he could've contacted me, too. I gave him my phone number the last time I saw him. I waited by the phone for weeks. I answered every unknown number, hoping it was him, but he never called. I didn't even know he was back in town until we ran into each other on Main Street."

"I don't know why Seth didn't contact you the minute he got back into town, but if I had to make a guess, it's because he's a planner. He probably wanted to have everything perfect before approaching you."

"Look, I can completely understand why Seth is

angry, but I would bet he's more hurt than anything," Vance chimes in as he takes a seat next to Selina. "Hurt by *all* of us."

"Not me. I had no idea about any of this. I only came for the free food." Brady holds his hands up in surrender. "But Seth called you pretty much every week when we first left, hoping you wouldn't forget the boy who promised to love you forever. After about a month, he tried to hide it, but he was still calling you occasionally, usually after a mail call when someone got a package or photos from home."

Tears once again pool in my eyes as I listen to him tell me about how heartbroken Seth was. "How did I not know?"

I cover my face with my hands as my mind goes through all the mistakes I've made over the last year. I should have contacted Seth to let him know about Rebekah as soon as I found out I was pregnant. Now, with the thought of not having him in either of our lives as a real possibility, my reasoning seems irrelevant.

"Oh, shit!" Selina shouts, making everyone in the room jump in surprise.

"Sorry," she says bashfully, before turning her attention toward me. "Do you remember those weird phone calls you were getting?"

"The unknown numbers," I whisper. "At first, I answered them religiously, hoping he would call, but after a while, I stopped, brushing them off as a wrong number or a telemarketer trying to sell me something. I never imagined that they could have been Seth calling me from overseas."

"Yeah, the satellite phones they give us come up with a restricted or unknown number. They say it's for OPSEC purposes, but I think they're full of shit." Brady pushes up from the chair and heads for the front door. "I'll go talk to him."

He walks out of the room without a second glance. I want to follow him and demand he take me to Seth. I want another chance to explain myself, to make him understand why I did what I did in the first place. But I know now is not the time. Brady's right. Not only have I betrayed him, but he probably feels like a sizeable group of his friends knew about Rebekah and didn't tell him, as well.

"We're coming, too!" Vance shouts as he stands up and jogs after Brady. "We need to apologize, and I'm sure he has questions."

Connor looks over at Vance and nods as he kisses Audrey on the head before following Vance out of the room.

"How the hell am I going to get out of this mess?" I look at two of my friends, hoping that they have the answer to all my problems.

"I don't know, Bri." Audrey grips my hand tightly and squeezes. "But let the guys have a talk with him, and he'll be back."

"I'm not too sure."

"Let's not forget that the man professed his undying love to you just seconds before everything imploded," Audrey says as she leans back in the chair and crosses her legs, as if she's just dropped a major truth bomb on the room.

"I thought you didn't hear anything." I shake my head at my friends as Selina places her hand on her belly.

"I said we heard enough. I didn't clarify how much or little we did hear." Audrey jokes.

"Vance and I are proof that love can survive anything," Selina murmurs. "You may have a few things to repair, but if he loves you the way we all know he does, then everything is going to be fine."

We all nod in agreement. Selina and Vance went years without seeing each other before getting back together and finding their happy ending. Who's to say that isn't possible for me and Seth?

With the newfound kernel of hope provided to me by my own friends' love stories, I try to imagine how life will be once Seth and I find our way back to each other. We can have family dinners and picnics in the park with Rebekah. He'll be there to rub my feet after a hard day at the studio or bring me lunch when I forget to pack one. We can spend rainy days watching Disney movies with Rebekah tucked tightly between the two of us. He'll be around to help me with the late-night feeding before wrapping his arms tightly around me to fall asleep at night.

Wait. I can't get ahead of myself. He may accept that he is a father, but what am I going to do if he wants nothing to do with me? The same feelings of dread I felt every time I tried to tell Seth suffocate me once again. I don't want to think about spending my life without Seth, not again, but if the only way I can have him is through our daughter, I'll learn to deal with it. I will always do what's best for her, even if it breaks my heart in the process.

"I know that look." Audrey slips out of the chair and kneels in front of me. "We'll cross that bridge if we come to it. Right now, we need to figure out a way for you to at least get Seth to speak to you again."

"Food and promises of sex always seem to work for Vance," Selina chimes in.

I give her a weak smile.

"Sex got her into this mess," Audrey quips.

I scowl in her direction, and she lifts her hands in surrender, but she clearly doesn't regret her statement one bit.

"You need to show him how you feel. That you see him as a life partner, not just as Rebekah's father," she adds.

I nod my head and look each one of my friends in the eye. We may not all have the same relationship status, but each of them has been to hell and back and found love again.

"Just like women, men want to feel loved and cherished." Audrey leans in and motions for all of us to lean in closer, as if she is about to impart some major revelation on the male psyche. "But you can't tell anyone their secret."

We all giggle, and for the first time since Seth drove away from me, I feel as if things could turn out okay for both of us. I just have to hope that my instincts aren't leading me in the wrong direction for a second time.

seventeen

seth

I drive around town aimlessly before pulling into the driveway of my empty house. As I turn off the ignition, I imagine how differently tonight would have gone if my curiosity hadn't gotten the best of me.

I wanted to find a place to escape the pain that was radiating through my body, but I ended up where I planned to make all my dreams come true. Bristol and I would probably be snuggled together on the couch in front of a roaring fire, making plans for the future. Today was supposed to be the day that I laid my heart on the line and told her how I felt, finally making her mine once and for all. But then it all went wrong. Completely and utterly wrong.

I know I wasn't delusional to believe that there was something between Bristol and me. I saw it in her eyes and in the way her entire face lit up whenever we saw each other. I could hear it in her voice when we said good night to each other every night during our phone calls. But for some reason, she's still afraid to open her heart to me.

I've done everything I know to show her how I feel. That I want her to be happy. To choose to love me, marry me, start a family with me. Maybe we did those things out of order, but it's still what I want. Seeing Bristol's belly swollen with our child *would* make me happy beyond my wildest dreams, but I missed the chance to see that. I'm sure there are pictures somewhere, but it's not the same.

I lean my head back on the seat and close my eyes, taking the time to think about where I want to go from here. Bristol and I have a child together, but can we salvage whatever is between us? Images of my life without Bristol next to me filter through my mind. It's only been a few minutes, but it feels like an eternity. Everything feels flat and lifeless now that things with the two of us are so up in the air. As far as I'm concerned, this isn't the end between the two of us, but how things proceed from here is up to Bristol.

I've been telling her repeatedly that I'd do anything to be with her, and I mean it. I've retired from the Marines, not completely because of her, but I'd be lying if I said she didn't have something to do with it. I moved to Tyson's Creek and have planned a life here for us. I was just waiting for the last piece to fall into place, for every part of my plan to be laid out before saying anything to her. But maybe that wasn't the right thing to do. Maybe she would've felt safer telling me about our daughter and letting down the last walls around her heart. Maybe. Maybe. Maybe.

"Fuck!" The sound of my voice echoes through the cab of my truck as I slam my palms on the steering wheel.

I take a deep breath and let it out slowly, momentarily quelling the raging emotions running through my body before opening the door and sliding out. The porch light is on, likely switched on when Mrs. Thomas accepted the flower delivery earlier this afternoon. I stride toward the front door, stick my key in the lock, and turn it. The door opens slowly, and I step inside, pushing it closed behind me.

Mrs. Thomas did an amazing job making the house perfect with the few items I've been able to buy in such a short time. She decorated the entire entryway with sunflowers and daisy bouquets and candles strategically placed to make a path toward the living room, the only completely furnished room in the house. I have a bed and dresser in the master bedroom, but I had planned for Bristol to help me with everything else.

As I turn the corner, my heart aches at how perfect it looks. Vases full of daisies and sunflowers cover every flat surface and candles of all sizes are placed near them. The setting sun filters through the windows, filling the room with a golden hue.

"This would have been perfect," I mumble as I pace back around the room, trying to wrap my head around the information I learned this afternoon.

My emotions are a mess, but the one that constantly keeps bubbling to the surface is betrayal. Almost everyone I call a friend had to have known about Bristol and Rebekah. No one said anything to me or even hinted that Bristol had a child. Maybe they wanted to give us space to figure things out together. Did she ask them not to tell me or to keep it a secret?

No matter how hurt and betrayed I feel, I can't be angry at them. If I was in their position, I'd have done the same thing. They barely know anything about me, and that's my fault. I keep to myself, and I appear moody to most people. I speak when spoken to, but I only give people the bare minimum of information about me. The few details I shared with them during the few months I spent visiting here before leaving on deployment were all superficial things. They had no idea of the man I was or am, taking Brady's word that I wasn't a complete asshole. They protected their friend.

The one thing that drew me to Tyson's Creek in the first place was how everyone takes care of each other. How no matter if you've been here a few times or lived here your entire life, you're welcomed with open arms. Everyone in this town is family. And family sticks together. And no one would betray someone they call family.

But why hadn't Bristol said anything to me before now? Once we got back in contact with each other, there were so many times when she could have told me about our daughter. We even talked about having children together someday, and that would have been the perfect opportunity to bring up the subject. But again, she said nothing.

I need to think. To find a way to quiet the noise in my head, giving me space to think all of this through. I need to go for a run. I head toward the back of the house in what will be my bedroom to grab the gym bag Mrs. Thomas dropped off for me earlier. I find the bag sitting in the center of the bed and reach inside. It takes a few minutes, but I find a pair of gym shorts and my sneakers at the bottom of the bag. My body moves on memory as I will my brain to shut down, to let the repetitiveness of my movements soothe the frayed edges of my mind. I walk into the bathroom and change quickly, leaving my clothes on the floor.

My heart squeezes inside my chest as I head back into the living room and take a seat on the couch to pull on my sneakers. The moment my feet hit the edge of the driveway, I make a left and start running. I breathe in and out slowly as the sound of my feet hitting the pavement echoes through my ears, and I relax into a steady breath. Beads of sweat collect on my brow as my emotions melt away, clearing my head and allowing me to think for the first time since leaving Vance and Selina's place.

After eavesdropping on their conversation, I was prepared for Bristol to tell me she had a baby with another man. I can't pretend as if it wouldn't have hurt knowing she was with another man while I was gone, but since we never officially said we were a couple, I would have accepted it. Honestly, I wouldn't have had a choice. I told her I was coming back from the desert to make her mine, but did I ever give her a reason to believe me?

I promised her I was going to come back, but again, we barely knew each other. At the time, to her, they were nothing but words and promises that could be broken at any time. She didn't have faith in me, in us, and the thought of that makes my soul ache, but I can understand it, too. If she had moved on, I couldn't have blamed her. But I never would have imagined that she was keeping this monstrous secret from me, a secret that would change the course of my life forever.

A little girl.

I'm a father.

My feet pound hard on the pavement as I pick up speed. Sweat soaks the front of my shirt as I push myself harder, shame washing over me in waves as I think about how hard the last eight months have been on Bristol. I can't imagine all the nights she spent worrying about our baby girl, wondering if what she was doing was enough. The late-night feeding and sleepless nights she must have endured with no one to share the load.

Anyone who knows Bristol knows she would rather die than ask for help, not wanting to be a burden. But I could have been there for her. The military gives expecting fathers paternity leave, and although it's hard to get approved through the command, I could've tried. I wasn't there for her when they needed me, and that's something I'll regret for the rest of my life.

Wait. Anger bubbles in my veins as I pick up the pace even further, practically sprinting down the road, trying to release all the anger flowing through me. No matter how bad I feel for her, this was a choice she made. Bristol could've gotten in contact with me to let me know our daughter existed. Allowed me to help her come to grips with being a mother, to support her in any way she needed, but she kept her hidden away from me. She *chose* not to share our daughter's existence with me. She *chose* not to allow me to be a part of either of their lives. It was a choice, no matter how I try to rationalize it.

I slow my pace to a jog as I allow my breathing to even out. I inhale through my nose and exhale through my mouth as I allow all the anger to seep from my veins. Running not only clears my mind, it also helps me clear my emotions. I'm still angry and hurt, but the feeling is more under control than before I started running.

As my pace slows even further, I notice the sun slowly disappear beyond the horizon and turn around. I need to head back toward my house before it gets too dark. Connor warned me that there aren't too many lights around the area, making it easy to get lost if you don't know where you're going. I don't really know the area well enough to be running aimlessly.

I walk through my front door just as the sun disappears behind the horizon. The smell of freshly baked apple pie fills my nostrils, reminding me once again of what tonight was supposed to be. Instead of going into the kitchen to see what Mrs. Thomas dropped off, I kick my sneakers into the corner before plopping down on the couch. I should probably shower, but I drop my head between my hands, realizing that I'm no closer to a solution to my problem than I was before I went for a run.

"Knock, knock."

My head pops up as Brady's voice reaches my ears. I notice him waving something white in front of him.

"I come in peace!" he shouts louder than necessary.

I shake my head. Brady has always been one for theatrics, even in the most serious of times.

"What are you doing here?" I grumble, not even bothering to get off the couch.

"Is it safe?" He peeks his head around the corner, and his eyes widen as he takes in the perfectly decorated room. "Man, don't you think you overdid it with the flowers?"

"At the time? No. But now? Probably." I snicker softly. "I really should text your mom and thank her for doing all this, even if it was a complete waste."

"I don't think it was a complete waste," Brady switches on the lamp sitting beside the couch before plopping down beside me, his nose instantly scrunching up in disgust. "You've been thinking, haven't you?"

"Yes," I deadpan. "And I'd like to continue to do so. What do you want?"

"Can't your best friend drop by your house unannounced? Do I need a reason?"

"Yes."

"I'm hurt." Brady clutches his hand over his chest, dramatically falling backward as if I wounded him.

"You really didn't know?" I ask my friend, hoping that someone wasn't keeping secrets from me.

"I did *not* know. I was in the sandbox right next to you, but I can't say I'm surprised." Brady relaxes against the couch, placing his right ankle on his knee as he looks at me. "I'm not surprised that she kept your daughter a secret. You were gone for a year, man. What was she supposed to do?"

"She should have told me," I take a deep breath to calm the anger I feel bubbling up inside me again. "She could've found some way to get a hold of me."

"I agree, but you two danced around each other for months. You spend one night together with no promises you would ever return."

"I promised her I was coming back for her."

"You and I both know that was a bullshit promise. We were off fighting a war where any number of things could happen. Do you really think she put a lot of faith into that promise?"

I open my mouth and slam it shut quickly.

"Right. She didn't know what your plans were once deployment was over."

"I told her how I felt before I left. I made it clear that she was the person I planned on spending my life with."

"But a year is a long time. People change, man. How was she supposed to know you would feel the same about her when you came back?"

"I called her."

"Did you ever bother to leave her a voicemail? An email address to get in touch with you? Anything?" He raises his eyebrow in my direction.

"She should have picked up the damn phone," I respond defensively.

"The numbers are restricted, jackass. How the hell was she going to know it was you?" Brady leans back onto the couch, laying his ankle on his knee. "Obviously, she didn't know you weren't a damn psycho."

I pause and think about what Brady said, replaying all my conversations with her in my mind. After that first night, I was head over heels for her. But I never *really* promised her anything besides my coming back. I called her every chance I got, but I was too much of a chickenshit to leave a message. I did the same thing I accused Bristol of doing before I walked away from her earlier. I was afraid of what would happen if I let her all the way in.

Bristol made it clear from the start that she couldn't see herself being in a relationship with a man in the military and never wavered. The military had been my entire life until that point, but I didn't have any plans past surviving deployment. It wasn't until Brady said something about retirement did the plan to move back to Tyson's Creek and searching for Bristol cross my mind. I knew I wanted to be with her, but I wasn't sure if there was a space for me in her life.

I was afraid that someone like me wouldn't be good enough for her. I didn't have a family or any prospects for a job. What did I have to offer her? The only thing I had ever known was being a Marine, but that experience doesn't really translate into marketable skills outside of being in the military. By not leaving a message, I gave myself the excuse to remain closed off from the possibility of being hurt. I knew I was a goner for her, but I had no idea how she felt about me. Bristol took the first step by giving me her phone number, but I didn't meet her halfway, putting all the pressure and blame on her if I came here and things didn't work out as I had hoped they would.

"Damn it. You're right." I groan as I lean back on the couch and cover my face with my arm. "She didn't know."

"Now you're seeing things clearly." Brady punches me lightly in the shoulder. "So, how do you plan to fix this?"

"Fix what? I did nothing except leave the situation before I said something I didn't mean." I turn in his direction, waiting for him to explain.

"Not that. Honestly, you handled that situation as well as anyone could expect. I'm talking about Rebekah. You have a little girl that you've never even met. What are you going to do about it?"

"I don't know." I give him the only answer I have.

I've always wanted a family of my own, but does she even want me to be a part of their lives? I don't have many memories of my father, and the few foster parents I had weren't the best. Yes, they fed me and kept a roof over my head, but they weren't the nurturing type. I don't know the first thing about raising a child. I've spent the last twenty years being told what to wear and when to eat and sleep. I have a routine, a certain way I prefer things to run and be done. How is that going to work, adding a little girl to the mix? Kids are messy and loud, two things that I can't handle on a regular basis, even before I joined the military.

I want to be a good father to our daughter. Be a shoulder for her to cry on when she needs me but also to help mold and guide her into becoming a beautiful young woman. But is that what Bristol wants? I understand her obligation to let me know I have a daughter, but what role does she want me to play in her life? Rebekah is almost a year old, and I've missed so much, so many milestones that a father should be present for, and I refuse to miss any more. But where is my place in their family? Bristol has a support network of people, friends and family, that will help her whenever she needs them. Does she really need me around?

"Don't get all doom and gloom, Seth. That woman loves you."

"I know, but I worry about where my place is with them."

"You worry too much, my friend." Brady claps me hard on the back, causing me to lurch forward. "Just take things one step at a time. Bristol and Rebekah will let you know what they need. Your job right now is to be there for them."

"Now that's one thing I know I can do." I smile brightly at my friend as my stomach rumbles. "I guess

I'd better find something to eat before I become very unpleasant."

"Already got that covered," Vance says as he and Connor come into view, each holding a pizza and a case of beer. "What's better than pizza and beer at an impromptu guys' night?"

I rub the back of my neck and laugh. "I think I have some paper plates and Solo cups in the kitchen, but that's all I can offer. I wasn't planning on eating dinner here."

"He planned to be eating other things," Brady snickers.

I cuff him on the back of the head and pin him in place with a stare. He mouths an apology as Connor places the pizza boxes on the coffee table before walking back out of the room toward the kitchen, probably to put the beers in the fridge to chill.

Vance drops the case of beer in his hand and rips it open, pulling a beer out for each of us and handing me one. "But first, we're sorry, Seth."

Connor grabs a can from Vance and cracks it open. "We knew Bristol had a daughter, but not who the father was. We assumed she was waiting to see where things went between you two before saying anything, but if we had known..." His voice trails off as if he was searching for the right words.

"You'd have done the same thing." I chuckle, popping my can open and taking a huge gulp. "Now that I've had time to think, I don't know if I'd done anything differently in your position."

"Thanks. For understanding, I guess," Vance says as he sets his beer on the coffee table and flips the pizza box open to grab a slice.

"Do you still love her?" Brady asks, taking a healthy pull from his beer and leaning against the couch beside me.

"What kind of fucking question is that?" I snap, crossing my arms defensively over my chest. "Of course, I fucking love her. Those feelings don't just disappear because we had an argument."

"This was a little more than an argument," Vance responds as he shoves a slice of pizza into his mouth.

"That's fucking disgusting." I snicker while taking another swig of my beer. "But I've been in love with Bristol since I first laid eyes on her over a year ago. I'll be damned if I let her or my daughter get away without a fight."

"Just what we wanted to hear." Vance claps me on the back. "But maybe take a shower first. You are ripe, my friend."

"I'm going now." I leave my beer on the coffee table before heading into my room.

When I came back, the guys have made themselves at home. Connor is sitting on the couch, staring at his phone with a soft smile on his face, while Brady is seated next to him on the couch, and Vance is sitting on the floor in front of him on the other side of the coffee table, a deck of cards laid out between them.

"What are you playing?" I ask before leaning over the couch between Connor and Brady to grab my beer.

"Go Fish," Vance's eyes never leave his cards.

"And I'm winning." Brady smiles, showing his hand to me.

"Sure. Sure." I chuckle, taking another sip of my beer. "You know I have a television, don't you?"

"Where?" all three men respond in unison as I grab the remote control from beside the light and point it toward the empty wall. A large projection screen drops from the ceiling.

"That wasn't there when Audrey lived here, was it?" Connor asks in awe as I turn on the satellite TV and drop the remote on the couch.

"Nope. This was something I bought just for me. I refuse to watch the game on a tiny-ass TV ever again."

"Every Sunday, Seth is having us over to watch the game," Brady says as he snatches the remote off the couch and starts flicking through channels before settling on some action movie.

"We'll see," is the only response I give him as I come around the side of the couch near the door and sit in the lone armchair by the window.

We all sit there and watch the television in silence for a few moments before Connor speaks up.

"So, what do you plan on doing now that you know about Rebekah?"

"I asked him the same thing earlier. Maybe he'll answer *you*," Brady grumbles as he shoves another slice into his mouth.

"First, I need to see both of your wives." I nod toward Vance and Connor. "I'm hoping for a crash course in all things baby."

"I raised a kid, too, you know," Connor grumbles, taking a long pull from his beer.

"You can come, too." I raise my now-empty beer in his direction. "I don't know a damn thing about babies outside of the little I learned in the foster homes."

"Seli asked Bristol and Audrey to do the same thing for her." Vance laughs, placing his bottle on the table in front of him. "She said what better way to learn how to take care of babies than from another mom?"

"After I wrap my head around having a daughter, then it's time to make sure my girl knows nothing has changed. She's it for me, and there isn't a damn thing she can do about it now. She's stuck with me."

"I don't think she'll have a problem with that," Connor says as he slaps me on the back and grabs another slice of pizza.

"Now that that's all settled, can we stop with all the feelings and drink some beer?" Brady grabs another beer, cracks it open, and chugs it. "I have no intention of leaving here sober."

"Can he sleep on your couch? I have no intention of dealing with his drunk ass tonight," Vance asks, eyeing Brady's swaying form skeptically.

Although this isn't how I planned for today to end, I can't say I'm disappointed. I may not have told my girl how much I cared for her, but I found out I have a daughter. Who could ask for anything more?

Now I just have to hope that I can be the man they both need.

eighteen

bristol

I pull out my phone for the millionth time today, open my messages, and sigh. Still nothing from Seth. Wanting to let him know I'm thinking about him, I open up a new message and type.

BRISTOL

Hope you're doing okay. Did you start work at the station yet? Maybe we can grab coffee or something. No pressure.

"Desperate much?" I mumble to myself as I set my phone down on the counter.

It's been almost a week since Seth found out about Rebekah, and I haven't heard a peep from him. I understand he needs some time to cool off and wrap his head around being a father. I just thought that after a few days, he would calm down and at least contact me, but he hasn't. I gave in two days ago and sent him a text message just asking how he was doing, but he never replied. Every time my phone chimes, signaling a new message, I jump, but it's never him. I wonder if it will ever be him again.

"Still nothing from Seth?" Audrey says from behind me as she wraps her arm around my shoulder, her eyes motioning toward my phone on the counter.

"Nothing. It shows that he read my text, but he hasn't bothered to respond." I grab it and shove it into my bag underneath the counter, crossing my arms. "He could've at least messaged me and told me to fuck off or something. The silence is killing me."

"I'm sure he's just trying to work through his feelings. It's a big deal finding out that you have a daughter you knew nothing about," Audrey answers with a knowing smile.

Not wanting to have the same conversation we've been having for almost a week, I change the subject. "I need a coffee. Want anything?"

"Nah. Seli and I are having lunch when I get out of here."

"Mind if I tag along?" I ask as I reach under the counter and grab my bag.

"Sure. We're meeting Vance and Connor," she responds brightly, and I cringe.

My heart aches at the thought of being around my friends and their significant others. I never used to be jealous of my friends, but now that I've had a taste of how things could be between Seth and me, I miss it. My heart yearns to have someone stand behind me and support me when I feel as if my entire world is falling apart. Too bad that person may never want to speak to me again.

"Suit yourself." Audrey twirls her hair around her finger, deep in thought. "Maybe we can grab dinner later this week. Give Leia a call. I'm sure she could use a break from everything going on with her dad."

"That's an understatement," I grumble, reaching for my phone, but I stop myself.

Mr. Armstrong isn't doing well. Leia hasn't shared all the details about what happened when he fell, but what she has shared with us isn't good. By some miracle, her father has agreed to turn over Tranquility Retreat to her, but only if she finds a husband.

"She has the solution to her problem, but she doesn't want to take it." Audrey jokes as I shake my head.

"If only it were that simple," I reply as my phone vibrates across the counter.

I dive toward it, almost knocking it off the counter. My shoulders tighten as I flip the phone over but immediately release when I see a text from my mom.

MOM

Hey, baby. Rebekah and I were out for a walk and stopped at Just the Drip for a snack. Want to join us?

BRISTOL

Let me check with Audrey, but I think I can make it happen.

I smile at the phone before turning to Audrey. "My mom brought Rebekah for a visit."

"Go. I'll text Seli and let her know I'll be running late for lunch."

"Love you." I smile at her over my shoulder before heading out the door. Thankfully, most of the classes for the day are finished, and I can run and hide for a little while.

Normally, I'd stop by the dance studio and shoot the shit with Selina for a little while, but since she's going to lunch with Audrey, I doubt she's there. With her belly growing every day, it's getting harder and harder for her to keep up with her students, let alone dance. Thankfully, Emersyn has stepped up and started teaching a lot of the classes, so Selina only has to worry about the more advanced ones.

The bell over the door chimes loudly as I stride into the coffee shop. I catch sight of Mom and Rebekah sitting in a corner. I wave at them before making a beeline for the counter.

"What's up, Bristol?" Katie says with a smile.

"Don't you ever take a day off?" I laugh as I drop my bag on a table near the counter.

"I work almost every day during the week, but you won't catch me in this place after dinner or on a weekend, unless it's as a customer."

"Can I get a caramel macchiato with extra caramel and whipped cream, please?"

"Coming right up," she says with a smile before turning to make my drink. "Here you go. I also added a butter croissant for the little one."

"You're too good to us," I reply before heading over to where my mom is sitting.

She's spending more time here this week than usual, more than likely because she heard what happened between Seth and me. I don't know how she found out, but I have a feeling that one of the girls gave her a call. And I'm glad they did, because right now, I need my momma.

"Hey, little one," I say, dropping to my knees so I can give Rebekah a kiss. She giggles softly, placing both her hands on my cheeks and squeezing them together. "Did you miss Mommy?"

"Of course, she did," my mom replies for her as Rebekah leans forward and plants a sloppy kiss on the end of my nose.

"Hi, Mom." I smile up at her before taking the seat right next to Rebekah. "Thanks for bringing her to visit. I needed a pick-me-up today."

"I know."

"Who called you?" I ask, taking a sip from my coffee.

"Audrey," my mom grabs the croissant off the plate and breaking it into pieces for Rebekah.

"Can I ask you a question?"

"Shoot."

"Have you ever messed up?"

Mom stills, probably trying to figure out where my question came from. "Um, you need to give me more information, Bristol. Everyone messes up, but it's never as bad as we think it is."

"I don't know if there's any way for me to fix things with Seth." I take another sip of coffee, trying to get my thoughts in order. "He won't respond to my texts or answer my calls, and it's been a week."

"I'm sure Seth understands you were protecting your daughter," she says matter-of-factly. "Anyone who spends ten minutes with you and Rebekah knows how much you love her."

I down the last bit of my coffee before shoving back from the table and heading toward the trashcan a few feet away.

"Does he know how you feel about him?"

I pause, my hand hovering over the trash as I think about her question. I open and close my mouth a few times before I spin around, my eyes wide in shock.

"No." I drop the cup on the floor and cover my mouth with both hands.

I never told Seth how I felt about him. Yeah, we have a daughter together, and I've been desperately in love with him for the last year or so, but he doesn't know that. Well, unless he's a mind-reader.

I've spent so much time guarding my heart and worrying about what he would say if he found out about Rebekah, but I've never let him know how much I love him. How my heart has yearned for its other half since the day I walked away from him before deployment.

Mom giggles softly before pushing back from the table and coming toward me. She bends down to pick up the cup and tosses it into the trash before speaking.

"There's your problem. That man moved heaven and earth to come home to you, but he doesn't know how you feel. Put that on top of finding out he has a daughter he never knew about? Any man would have doubts."

"I didn't plan on keeping her from him forever." Tears stream down my face as the weight of everything crashes down on my shoulders.

"I know, sweet girl." Mom wraps her arms around me and pulls me in for a hug. "We can't dwell on the past, but we should always keep our eyes on the future. You never know how things are going to work out."

"How do I do that?" I wrap my arms around her waist and squeeze her tightly.

"Do you love him?"

"Yes," I say with conviction as I pull back from her embrace.

"Then tell him. Men are simple creatures. Once he knows how you feel, if he feels the same way, everything will work out as it should." Mom runs her thumbs under my eyes, wiping away the tears, and cups my face.

Seth told me he loved me that day, but I need him to know that I see him as so much more than the father of my child. He is one of the most important people in my life.

"Thanks, Mom," I say with a smile, stepping around her and heading back to the table to grab my bag. I drop a kiss on the top of Rebekah's head before turning back toward her. "I have to teach a class, but thanks for the visit and the pep talk."

"That's what moms are for, Bristol." She kisses my cheek softly before patting it with her hand. "After you patch things up, you should bring Seth to have dinner with your father and me. We'd love to meet him and give him the once-over."

Mom and I both snicker as I reach for her hand and squeeze it tightly. There are no words to explain how much these past ten minutes have rearranged my outlook on my relationship with Seth.

"Now, git. I'll take Rebekah back to your place and put her down for her nap," she teases.

I give her hand one last squeeze before striding out the door with a little more pep in my step than when I entered. I make my way back to the studio and get ready for my next class. I need to get Seth to at least talk to me. Although I don't want to lay my heart out to him via text message, I may not have a choice.

I drop my bag onto the counter and fish around for my phone, grabbing it quickly.

"They say the way to a man's heart is through his stomach," I mumble into the empty lobby before typing out a text to Seth.

BRISTOL

I'm making enchiladas for dinner. Aren't those your favorite? You can stop by if you aren't busy. Just text me and I'll shoot you the address.

I hit send on the phone, and then I hesitate. Mom said I need to let him know how I feel. Easier said than done, but putting it in a text is a good start.

BRISTOL

I miss you.

I send that message and shove the phone into my bag before I change my mind. Now it's up to him to make a move. Hopefully, I haven't lost him.

* * *

I make it through my last class, close the studio, and head right home to relieve my mother. After shooing her out the door with promises to visit my parents next weekend, I make a quick trip to the grocery store and get back to my house in record time. It took some Herculean effort, but I only checked my phone twice to see if Seth texted back. Nothing. I shouldn't be surprised that he hasn't said anything, but now that I've accepted my feelings for him, it hurts so much more.

"What do you think, baby girl?" I say to Rebekah as I pull her out of the car seat. "Should we cook Daddy dinner?"

She coos softly at me before trapping my face between her two tiny hands.

"I'll take that as a yes."

I smile, leaning forward and brushing a kiss on her forehead before putting her on the floor with a few toys and getting to work on dinner. I absentmindedly begin assembling the enchiladas. Lucky for me, I know this recipe by heart, or I would be in trouble.

My mind is occupied with thoughts of Seth and how to make things right between us. I need to let him know how I feel about him. Not because we have a beautiful daughter together, but because he is the other half of me. There is no way I can convey my feelings in a text message, so I need to figure out some way to get him to talk to me.

"Maybe I can text one of the guys," I mumble to myself as I pour the enchilada sauce into the casserole pan and shove it into the oven.

If anyone would know the way to get back into his good graces, it would be them. Men are pretty much all the same, and at this point, I'm desperate, especially since my two best friends are preoccupied with Lord knows what. I'm not bitter. Nope, not even a little bit. I just wish I knew what was going on.

I quickly set the timer on the oven, wash my hands in the sink, and head back into the living room to grab Rebekah.

"How about we get you fed, little one?" I pick her up and head back into the kitchen, strapping her into the highchair before opening the cabinet beside me in search of something to give her. Not wanting anything too complicated, I grab a jar of sweet potatoes and some rice cereal, dump some of each into the bowl, and stir them together.

"Not the most appetizing dinner, but it's something, right?" I say as I plop down into the chair and begin feeding her.

We finish just as the timer goes off on the stove. Wanting to ensure she is occupied while I have the oven open, I pour some sweet potato puffs onto her tray. I turn off the timer as I open the oven door, and the smell of baked cheese and seasoning wafts through the room just as I hear a knock at the door.

"Coming!" I shout over my shoulder as I place the dish on the top of the stove and head for the door, wrenching it open.

My eyes widen in shock when I take in Seth standing before me.

"H-hi," I stammer, unable to say anything else. I assumed, based on his lack of response, that he had no intention of coming here for dinner, but here he is. "How did you know where I lived?"

"It took some convincing, but Audrey told me." He flashes me a crooked smile before stepping forward and kissing my forehead gently.

My eyes slip closed as I savor the feeling of his lips on my skin for the first time in what seems like forever.

"Is the offer for dinner still available?" he asks.

"Of course! Come on in," I respond overenthusiastically.

I step back, leaving enough space for him to come in, then close the door behind him and watch as he looks around, taking in all the pictures of my friends, family, and Rebekah that cover my walls. He comes to a complete stop in the center of my living room, his eyes focused on our little girl sitting in her highchair directly in front of him.

I open my mouth to speak, but nothing comes out. I had hoped that she would be dressed in her best outfit when she met her father for the first time, but her clothes are covered in parts of her dinner.

Seth quickly strides toward her.

"Hey, beautiful," he whispers as he grips her tiny hand in his.

My eyes fill with tears as she grasps one of his

fingers tightly. I have tried to picture this moment since I saw Seth outside the coffee shop all those weeks ago, but this is so much more than I could ever have imagined. The two of them just stare at each other in awe, as if they recognize each other.

"Although she's never met you, I've told her everything I could about you. Even more since you came back into our lives." I sniffle, not wanting to lose control just yet. "I'm sorr—"

"Bri," Seth's gravelly voice, full of emotion, cuts me off.

"No, I need to get this all out. I'm sorry for not trying to find you sooner. I'm sorry that you missed so much of our daughter's life because you were fighting for our country. You were right. I was scared. Scared of how much you meant to me and how heartbreaking it would have been if I lost you."

A loud sob bubbles out of my throat as two strong arms wrap around my waist. Seth pulls me into his chest as I grip the front of his shirt.

"Shhhh," he mutters as he kisses the top of my head.

I try to wrangle my emotions, but everything is too much.

He's here.

With me. With us.

He didn't run away.

Everything has led to this moment. Rebekah, Seth, and I are finally together as a family.

"Feel better?" His voice rumbles in his chest as I lean back, tipping my head up toward him.

I expected to see judgment in his eyes, but all I see is love. I want to tell him how I feel, that I love him in the deepest part of my soul. But as I open my mouth, he takes a step back and smiles at me softly, releasing me from his protective hold.

"Dinner is ready. The plates are next to the stove, and the silverware is here." I point at the drawer to my right as I step around him toward Rebekah. "Let me just give this little one a bath and get her into her pajamas really quick, and I'll join you." I pick her up and attempt to make my escape.

"Can I help?" He brushes his hand down my arm before pulling it back and lowering it to his side.

"Of course," I whisper as I turn and head down the hall toward the bathroom.

The thud of his work boots on the floor signals that he's following me.

Seth told me he loved me before everything hit the fan last week, but my lies have caught up with me. I knew things wouldn't go back to how they were immediately, but I hoped I still had a place in his heart. But judging by the way he shut me down just now, I have a lot of work to do before he will let me in again.

Not wanting to ruin this family bonding moment, I

put a cap on my emotions. Rebekah needs to be my focus. Although I'm desperately in love with her father, she needs to be my priority. I'm the reason she's spent the last eight and a half months without a relationship with her father, and I won't do that any longer.

nineteen

seth

We work in tandem as we get Rebekah into the bath. I run the water, checking the temperature frequently, as Bristol quickly undresses Rebekah and places her in the tub. I watch the two of them together as Bristol tickles her belly lightly before placing a few toys and a washcloth in the tub to keep her attention.

She gently leans Rebekah back in the water, splashing a little water onto her head to get her hair wet before sitting her back up. I kneel beside them, wanting to be as close to them as possible.

Bristol gives me a shy smile as she points beside me. "Can you hand me the shampoo?"

I turn and notice a yellow bottle of liquid beside me, grabbing it quickly and handing it to her.

"Thank you," she mumbles before opening the bottle and pouring a little into her hand. I watch as Bristol lathers the liquid for a few moments, letting it bubble, then rubs her soap-covered hand over our princess's head.

Wanting to be of more help, I grab the pink cloth hanging from a hook beside the tub and dunk it into the water. I glimpse a purple bottle of lavender body wash where I got the shampoo and pull the cloth out of the water, dropping a dollop of soap into it and rubbing the sides together. After a few moments, I reach under Bristol's arms and lather up Rebekah's belly, stopping to give her a tickle before running the cloth along both arms and then down her back.

"Where did you learn how to give a baby a bath?" Bristol's eyes widen in shock.

I chuckle as I run the washcloth down Rebekah's back, dunking it into the water to rinse it before going back and wiping the soap from her skin. "There were younger kids in some of the foster homes I was in. I never gave any of the girls baths, but I figure the general mechanics are the same."

"Yeah." She gives me a bright smile as I finish washing our daughter, then leans her back once again and rinses the shampoo from her hair. "I'd better give her some time to play, or she'll have a fit."

Rebekah squeals in delight as she smacks the largest cup into the water repeatedly, splashing me.

"I didn't plan on having a shower while giving you a bath, Princess. Can we cool it on the splashing a little?" I say, grabbing one of the other cups in the bath and filling it with water before dumping the contents into the cup Rebekah is holding.

She watches in wonder as the water fills the cup, spilling over into her little hands, and I refill my cup and dump the water into her cup again. After a few moments, she squeals in delight.

"I think you have a new fan," Bristol says softly as she reaches over my head for a hooded towel thing and grabs Rebekah with the other arm.

She whines in protest, but Bristol wraps her in the towel quickly, pulling the hood over her head.

"Mama has spoken, Princess. I'm sure there'll be more time to play in the water next time." I smile brightly at them as I push up to my feet and follow Bristol out of the bathroom and down the hall.

There is a room to my left that seems to be an office with large bookcases covering one wall. An oversized chair is tucked to the left of the window with a fluffy-looking blanket draped over the arm.

"Your favorite spot," I say to no one as I remember Bristol talking about her favorite spot, curled up in her favorite chair with a good book.

Not wanting to be left behind, I continue down the hall, peeking into a room directly across from the first, which is decorated in soft pinks and purples. Rebekah's name hangs above a beautiful white crib that's pushed up against the wall.

"Is this her room?" I question, wondering why we aren't continuing down the hallway.

"Yes. The girls helped me decorate it," Bristol says as she lays our daughter down softly on a changing table. "It took me forever to decide what I wanted, but as soon as I decided, Leia, Seli, and Audrey were here the next day with paint, and we got it knocked out."

"Those girls are a force to be reckoned with, that's for certain." Bristol raises her eyebrow at me. "That night, after I cooled off, I called Selina and Audrey. Between the two of them and Connor, I was able to get everything I needed to make sure my place was ready for you and Rebekah."

"*Your* place? How did Brady take you wanting to baby-proof your apartment?" She smirks at me as she quickly puts a diaper and pajamas on Rebekah before picking her back up.

"My house. I bought Audrey's old place."

I run my hand across the back of my neck. This isn't the way I wanted Bristol to find out about my preparations for her and Rebekah in my life, but she needs to understand I'm here for the long haul.

"I still need some furniture, but they made sure I had everything Rebekah needed. I set up a room for her and painted it a pale yellow color with sunflowers and elephants around the room."

"Sunflowers..." Her voice trails off as she lifts

Rebekah into her arms and snuggles her nose into her neck.

"Your favorite flower. And elephants... well, I chose those mostly because I thought they were cute." I take a deep breath and step closer, wrapping them in my arms.

A confused look covers her face before she sighs heavily. "That's what you've been doing the last week?"

I nod my head. "I wasn't ignoring you. Preparing is a better way to explain things. I just wanted to show you I was in this for the long haul. That I'm not going anywhere. You and Rebekah are my home."

Bristol steps out of my embrace and stares at me, searching for something, but doesn't say a word. Unable to take the silence any longer, I speak again.

"Don't be too mad at the girls. I swore them to secrecy. I wanted it to be a surprise," I say, wanting to make her understand.

"I hate surprises," she grumbles.

"Good to know."

"Do you want to hold her?"

"Yes," I say quickly, a little louder than expected. "I mean, that would be great, but I need you to show me how. My experience is limited to baths and putting some pasta things in the microwave to warm."

"Have a seat in that chair. It'll be easier to keep her from squirming. Since she's not a newborn anymore, you don't really have to worry about anything. Just make sure she doesn't crack her head open."

I nod and stride toward the chair in the corner. It's covered in light pink fabric with large white polka dots all over the entire thing. A small white end table is sitting beside it, with a unicorn lamp on top. I lower myself into the chair, and she places Rebekah in my arms.

"Hey, Princess," I murmur as my daughter spins around and gives me a huge smile. "She's beautiful." I lower her down into my lap and brush my hand across her soft curls.

"We did good, didn't we?" Bristol says.

I just nod my head, unable to believe that we created such a perfect little girl.

"I just need to run to the kitchen and warm up some milk. I won't be more than five minutes."

"Sure thing. We'll be here when you get back." I hold up Rebekah's small hand and wave at Bristol as she heads out of the room, leaving the two of us alone for the first time.

"Hey there, Princess. I'm not sure if you know this or not, but I'm your daddy." I grind my teeth together, overcome with the love I feel for this little girl. "I thought your mama was gonna be the only woman I loved for the rest of my life, but then you came along. I promise, you two are the most important people in the world to me."

Rebekah lays her tiny hand on my cheek as her eyes droop shut before flying open. I chuckle as she struggles to stay awake, afraid she will miss something in the few hours she is asleep. "Relax, little one. I'll be here when you wake up, and every day after that."

"You mean it?" I hear Bristol's voice and turn in her direction as she comes into the room, a small bottle in her hand.

"Of course, I do, Bri. I have spent my life waiting for both of you. I don't plan to waste another minute without you in my life. However you want me."

I reach out and grab the bottle from her, then slide it between Rebekah's lips. She wraps both of her small hands around it, sucking greedily as her eyes droop shut one more time.

"Give her a few minutes, and she'll be out like a light." Bristol runs her pointer finger down our princess's cheek before taking a seat on the arm of the chair I'm sitting in.

"I meant every word, Bristol," I say once again, turning in her direction as her eyes fill with tears. "I need you to know that I've loved you since the night we finally gave in to our feelings, connecting our hearts forever. I told you that day that I was falling for you, but today I can say with certainty that I am completely and utterly in love with you. Both of you."

Tears stream down her cheeks now. "I was so afraid

when you didn't answer any of my calls or texts over the last week that we had lost you forever."

"Never," I respond with conviction as I look down at our little girl.

Bristol giggles softly, sliding her arms beneath Rebekah and gently lifting her out of my arms. "I think this one is down for the count. I'm sure dinner is cold by now but thank God for microwaves."

"Dinner can wait." I have a much more pressing matter to attend to now... or as soon as I can get out of my daughter's room. I plan to show Bristol exactly how much she means to me.

"My room is across the hall." She motions toward the door as she lays Rebekah down in her crib. I turn and walk across the hall, taking in her room. It's decorated simply with a portable crib tucked into the corner near the window.

"I just started putting her in her room at night. She's been mostly sleeping through the night for over a month, but I wasn't ready to be apart from her yet," she whispers, her eyes drifting from my lips to my eyes every few seconds. "Thank you for giving us a second chance."

I sigh as I tuck a piece of hair behind her ear. "Bri, when are you going to learn how irrevocably and unconditionally I love you?" I whisper before kissing her gently.

My heart races—no, gallops—in my chest as

emotions swirl through my mind. Yearning to feel the softness of her skin against my calloused fingers as I make her mine, ruining her for any other man who dares to lay his hands on her.

"Are you ready to stop running from me?" I groan as she pushes gently on my chest, and I fall back onto the bed.

She swings her legs over mine before lowering herself and straddling my lap. I swipe my thumb across her cheek, her skin feeling like silk beneath my calloused fingers. I stare into her eyes, committing this moment to memory.

"I love you, Seth. With every part of my being," she murmurs as she grips the base of my neck, pulling me closer to her. Our lips brush gently against each other, and I groan.

I rest my head against hers, closing my eyes tightly as I fight for control. My mind and body are at war with each other as the magnitude of her words sinks in. A possessiveness unlike any other rages through my mind as the desire to claim her, mark her as my own, becomes almost overwhelming.

"Fuck," I growl, nuzzling my face into her neck and nipping at the sensitive flesh below her ear. "Say it again."

"I love you, Seth. Now, make me yours." Unable to resist her allure any longer, I lean forward and capture her lips with mine, pulling her body flush against mine.

Her body presses against mine, her nipples brushing against the fabric of my shirt as her hips rock back and forth against me.

My fingertips dig into her skin, holding her flush against me in fear that she'll push me away. Not that I'd ever let her, not after everything we've been through. We've fought hard for this chance to be together.

Electricity pulses in my veins, turning into a burning need as one of her hands slips beneath my shirt. Her fingernails scratch across my skin, sending shivers of pleasure down my spine before she places her hand above my heart. The heat of her palm against my skin brings a moan from my mouth.

"Seth, I need you." The wantonness in her voice caresses my skin, making goose bumps pebble on my flesh. "Love me in a way only you can," she mutters against my lips before pressing them against mine more forcefully.

I quickly flip us over, laying her down on the pillowy surface before standing back to my full height. I quickly shed my clothes before joining her again on the bed. I snake my hands up her body, gripping her breast hard through her shirt.

She mews in pleasure as she sits up, grinding herself against my knee, her juices seeping into my pants. As soon as her shirt and bra are off, I attack her breast, sucking hard on her nipple. A sweet taste enters my mouth, and I pull back slightly.

"Breast milk," she mumbles as she tries to cover herself up.

I grasp both of her wrists and pin them at her sides. "The most delicious thing I have ever tasted."

Bristol pants softly as I take her nipples into my mouth once again, nibbling gently on the pebbled nubs. Now I understand why she had the large wet spot on her shirt the night she stayed at my place.

"Drool, huh?" I chuckle as she gasps in pleasure, unable to say anything else, and I use my free hand to reach into the yoga pants she is wearing.

"Off," I command as I slide off the bed once again and watch as she shimmies out of her pants and tosses them to the side. "You're so fucking beautiful."

"Please," she begs, the tips of my fingers brushing against the fine hairs covering her clit. She rocks into my palm as she reaches down to grab my cock.

"Patience," I hiss, pinching her clit between my fingers. Bristol's back arches off the bed as I slide one finger inside her, gently pulling it out before slowly sliding it back in. My eyes remain focused on hers as she teeters on the edge of an orgasm. I can feel our hearts pounding in unison as if they have finally found each other again after all these years.

"Tell me what you want," I demand.

"You. Just you." She whimpers as I pull my fingers from inside her and slide between her legs. I nip at her flesh, slide my hand into her hair, and capture her lips once again, nibbling before sweeping my tongue into her mouth. Gripping her leg tightly, I lift it up near my waist and slide my cock between her folds. Her juices help my shaft glide back and forth, bumping her clit with the head with each pass.

My chest rises and falls quickly as I thrust forward, my cock sliding deeper with each pass. Bristol's mouth latches onto my shoulder, biting down hard as she moans. Her arms wrap around my neck, her nails digging into my back, anchoring herself to me as she pulls her body flush against mine. Her clit grinds against me, causing my legs to tremble. My hips rock back and forth in time with my movements, both of us desperate to come.

"That's it. Take what's yours," I whisper into her ear before pulling the lobe into my mouth and biting down on it.

"You're so fucking perfect," I grind out, my thrusts becoming more erratic, losing the smooth glide I once had. "I need you to get there, baby. Come all over my cock," I growl as my balls tighten, ready to release.

"I'm close," she whines.

I slide my hand between us and rub her clit, and her pussy tightens around me like a vise grip. My mind can no longer process words, only actions. The arousal racing through my body is climbing towards an impossible end. Higher and higher, clenching so hard around the intrusion that's controlling every aspect of my life in this moment.

"Fuck!" I roar, slamming into her only twice more before spilling my seed deep inside her. My muscles twitch from the strain as I slow my pace, pumping in and out of her as I draw out her orgasm. Her body quivers slightly as I roll to the slide and slide out of her with a groan.

Bristol lays her head gently on my chest as I pull the covers up and over us. My lungs can't pull in enough air. I can barely hear anything over the sound of my heart pounding in my ears, but I am acutely aware of her. "I've been waiting my entire life for you," I whisper into the darkness, pulling her tightly against me just as my stomach rumbles.

"I guess we should go have some dinner." Bristol giggles as she tries to wiggle out of my arms.

"Thank God for microwaves," I say before pressing a kiss to her shoulder and releasing her. I throw my legs over the side of the bed and grab my boxers. "I plan on having you for dessert. No need for too many clothes."

I toss Bristol my T-shirt, and she shakes her head at me, but pulls it over her head and saunters out of the room.

I'm not sure what the future holds for us, but I know one thing for sure: it's going to be an adventure. I have spent my entire life trying to find a family and a place to belong, and I've finally found both with her.

twenty

brady

"You'd better keep your damn hands to yourself, Brady," Beckett growls as we come to a stop in front of his car.

"You act like you don't know me at all." I shove my hands into my pockets, willing myself to calm down and not beat the shit out of one of my best friends. "I'd never do anything like that to Emersyn."

"I used to believe that. Until I caught you taking advantage of her at your going away party last year."

"Give it a rest, Beckett. I had every intention of telling Emersyn how I felt about her that night. Sex was the furthest thing from my mind."

"Could have fooled me."

"Look, I came over here to shoot the shit and get things back to how they were. I miss my friend."

"Why aren't you hanging with your buddy Seth?"

"What are you, jealous?" I chuckle, causing Beckett to scowl in my direction. "I got tired of being the fourth wheel." I hold my hand in his direction.

Beckett stares down at my hand for a few moments before giving it a hard shake. "Sorry, man. I missed you, too." He pulls me in for a one-armed man hug, then steps back. "You know I see nothing but red where my baby sister is concerned. I need to protect her."

"From what I can see, she's done a pretty good job protecting herself." I glance to the side and notice Emersyn propping up the hood of her car.

She catches sight of us staring and wiggles her fingers at us, letting us know she's good.

"Tell me about it. She just chewed my ass out for treating her like a child." His eyes soften as he looks over my shoulder at his sister. "I want to protect her from everything. I don't want to watch her cry from heartbreak again."

"Again?" I question, seeing the perfect opportunity to find out how Emersyn has taken my year-long silence. "Because of me?"

"Of course, asshole. Did you have to cut off all communication with her? The first few weeks after you left, she cried herself to sleep, wondering what she did wrong to make you turn your back on her. Then it turned into months of worrying if you were all right. Thankfully, your mom kept us up to date on what was going on with you, but not hearing from you took its toll."

"I tried to keep my distance, like you said, but it was hard. My resolve broke a little more with each email and package she sent, but then one day, they just stopped."

"It was for the best, Brady. By leaving her, you let her grow and become the woman she is today."

"But I'm home now, for good."

"And?" He raises his eyebrow at me before unlocking his car and opening the door. "Look, I'm glad you're home safe and sound, but we've been friends since I was five years old. You're not good enough for my baby sister."

Beckett ducks into his car and slams the door in my face, ending the conversation.

I step out of the way as I hear the ignition turn over, and he pulls out of the spot, beeping the horn at us and waving out the window as he drives off toward the bar.

"Sorry. He's an asshole."

Emersyn's voice startles me, and I spin around, taking a step back.

"What are you apologizing for?"

The air crackles between us as I stare into her eyes. Her honey-colored skin glistens in the sunlight as she brushes some curls off her face.

I can't stop my eyes from roaming down her body. Her pert nipples peek through the thin cotton shirt she's wearing, tucked into a painted-on pair of jean shorts that should be illegal.

"Up here."

My eyes snap up to her, and I smile. No sense in trying to hide the fact that I was checking her out.

"I would apologize, but I'm not sorry." I brush past her and head right for her car, bending over the front end while looking inside. "What seems to be the problem?"

"The check engine light came on when I was leaving this morning, and I didn't want to drive it all the way to my parents' house, so I came to Beckett's place instead." Emersyn turns and leans against the front bumper, staring off into space.

"It may be a clogged filter, but that's an easy fix. I can head to the auto parts store while you're at work and change the oil and put in new filters. If the light comes back on, I can hook it to the diagnostic tool and find out what's going on."

"When did you learn so much about cars?"

"We did a lot of our own maintenance overseas. I wouldn't say I'm an expert, but I know how to fix the basics." I unhook the prop rod from the hood and slam it shut.

"What's on your mind, Em?" I stand to my full height and turn toward her.

I have a feeling things are going to get uncomfortable quickly, but we need to talk things out sooner rather than later if there is any hope of us starting over.

"Why did you leave without a word?" Emersyn whispers, wrapping her arms around her waist as if protecting herself from my answer. "I know you had a war to fight, but you could have at least returned an email or a letter. I doubt they had you so busy over there you couldn't send a simple note saying, *I'm not dead.*" She pushes off the front end of the car and begins pacing back and forth. "I told you have I felt aboutv you that night, and you just left. You didn't even have the decency to tell me goodbye. You just vanished without a trace."

"Em." I reach out, wanting to pull her into my arms and tell her everything I've been feeling over the last year.

"No, Brady." She steps out of my reach. "You don't get to come home and make everything better with a smile and an apology."

"I *am* sorry, Em. So sorry." My voice breaks toward the end of my sentence, suddenly overcome with the realization that she may have moved on and forgotten me—as I'd hoped.

"I told you I loved you! I poured my heart out to you before you went off to war without the promise of return. And you said *nothing*." Angry tears stream down her face, but she swipes them away quickly. "What makes matters worse is you made me believe you cared. That you had been dreaming about our first kiss for as long as I had, if not longer."

Emersyn spins on her heels, storming toward Beckett's apartment, but I follow her. She started this conversation, and I'll be damned if I let her get away without hearing my side of the story. The only thing on my mind is finding some way to make this up to her and show her how much she means to me, that she deserves so much more than what I just gave her.

It isn't until I'm sitting in front of the auto parts store that I realize what a colossal mistake I've just made.

epilogue

bristol

eighteen months later

"Are you kidding me?" I screech as I flop down on the couch in Seth's living room.

Although it's been over a year since Seth and I finally became a couple, we're still living on opposite ends of town. Seth has been hinting at wanting to sell one of our houses and move in together, but I'm just not there yet. It's not that I don't love him with every fiber of my being, but I want to have a ring on my finger first. Call me old-fashioned, but I want our lives to be tied to each other in every way before we take that next step.

"What are you grumbling about?" Seth asks as he comes around the corner into the living room, followed closely by Rebekah.

"Audrey just canceled. She said she can't watch the little one today," I grumble, shooting off a text to Selina, hoping she'll be able to watch her for a few hours.

Seth and I were going to spend today planning our little girl's second birthday party, and we were hoping to not have the distraction of our toddler for a little while.

"I'm sure she wouldn't have canceled at the last minute for no reason." Seth kisses my forehead gently before turning around and wrapping his arms around Rebekah.

She squeals in delight as he lifts her in the air, blowing raspberries on her belly. These two have been thick as thieves since they first laid eyes on each other. I have a feeling that if I wasn't the one with the milk, she'd have completely forgotten that I even existed. It's taken some getting used to, but having Seth here for us whenever we need anything has been amazing. Having a partner to share worries with and celebrate the happy things is something we were both missing. With his job at the sheriff's office, Seth has been here for mostly all her major milestones. He even makes sure he's home every night for dinner, even when he's on duty. He wants to ensure that both Rebekah and I know we're the two most important people in his world, and he would do anything to make us happy.

And he has. Made us unbelievably happy, that is. Now, if he would just get off his rear and propose, everything would be perfect. It's not that we haven't talked about marriage, because we have, but something is holding him back from popping the question. I've tried talking with the girls about it, but they all assure me he is just waiting for the perfect moment. When is this man going to learn that I don't want perfect? I just want him to be mine... forever.

"I have a feeling it has something to do with the guys having a day off today for the first time in months." Seth takes a seat on the couch, placing Rebekah on his knee.

He bounces her up and down a few times before she crawls between the two of us, snuggling into my side as her eyes droop.

"Audrey and Connor never got a honeymoon. Let them have some time together. I highly doubt they get any alone time with two teenage daughters in the house." He leans back on the couch, draping his arms across the back.

Vance and Connor's construction company has been doing even better since they finished the project in Magnolia. Leia also convinced them to do some renovations to the cabins at Tranquility Retreat last year. Both those projects helped them land a few huge contracts to build custom homes on the empty land outside of town, a big deal for them and the town.

"Connor was complaining about the boys coming around for his girls recently." We both laugh as Seth plays with the tips of my hair. "I guess I can cut him some slack, but he needs to let those girls be teenagers. They both have good heads on their shoulders. Neither of them has to worry about Jade or Love doing anything too reckless."

My phone chimes, and I unlock it. "Dang it."

A text from Selina is waiting for me, telling me they have plans to head to The Willis Farm Sunflower Field about two hours east of us. But at least she invited us along, too.

"Seli asked if we wanted to go to the sunflower field with them. She promised a picnic and said she'd watch Rebekah for us for a few hours when we get back."

"Sounds like a plan. We planned on taking Rebekah there after her birthday anyway." Seth smiles at me, then slides his arm off the back of the couch, and heads toward the back of the house. "I'll go pack her a bag to take to Seli's house, and then we can grab some lunch on the way out of town. Hopefully, the princess will sleep the entire drive and save us some tears."

"Okay, sounds like a plan to me," I say with a smile as I quickly text Selina back. Although this isn't going how I originally planned, things seem to be looking up.

It doesn't take us long to get the truck packed up, buckle Rebekah into the car, and make a stop at Culver's on the way out of town, and we take the two-hour trip to reach the sunflower fields. Thankfully, today is a perfect day to be out in the fields. The sunflowers are in full bloom, and a light breeze blows around us. There aren't too many families here, which is great because, with just our two families and strollers, we are a force to be reckoned with.

We walk around the field for a little while before the girls get fussy, and we stop to take a break.

"Picnic time!" Vance shouts, rubbing his hands together in delight.

"You would have no idea I fed this man on our way here." Selina shakes her head at him as she pulls containers of fruit from the picnic basket.

Since it was already past lunchtime, we decided to just pack some snacks for the kids and finger foods for us.

"We're growing boys. We need to eat frequently."

I spin around at the sound of Connor's voice as Audrey takes a seat beside me on the blanket.

"I thought you couldn't babysit today?" I squint my eyes at my friend.

Something strange is going on, and I'm determined to find out what it is.

"No one could babysit today because Seth asked us all to be here," Jade chimes in as she unstraps Rebekah from her stroller, propping her up on her hip, while Love grabs Vance and Selina's daughter, Brittany.

"I don't understand." I look at all my friends for a hint as to what is going on when I feel a light tap on my shoulder.

I spin around quickly and come face-to-face with a huge sunflower. Tears fill my eyes as the light shimmers off a heart-shaped diamond ring sitting perfectly in the center.

"Bristol, I have traveled the world searching for the piece of my soul that was missing, but I never imagined I would find it in a small town in Tennessee." Seth grips the ring in between his fingers and lowers onto one knee, holding it out to me as a gift. "Now that I finally have you and our princess, I will never be alone again. Will you please do me the honor of being my wife?"

"Yes! Yes! Yes!" I shout before launching myself at him, and we both go tumbling over on the blanket.

My lips instantly connect with his as I pour all my happiness into this one kiss. Our friends erupt into cheers as we celebrate our happily ever after, but I'm not ready to face them just yet.

"Good reason to cancel on babysitting, don't you think?" Seth whispers in my ear as he pulls me tightly into his chest.

"You can say that again." I giggle as I bury my nose in his chest, but something suddenly occurs to me. "Where's Leia?"

"She got stuck in traffic but should be here soon." Seth sits up, lifting me with him and placing me in his lap.

I know that our beginning was far from the typical romance, but now we'll finally have our happy ending.

the end

I hope you enjoyed *Waiting to Love You*! Wondering what happened to Seth, Bristol, and Rebekah after the end? Scan the QR code for instant access to a bonus epilogue for your new favorite couple.

Already subscribed? Just check your last newsletter for the link to my bonus material! If you can't find it, you can simply resubscribe and the scene will be yours in minutes!

USA Today Bestselling Author AJ Alexander has been writing romance since 2018. She loves writing small town romances with found families and all the nosey nellies that help her characters find their happily ever afters! She lives in Arizona, otherwise known as the surface of the sun, with her husband, two daughters, two cats, and a lovable golden retriever.

When she isn't writing you can find AJ reading, binging the latest true crime documentary on Netflix, or binging the latest Korean Drama or Anime that's released. AJ is a cynical hopeless romantic that believes in love at first sight, that bigger is always better, and everything should be put off for a nap.

Come find her in the wild! There's nothing she loves more than connecting with my readers.

www.ingramcontent.com/pod-product-compliance
Lightning Source LLC
La Vergne TN
LVHW091249110826
845146LV00002BA/590

* 9 7 9 8 9 8 9 8 2 5 0 5 9 *